Armed
and Dangerous

JAMES KENNEDY

Armed
and
Dangerous

HEINEMANN : LONDON

First published in Great Britain 1996
by William Heinemann Ltd
an imprint of Reed Books Ltd
Michelin House, 81 Fulham Road, London SW3 6RB
and Auckland, Melbourne, Singapore and Toronto

Copyright © James Kennedy 1996
The author has asserted his moral rights

A CIP catalogue record for this title
is available from the British Library
ISBN 0 434 00354 9

Typeset by Falcon Oast Graphic Art
Printed and bound in Great Britain
by Clays Ltd, St Ives plc

To David O'Leary

who first posed the vital question,
what if . . . ?

PART ONE
Tuesday

ONE

1

At eight-fifteen that evening, a couple of minutes after the Category As had filed into the exercise yard for their recreation period, Woolly Barr was told he was going over the wall with the rest of the IRA prisoners.

The whole population of that special secure unit. They weren't trotting meekly back to their cells tonight. They were breaking out.

Woolly knew a lot about Whitemoor prison, where he'd spent the last five years.

He knew that the fence around the special secure unit was monitored by searchlights and closed-circuit tv.

He knew that the perimeter wall, if anyone ever got that far, was thirty feet high.

He knew there was a moat the other side.

And he knew that the surrounding countryside was flat and marshy, the worst kind of all for heading across on the run.

So Woolly said immediately, 'You can't!'

Sean McDaid, who'd broken the news and was now walking beside him in the yard, laughing for the benefit of the watching prison officers, snapped at him, 'Get yourself ready! Look for Danny Boyce! Wait for the order!'

He ran his fingers through his short, curly hair. The way he always did when he felt crossed.

McDaid was officer commanding, IRA prisoners in Whitemoor, and maybe knew something no one else was in on.

Woolly still wasn't convinced, but didn't risk an argument.

Because McDaid wasn't someone you questioned. Unless you could match his violence.

And the fact was, Woolly didn't even *look* like a Category A prisoner any more. Five foot five in his best shoes, he was smaller and slighter than the others.

They said he'd softened during the decade in prison, the hardness gone from his dark-brown eyes, the lips slacker than they might've been, a little too much fat on his round face. Time to time, when it suited him, he still limped from the bullet he'd taken in the right knee when he'd been captured in Birmingham.

And he said now, 'What about my leg?'

But McDaid had already moved on, urgently whispering orders to the next man, and Big Danny Boyce, all six foot two of him, had slipped in beside Woolly.

'You've got to smile, Woolly,' Boyce warned. 'Stop shaking. Relax. This is recreation.'

So Woolly smiled and said again, 'What about my leg?'

'What *about* your leg?'

'My bad leg. I can't get across the marsh.'

'You're not *going* across the marsh,' Boyce told him. 'Soon as the signal goes –'

'What signal?'

'Will you listen to me, man!'

'Sorry, Danny. It's just –'

'We'll not all get away from here. We know that. So we're to act as decoys. Most of us. Get in the way of the screws. Give the lads a free run on the first leg.'

'Which lads?'

4

'Not our concern, Woolly. Just stick with me. I'll see you all right.'

'But what's the signal?'

'Quiet, now!'

Woolly started shaking again. Because he was scared. And didn't want to go.

'Cold,' he said to Danny Boyce.

He pulled the collar of his heavy lumberjack coat around his ears and sank his head into it, blowing frosted air all the time, trying to say it was the sharp winter evening that had him shivering.

'Cold,' he said, his voice breaking with fear.

And his trembling legs not holding him steady any more.

Passing the prison officer down in the left corner of the yard, Sean McDaid came again and took Woolly's arm and squeezed the bicep. Squeezed it hard, almost forcing out a cry of pain. Whether as a warning or encouragement, Woolly didn't know.

Five seconds later, Woolly was still feeling the pressure, throbbing away in his muscles, when the atmosphere in the yard shifted quickly.

Everything went suddenly quiet. The laughter died. Voices broke into silence. Even the footsteps fell away. In the stillness, a guard dog got restless and whined, shuffling on its hind paws.

And then Woolly heard the gunshots.

For an instant he thought they were meant for him. Because he hadn't known there were guns in the unit. Because it meant the others had kept it from him. And usually, there was only one reason for concealment like that in the cage.

Execution.

But Woolly wasn't hit.

Instead, a little behind him and to his right, a prison officer went down, screaming and clutching at his shoulder.

Woolly swivelled. He saw it was Roger Warfield on the

5

ground, the blood oozing through his fingers. And he started thinking he was happy about that, it wasn't fatal, because Roger Warfield . . .

He never finished the thought.

Danny Boyce, reaching him again, grabbed his arm, yanked him away and pushed him forward, forcing a fast pace across the yard.

To Woolly, stumbling in front of Boyce, the scene around him now was a nightmare. It was chaos. Madness.

Because everyone else had a role. Everyone except him.

Some held the other prison officers and their dogs captive. He saw an Alsatian going down under a blow from a heavy wooden baton wielded by a prisoner. He saw another being brought to heel by its handler.

Two men with wire cutters were kneeling at a corner of the inner fence, quickly hacking away an opening.

As they ran towards this gap, behind Boyce and Woolly himself, others took lengths of a pole from their clothing and started screwing them together.

Everyone knew their place and knew their function. Except him.

And everyone, except himself, was shouting, had a slogan or a threat or an order or a warning. Of all the struggling crowd of prisoners and officers in that small yard, only Woolly was silent. Whimpering inwardly.

Over at the unit's second fence two prisoners were crouched, their hands locked together, making a human stairway over the obstacle.

Danny Boyce reached them first and was instantly over.

But even for that second or so, while Boyce was out of sight, Woolly wasn't free to cop out. As soon as Boyce released him in front, someone came from behind to hold his shoulder.

Woolly turned and saw it was Denis Reilly, a tough, unhappy kid with skin so poor and lips so thin he couldn't even manage a smile without being threatening.

And it was Reilly, half carrying him, who stayed with Woolly from the fence to the perimeter wall.

Danny Boyce had vaulted the thirty feet and was already sitting on top of the wall itself, covering the drop to the other side with a revolver and frantically gesturing the others up. He'd secured and lowered a makeshift ladder of rolled and sewn bedsheets with short pieces of metal for rungs.

Woolly felt sick. He felt weak in both his knees and couldn't really remember right then which of them had once been shattered by a bullet.

He must've fainted, he reckoned later.

Because the next he knew, he found himself kneeling in water, sinking in the moat the other side of the perimeter wall, and couldn't remember whether he'd braved that thirty-foot climb and drop or whether Reilly had carried him up and carried him down again.

Five, six, seven others were out as well by now, scrambling from the moat beside him. They looked like wild, savage creatures. Panicked by something in the water.

Apart from Sean McDaid, he couldn't tell who they were, if Boyce or Reilly was among them.

McDaid was shouting at him now, ordering him on, but Woolly couldn't hear the words.

He could hear the sirens. He could hear the gunshots and the noise of his own sobbing and the barking of the prison officers' German Shepherds coming at him from right and left.

Terrified of the dogs, he pushed up his hands in a useless gesture of surrender, wondering wildly if the animals had been trained to recognise that too.

It wasn't teeth that grasped his wrists, though. It was other hands. Two on his left. Two on his right. They dragged him from the water, on to his feet in the high grass and reeds on the bank.

7

He looked up. And saw with relief that he'd been captured. It was two prison officers who'd pulled him out.

He held out his hands for the cuffs.

Instead, two other prisoners launched themselves at the guards from the front, knocking them backwards into the moat.

Behind him, then, Woolly heard one of his rescuers being brought down by a snarling dog, and the man's screams of pain panicked him.

He sprinted blindly. Trying to get away from the panting, slavering animals. Sprinted as he hadn't done for more than ten years. Out of the floodlights surrounding the prison, somehow finding a firm pathway through the darkness and the marsh.

A searchlight picked him out, though. And tracked him all the way.

Set loose by their handlers, two dogs bounded after him from the perimeter. Their huge strides eating up the gap and closing quickly.

And Woolly's body shook with sobs as he ran. He cried with terror. Knowing that he'd be brought down whether he stopped or not.

He heard gunfire close behind and for the second time that night thought it was meant for him. Thought the prison officers had been armed.

For an instant, as darkness enveloped him again and he felt a stab of pain in his left calf, he was certain he'd been hit.

But he was still running.

And it was a dog who howled in agony.

Woolly didn't dare turn. And he was too terrified to think straight. But he realised that it must've been the searchlight and a German Shepherd which had taken the hits.

The heavy panting stayed close behind his heels, though. Convincing him that the second chasing beast still kept pace

8

with him.

Until a human voice gasped, 'Ease up, Woolly! Christ sake! Ease up a little, man! Got to tell you where we're going.'

And Woolly realised it was Danny Boyce, not a guard dog, close at his back.

Woolly stopped. And sank to his knees, sobbing uncontrollably.

Boyce yanked him upwards, half carried him on. 'Come on! Got to show you where we're going.'

2

Jennifer Crooks took the saucer and teacup from the table and walked with them over to the front window of her living-room.

The curtains there were already open.

Beyond the row of houses opposite, over the marsh between the prison and the village, she could see the powerful beam of a police helicopter searchlight sweeping the area.

Even at that distance, even through the closed window, she could hear the rotary blades and occasional shouting from the policemen searching on the ground. The cold night air carrying the noises through the darkness.

She looked at her watch. It was almost eight-thirty.

She wondered how many prisoners had escaped, how many were still free.

She wondered then if she'd locked the back door or left it open after coming in from the garden earlier.

Usually, winter nights anyway, she had this routine. Turn the key in the lock and take it out and hang it on the free hook above the sink.

Habit. The great deadener. You don't even know you're

doing it any more.

The thought made her nervous. So nervous that she couldn't think straight, couldn't remember how the hell she'd left the back door.

Better go and check.

She put the cup and saucer on the bare floorboards to the side of the window, not bothered for once by the effects of heat on the varnish and the stain.

She quickly pulled the curtains closed then and was stooping to collect the cup and saucer again when she was aware of movement behind her.

She turned.

Two men were standing in her living-room. Both were wet and cold. Both looked exhausted and in pain, struggling to catch a breath between clenched teeth. And both were carrying revolvers in their right hands.

The younger one, a big, raw, red-faced fellow of nineteen or twenty, and looking like a farmer's son, had thin lips that made his mouth look like a dark gash across the bottom of his face.

He had hungry eyes. Eyes that hadn't seen a woman since they'd locked him away.

They stared at her now, devouring her.

She felt them eating through her clothes. Under the white shirt and blue jeans she was wearing.

The other prisoner, his light-brown hair styled short and curled, his face shaved clean, his blue eyes soft and moist, looked more like a clerk than a criminal, more like a thinker who'd strayed to some survival course.

'You know who we are?' the clerk asked her.

His accent, heard the last twenty, twenty-five years on news bulletins, was from Northern Ireland. Deceptively soft. Almost musical.

She nodded. Her mouth dry. Not able to answer for the moment.

10

He raised the hand-gun to her. But only gestured with it.
'Let's move!' he ordered. 'Now!'

She walked towards and past them.

Still not able to talk.

She led them out of the room, to the wooden stairway in
the hall, and then up, to where a metal step-ladder stood on
the landing under the narrow opening to the attic.

The younger one climbed and squeezed through the trap.

When he looked down again it was directly at her, into the
gap where the top button of her shirt was open.

The older one followed. Blocking the view. Getting in with
less trouble. Immediately dropping the door back in place
from above.

And Jennifer Crooks went quickly back downstairs, mop-
ping up the water that had dripped from the men's clothes as
she went, and back to the living-room, to wait for the second
pair.

Knowing now that she hadn't been sucked in by habit that
night, that she'd left the back door unlocked the way she'd
been ordered to.

3

Jody Stafford and Junior Doherty, with two IRA volunteers
named Crawley and Sheehan in the back of the Vauxhall Astra,
drove into Belfast from Armagh at nine o'clock that evening.

They were, effectively, an officer unit of the IRA's own military police, enforcing the ceasefire that the organisation had
held since late the previous year and investigating possible
breaches.

Tonight they were on their way back to see a man they had

11

captured a few days earlier.

His name was Tommy Brennan. The week before, he'd knocked over a bank and wounded a teller, setting hard questions about the IRA's control of its own volunteers during the ceasefire.

Now he'd just been sentenced to kneecapping, and been given the present of continuing life on condition he handed over the loot from the job.

'A problem with an individual volunteer is being rectified,' as the official statement put it.

A week ago, Tommy Brennan had been a personal friend of some of those now travelling in the car to punish him.

'We're paying a high price for this fucking peace,' Junior Doherty swore.

Jody Stafford, sitting beside him in the passenger seat, nodded in the darkness.

'Good men being shot by their own,' Doherty went on bitterly. 'And nothing much to show for it yet. Nothing that I can see anyway.'

'What you mean', Stafford said, 'is that we were gaining more at less cost before the ceasefire. Isn't it?'

For the moment, it was still only a question in each of their minds. Without an answer one way or the other.

Brennan, the bank robber whose actions had sharpened that question, was being held in the basement of a house on the Falls Road.

He looked up sourly, almost with contempt, as Stafford and the others came in.

'Well?'

'You've been found guilty –'

'Just tell me if you're going to kill me to keep your new friends happy. And tell me if you're going to be the one to let my kids know as well.'

The telephone interrupted Stafford's answer.

12

Junior Doherty picked up the receiver and listened, put his hand over the mouthpiece while saying, 'Red Hanrahan wants to see you, Jody. Says it's urgent.'

'Where's the call coming from?'

'Your home. He's been trying to contact you the last while.'

Stafford sighed.

The British and their *Boy's Own* dramatics, he thought wearily.

Hanrahan was the code name of his MI5 contact in Belfast. According to a scheme they'd agreed on, the colours indicated the problem. White for a bomb explosion. Black for a fire fight.

Red was for a jailbreak.

'The execution of your sentence is deferred, Tommy,' Stafford said to the bank robber.

'What the hell does that mean?'

'It means you'll have to wait. Not to hear your sentence, though. No one is going to kill you.'

Stafford left the bank robber to Junior Doherty and the others and drove alone from the Falls Road, turning south when he hit the M1. The rendezvous was a roadside motel a few miles down the motorway.

Hanrahan, looking like a middle-aged businessman in a white shirt and pin-stripe navy suit, was waiting in a bedroom for him.

Stafford took the offered whiskey, but couldn't taste it. His nose was blocked and his palate dead. He'd had a slight headache, too, since early that morning.

He sat down on the only chair in the room and asked, 'Who's out?'

'Mr Rawlings wants your immediate presence in London,' Hanrahan said.

'Does he now?' Stafford asked drily.

'I need not remind you that as IRA liaison officer, the

13

Tuesday

...d to any perceived breaches of your ...of military activities is yours.'

...Who's out?'

...explained to you in London. You're to ...rse.'

...at our headquarters on Millbank, London, to one o...on heads.'

He took a card from his wallet and passed it to Stafford, who slipped it casually into a pocket without looking at it.

'That's her telephone number,' Hanrahan explained. 'It is exclusively reserved for your use. Once you report, Miss Maybury will brief you comprehensively on your role.'

Stafford had tensed, the indulgent smile dying on his lips, his eyes hardened with distaste. 'Maybury?' he repeated.

'The officer in charge of the case.'

'*June* Maybury?'

'Have you met?'

'I asked you a question. Is it *June* Maybury?'

'Yes, of course, but –'

Stafford came out of the chair and advanced on Hanrahan. His lips had curled with bitterness. 'You can tell Rawlings', he said, 'that I'll not be dealing with June Maybury. Do you understand?'

'I'm afraid –'

'Do you understand? Anyone else. Anyone who hasn't already dirtied their bib in Northern Ireland. Now. I've no fucking intention of sitting around here sipping bad whiskey all night. So for the last time. Who's out?'

'You understand I'm not empowered to divulge –'

'Just give me the names!'

'Well, so far,' Hanrahan said, 'Sean McDaid and Denis Reilly. There may be others.'

'McDaid?'

14

'Do you know him?' Hanrahan asked.

'Vaguely,' Stafford lied.

Time was, himself and Sean McDaid had run the most efficient and the most feared active service unit in Northern Ireland. But they'd parted somewhere, back about three years before.

Harahan was saying, 'I have a car waiting outside for you now. You'll take a military flight –'

Stafford pushed the empty whiskey glass into Hanrahan's stomach and turned away. 'I'll be back.'

Hanrahan followed, pleading. 'I'm afraid you can't leave other than in the waiting car, can't communicate other than with myself until we reach Headquarters.'

'Look,' Stafford said, 'I've got something else in the same line to deal with first. If I don't, it won't matter a damn whether you find your escaped prisoners or not. You understand?'

'Yes, but –'

'I'll ring you. Let you know when I'll be back. Okay?'

They didn't put a tail on him, back up the M1 and into the Falls Road again.

It meant they hadn't the manpower themselves and hadn't yet brought the RUC or the Army in on the act. They were keeping the jailbreak quiet for the moment.

Junior Doherty was still baby-sitting the nervous bank robber in the flat.

Stafford took Doherty from the room and told him, 'I want Crawley and Sheehan and yourself ready immediately. We've got to leave for England. Quickly. The next flight out of here. I want somewhere we can use there. Close to London. Go. Get it organised.'

When he came back afterwards he looked a bit more kindly than before on Brennan.

He sat down and smiled and said, 'Want to save the old limbs, Tommy?'

15

'How do you mean?'

'You worked with Sean McDaid, didn't you? I mean, over the last three or four years. Before he went over to England.'

The contempt and the studied boredom fell from Brennan's eyes and were replaced by an anxious curiosity.

'Sean?' he said. 'He was in Whitemoor. The prison.'

'Was?' Stafford repeated.

'Is. I mean, is.'

'No,' Stafford said quietly. 'Was.'

'You mean he's really out?'

'Why? Were you expecting him?'

'No. Jesus, no. It's just, you know, I heard the word he might be trying something around this time.'

'Right,' Stafford said. 'Say it to anyone else, Tommy, and you're a dead man. But if you keep your mouth shut and if we manage to tuck McDaid back in nice and quietly, we'll wipe the slate clean of your own mess. You know what I mean?'

Brennan seemed to have a struggle, weighing the health of his knees against his gamble on McDaid.

He said finally, 'I always heard Sean had a safe house organised near the prison. Somewhere to go to ground quickly.'

'Where?'

'I don't know. I don't know the address or anything like that. Maybe I could find out.'

'Maybe,' Stafford agreed. 'What else? Do you know what mission he was on in England when he was picked up a year ago?'

Brennan raised his eyebrows. 'You mean it wasn't sanctioned?'

'What do you know about it?'

Brennan shrugged. 'Nothing.' His hand went unconsciously to rub his left knee and he said desperately, 'I might be able to find out, though. I heard Dixie McDaid, Sean's brother, was in on it. He was already in England. He lives in London.'

16

Stafford nodded, not surprised at the news.

Three years before, a squad of men had taken Dixie McDaid from a high-rise flat nearby, down the narrow stairway and into the waste ground behind the block, where they'd broken both his arms with baseball bats.

Jody Stafford had been in charge of that punishment squad.

Even though he'd accepted that his brother Dixie had been lining his own pockets with IRA funds, Sean McDaid had never worked with Stafford afterwards.

Brennan was asking anxiously, 'How about the deal?'

Stafford nodded again. 'Get me the address of McDaid's safe house and we'll square things up when I see you again. Don't think of trying anything, though. Two of the lads will be keeping you company all the time.'

Five minutes later Junior Doherty was back with a list of flight times and destinations from Aldergrove Airport and Stafford was on the phone to the motel down the motorway, asking for a connection to the room Hanrahan was using.

Stafford checked his watch and underlined the details of the next flight to Manchester as he said to Hanrahan, 'I've almost sorted out my little problem this end. I'll be back with you again in a couple of hours. Okay? What? No, *two* hours. Good. Try and get a better whiskey, will you?'

4

The way Sean McDaid had instructed the hide-out to be organised, long before he imagined he'd need it himself, a little buzzer sounded in the attic whenever someone rang the front doorbell from the street.

A lot of other things had been thought of too, of course.

17

There were food and clothes and books stacked up there. Even fresh ammunition for the .38 revolvers. And Jennifer Crooks had heavily insulated the walls and flooring so that the sounds wouldn't carry to the neighbours on either side.

But the prisoners liked the little buzzer best. It let them know when they could relax and when they had to tighten up. It watched their backs for them. It made them feel *free*. The first time in a decade for some of them.

It was eleven-thirty that night and the four who'd made it, McDaid and Denis Reilly, Danny Boyce and Woolly Barr, had all dried off and changed and eaten and were now taking it easy, reading and chatting, when the buzzer finally sounded.

'Police,' McDaid said softly.

Woolly Barr, who hadn't really eaten or talked very much the last three hours, stood up suddenly and stayed there, shivering and staring wildly at the attic's door, until Danny Boyce eased him back down again.

'It's only routine,' Boyce told him. 'Just a routine call, Woolly. Nobody knows we're here.'

Just in case, though, he kept his big hand on Woolly's forearm, half comforting, half threatening . . .

5

Jennifer Crooks let the doorbell ring again, for the third time, before getting up to answer it.

As if the damn thing had woken her from a nap in the armchair. But of course to give the four in the attic time to settle, time to arm themselves.

She had a last look around the living-room.

There was no water that might've dripped from the

fugitives' clothes. No mud from their shoes or boots.

She took a newspaper from the coffee table. Opened it. Refolded it. And dropped it on the armchair she'd just risen from.

She finally went to the hallway then, hitting the light switch on her way, checking the floorboards out there, the stairs going upwards.

As soon as she pulled the lever to release the lock and opened the door, though, she knew that she was already in trouble. Already making mistakes.

Although it had to be the police out there, she should really have *asked* who it was.

And the bolt on the door should've already been in place. She was supposed to be the nervous housewife.

Even worse, though, the local constable who stood out there in the street, blowing on his bare hands to keep them warm, was Roddy Wark.

They'd been dating on and off the last six months, herself and Wark. Jennifer Crooks stringing him along with occasional sex, picking up what she could from his loose talk.

Except it was a two-way thing, as she found now, just like everything else. He knew the inside of *her* house as well as he knew the interior of his own. Apart from the attic.

Wark stepped past her now, not waiting for the invitation.

He said, 'I can't really stay, Jenny.'

But he walked along the hallway, glancing up the stairs, and turned into the living-room.

Saying, 'Keep the doors locked and bolted, love. No need to panic. Just be alert. Report anything you see.'

Jennifer Crooks closed the front door and followed him, having to moisten her mouth again.

'What's going on, then?' she asked.

He hadn't answered her by the time she reached the living-room.

She stopped in the doorway, wondering what was distracting him. She realised then that his eyes had been caught by something on the floor. She saw his body tensing, trying to figure something out.

All the preparations they'd made, but nobody had told her what to do, how to warn the fugitives in the attic, if someone was suspicious.

She moved a little, into the room, searching for the angle his face was at, trying to locate what was bothering him.

And then she saw it.

It was the unwashed cup and saucer she'd left abandoned on the floor near the window, half hidden by the curtains.

Nothing, really. Nothing to link her with the fugitives. But she had this reputation for being houseproud, almost neurotic. It was something he ribbed her about.

She heard the blood suddenly pounding in her ears. Through it, she thought she heard a noise from the attic, something brittle being stepped on or fallen on and snapping.

Again her mouth was too dry for excuses, for distractions. She waited.

Watching his troubled face.

And then the doorbell rang again.

6

Up in the attic, sitting tense and silent in the darkness, they heard the second buzzer and tried to make sense of it.

Maybe it was Jennifer Crooks, they thought, giving them a signal that the coast was clear? But they hadn't agreed on any signal.

Then maybe it was a neighbour, complaining about strange noises?

20

Or more cops?

Maybe.

Sean McDaid joined his slim, pale hands together, the fingers interlocking, and bowed his head. To his left, he could still see the silhouettes of the others.

Reilly, always half hoping for the worst, had raised his .38 revolver. His hand was already tiring from the weight. His finger was stupidly on the trigger.

Reilly might be a mistake, McDaid conceded now.

A week before, McDaid's lieutenant in Whitemoor had been brought to hospital with a perforated ulcer. *Someone* had to replace him on the break. Someone tough and strong and quick with a gun.

Someone like Reilly.

But perhaps not Reilly himself.

McDaid looked beyond the youngster, to where Danny Boyce had his left arm tightly around Woolly Barr's shoulders. Maybe to comfort the little man.

Maybe not.

Woolly had just sobbed loudly at the second buzzer and the huge palm of Boyce's right hand was now locked over his mouth and nose. He appeared to be struggling desperately for breath, seemed about a minute away from suffocating.

That was Boyce, McDaid thought.

He had feelings and he had strength. But instead of brain cells he just had loyalty. Someone else always had to guide that raw power of his.

McDaid leaned across in the darkness and prised Boyce's forefinger away from Woolly's nostrils.

He didn't hear the sharp, urgent intake of breath through Woolly's nose, though.

A joist creaked under his own shifting weight.

He stopped, not wanting to risk repeating the noise by moving again. And found himself trapped in an awkward

21

position, leaning to one side without any support.

A couple of seconds later he heard the metal step-ladder being put into place beneath them.

Someone mounted the first rung. And paused there, probably looking upwards, before they climbed again. But they came rapidly now. With an even rhythm.

McDaid glanced once more at the others.

Woolly Barr, finding himself suddenly freed from Boyce's bear hug, now voluntarily held his breath.

Reilly pointed the revolver's muzzle at the still unmoving trapdoor. But his hand had little strength left. The gun's sights kept dropping below the target.

And then, too late, Reilly realised that he was on the wrong side of the trap. Whoever was climbing was also pushing the door upwards towards the gun, still shielded by it, still hidden behind it.

Reilly stood up.

But Sean McDaid's sharp voice suddenly cut through the tension. 'Put the gun away!'

Reilly didn't. Not immediately, anyway. Not until Jennifer Crooks's straight, blonde hair came into his own view.

'It's all right,' she told them. She coughed drily. 'They've gone now.'

'Who was it?' McDaid asked.

'Just a local constable.'

'The second caller.'

'His mate.'

McDaid nodded. 'What time do you normally go to bed?'

'In about half an hour. Midnight.'

McDaid said nothing more. But wondered.

Why had the two cops separated? To cover as many houses as quickly as possible?

Then why had the first one stepped inside, wasting time with pleasantries? Why did his mate have to drag

22

him out again?

Were they searching all the houses?

Or was it that . . .?

McDaid looked again at Jennifer Crooks, who was still standing on the ladder, half in, half out of the attic.

Looked at her in a way he found a bit repulsive. Her short, blonde hair and lively face. The brown leather belt around her slim waist. The pale flesh of her neck and upper breast at the open shirt collar.

Three years he'd argued with the IRA's Army Council back in Northern Ireland, trying to persuade them to see it his way.

Get some safe houses near the high security prisons. Inconspicuous people. English born, maybe with Irish parents, but anxious to work for the cause. Sleepers.

He wasn't going to have it all blow up in his face because of a woman.

He asked her, 'Have you got a portable radio?'

She nodded. 'Yes.'

'Is it working? Batteries all right?'

'Yes.'

'Go back down now,' he told her. 'Go to bed at your usual time. Leave a small light on somewhere. We'll need breakfast early in the morning. Bring the radio up with you.'

When she was gone, he didn't bother switching on the light in the attic again. He groped across to his sleeping bag, unzipped it and climbed in, fully clothed.

'Get some sleep,' he ordered the others. 'We're moving out tomorrow.'

And he fell instantly asleep afterwards.

Danny Boyce was the only one to follow him quickly. Because Boyce, too, felt pleased with himself.

The rest of them, they had him marked down as an old ox. Strong. And willing. And dumb. Big Danny, the champion athlete. As loyal as he was powerful.

23

Boyce knew it all. And didn't mind.

In fact, he found it better like that.

Skittish thoroughbreds are always closely watched, he told himself. Oxen aren't.

And behind that reputation of his, Boyce himself could watch the others. And see how things were going. And wait for his chance.

Back in Northern Ireland, he had a wife and a daughter in her early teens. The only things he now cared about in the world.

Prison had been hard on him, forcing separation from those two. So hard that he'd lost his faith in the cause while inside.

But he'd kept his mouth shut and made himself indispensable to any escape attempt. And he'd made his plans with his wife. Soon as news broke of an escape, she was to travel with their daughter south to Dublin and from there to France, where her relatives lived, to wait for him.

And here he was now, free at last, turning happily into his sleeping bag and muttering, 'Night, lads.'

No one answered him.

Denis Reilly was lying on his back, his eyes open, nursing his resentment.

He was out of prison. Just like he'd prayed for.

But there was a woman only a short distance away from him and he still couldn't have her. He still had no money in his pockets. Still had no prospects. Still had no hope without the IRA.

All his life, growing up poor in deprived Belfast estates, he'd kept himself awake at nights, dreaming of women, of money, of fast cars and excitement . . .

And he was still dreaming. And still awake.

So was Woolly Barr, although he'd given it his best shot, counting sheep and thinking of beautiful women. He just couldn't keep his eyes closed.

24

Because Woolly was still scared. More scared now than he had been before.

He didn't want to be stuck in this dark attic with three desperate fugitives. He wanted to be back in his cell, back on his bunk, playing out the rest of his sentence at a nice pace, with the comforting old sounds, the sounds of keys and shutters and footsteps, lulling him to sleep.

And besides, things were worrying him. Things he didn't understand. Things like . . .

He looked across at Danny Boyce, who was lying on his right. But Boyce's eyes were already closed in sleep. So he rolled over to look at Reilly on the other side.

'How many more?' Woolly whispered.

Reilly grunted. 'Eh?'

'Got out,' Woolly explained. 'How many more made it out?'

'No more. This is it,' Reilly said.

'Are you sure?'

'Look, Woolly. It was like American football. That was the idea.'

'American football? I don't get you.'

Reilly sighed impatiently. 'All the fellows blocking the tacklers while the guy with the ball gets a free run through. See? None of the others were ever going to break out tonight. They were the blockers.'

'Yeah,' Woolly whispered bitterly. 'Bit of a cock-up, though.'

'What? What cock-up?'

'I was supposed to be one of the blockers, not a runner. Danny told me.'

Reilly was silent a couple of seconds. And then he laughed. A short, derisive laugh. A week before, he'd been one of the blockers too. Until McDaid promoted him.

'Go to sleep, Woolly,' he said.

But neither of them could.

Five minutes later Reilly raised himself on one elbow and turned again towards Woolly. Not laughing any more.

'Think she's asleep?' he asked hoarsely.

Woolly was baffled. He'd been thinking about the ladder of sheets and metal bars that had been constructed in the prison workshop. Thinking about the pole for Danny Boyce's vault. He'd been wondering how, and why, the making of these things had been kept from him.

He asked vaguely, 'Who?'

'Down under us,' Reilly said. 'You think she's asleep?'

He was breathing hard now and restless inside the sleeping bag, racked by desire.

'Shit!' he groaned. 'She's not asleep. I can *feel* it! She's lying under the covers with nothing on, but she's not asleep. You hear her taking her clothes off a while ago?'

7

Coming in to land at Manchester Airport, Jody Stafford glanced at his watch.

It was a little after midnight.

Back in Northern Ireland, he reckoned, inside the motel down the M1, Hanrahan should be getting restless by now. Getting suspicious. Maybe making phone calls.

Stafford said to Junior Doherty, who was sitting beside him, 'If they've twigged and they're waiting for us at the airport, I don't want any trouble. You shrug your shoulders, go quietly.'

'Okay.'

'We go through customs separately. Crawley first, Sheehan, then you. I go last.'

'What happens if you get picked up and the rest of us get

through?' Doherty asked.

'You go ahead as we worked it out. Even if only one gets through. Go ahead. Have you got transport lined up?'

'The car's okay.'

'Weapons?'

'Not until we get to London.'

'What's the house like?'

'It's just outside London, near a village called Radlett. A farmhouse. Isolated. The couple who live there, they went on a winter holiday last week. It's okay.'

They were silent for a while, looking down on the runway lights below them.

Stafford glanced again at his watch.

How long would Hanrahan wait? How long does it take for a phone call from Northern Ireland to England? How long would it take to get Special Branch in place at the airport?

'What are we going to do?' Junior Doherty asked suddenly.

Stafford looked at him. 'How do you mean?'

'You know,' Doherty said awkwardly. 'When we catch up with Sean McDaid. What are we going to do? Are we going to help him or what?'

'That's the question,' Stafford admitted. 'Isn't it?'

'I mean, it would be the end of the ceasefire if we did, wouldn't it?'

'Yes.'

Doherty was reluctant, not wanting to push it too far.

But he said anyway, 'If it was straightforward, you know . . . I mean, if you just wanted McDaid back in prison, you would've stayed with MI5, wouldn't you?'

'I suppose,' Stafford conceded. 'So I suppose it's not straightforward. I don't know. We'll take it as it comes. All right?'

Ten minutes later they were touching down.

They had little luggage, only a holdall each, and didn't

27

expect to be delayed by customs.

Lingering near the tail of the queue, Stafford searched for signs of an alert, of increased security.

He didn't see any.

He watched Crawley and Sheehan and Junior Doherty passing through and then took his own place for inspection.

The customs officer frowned as he looked at Stafford's face. Trying to place it. Because there was something familiar about the features, something he had seen before.

He started to form a question. 'Don't you . . .?'

But then gave it up. And smiled. And let Stafford through.

8

They called him the minister. Not because he held so menial a seat at the Cabinet table that his title didn't deserve a capital. But only because once, for eighteen months of his distant youth, he'd strayed into a seminary.

Now he was grey-haired and walked with a cane and only served the state. But the nickname had clung.

His real name was George Rawlings.

He was the current Director-General of MI5. He'd been appointed less than six months before, from outside the service. And his position had still to be secured against internal opposition.

Late that night he stood in his office, leaning on his cane and waiting for his private secretary, Nicholas Orrinsmith, to leave the room.

While he waited, he considered the pair he had summoned. They were sitting the other side of his mahogany, kidney-shaped desk, facing each other rather than him, both tense, both impatient to react to the first slight. Like two heavy-weights either corner of a boxing ring, the minister thought, waiting for the bell.

Heavyweights of different genders, though. So the usual rules didn't hold.

The man was Superintendent Geoffrey Gilston from Special Branch and seemed the more belligerent, the more eager to get a scrap started. The woman was June Maybury, one of Rawlings's section heads in MI5, although appointed by his predecessor, Sir Andrew Pinnington.

The woman was young, in her mid-thirties, and she was modern, with close-cropped, jet-black hair and wearing a bulky, bright sweater and black jeans. The man was old, in his late fifties, and old-fashioned with it, his sparse, brown hair neatly parted over a rugged face, his dark jacket and trousers dull and unloved.

A difficult pair.

Rawlings sat down, crooking the handle of his cane over the armrest of his chair. He lightly tapped a pencil, three times, on the surface of his desk and said, 'I've already spoken to the Governor of the prison, Sir Robert Silverton . . .'

And there he paused a moment. To pay his last respects.

Poor Bob, he thought. Wouldn't survive all this, of course.

Guns smuggled into his secure unit. There was already talk of the metal detector being set too low to register firearms because its location near some underground pipes was constantly setting it off.

Probably some of his prison officers corrupted also.

But certainly, unsatisfactory procedures supervising the exercise yard and the workshop and the visiting areas. Makeshift ladders and poles constructed out of sight of the staff. Visitors and inmates left alone behind closed doors.

Poor Bob. In the morning he'd take a visit from the Director-General of Prisons. Later he'd have the commission of enquiry

29

ordered by the Home Secretary.

Have to carry the can, of course. Even though the orders for easing back on surveillance of IRA prisons must have come from higher beings concerned about the continuation of the ceasefire.

Rawlings sighed. He said, 'From what one can gather of the expressions of disappointment and other exchanges between prisoners and from what little informal questioning of inmates has already been managed, it seems that two of the four prisoners should not have escaped.'

Gilston raised his eyebrows. 'Surely none of them should have escaped, sir?'

And realised immediately that his cleverness was a mistake.

Rawlings, he had been warned, was touchy about missing out on a University education. Gilston himself, like many of the other officers in MI5, had an honours degree from Oxford.

'I'm expressing myself poorly, of course,' Rawlings conceded sarcastically.

June Maybury crossed her legs impatiently and sat upright. She said, 'Apparently the break-out was organised so that only four inmates should escape, the remainder occupying the prison staff during the attempt. The number is significant. It suggests an active service unit. It also suggests an objective other than simply gaining freedom.'

'Do you believe this, sir?' Gilston enquired.

Something nettling him. How did Maybury know so much, so early? They had arrived at the building within seconds of each other and had entered this office together.

Women, he reflected. Something else he had been told about Rawlings. He had a weakness for women. Nearly cost him his life once in Eastern Europe when he was attached to MI6.

Rawlings sighed again. He carefully took some sheets of A4 paper from the pile in front of him and handed one each across the desk to the others.

'Let's have a look at the profiles of those who have escaped, shall we?' he suggested.

He took a pair of spectacles from the breast pocket of his jacket and put them on and read from the paper. 'Sean McDaid, serving twenty-five years for conspiracy to cause explosions. Daniel Boyce, serving twenty years for a similar offence. Denis Reilly, sentenced to life imprisonment for the murder of a police constable. And William Barr, fifteen years for armed robbery. McDaid, the prisoners' O/C, is quite clearly the leader.'

'Which two were part of the original escape plan?' Gilston asked.

'The two explosives experts. McDaid and Boyce.'

'I see.'

'Furthermore,' Rawlings said slowly, 'this, as you well know, is one of the very few prisons in Britain or Northern Ireland or the Irish Republic in which the Republican inmates have not yet issued a statement of support for the IRA's cessation of military operations. I'm afraid we have no option but to believe that this group's objective is none other than to destroy the ceasefire and resume the military campaign against Her Majesty's Government and forces.'

Rawlings paused. He shuffled his papers again, finally coming up with the one he needed.

He said, 'There is a further point, Geoffrey. Almost three months ago, we received information from a reliable source within the prison that a break-out was imminent, that it would be led by Sean McDaid as a move against the ceasefire and that his specific objective was to complete the job he had been sent to England to perform. As you know, McDaid was arrested almost exactly a year ago, but only with detonators and fuses. No explosives. One of the terrorists in this three-man unit was killed by police at the time. The other was murdered

by his own people in prison, presumably because they sus-
pected that he had been the informant. He hadn't, of course.
The unpleasant consequence, however, is that only McDaid
himself now knows how he will strike at his target here in
England.'

'Is he acting alone, sir, a maverick operator, or with the support of other IRA terrorists disillusioned with the ceasefire?'

'We do not know.'

'Then what of the people who sent him from Northern
Ireland originally? I realise we are not officially talking to the
IRA, but surely in the circumstances –'

'Everything that can be done in that area is already under
way,' Rawlings assured him.

But Gilston went on, growing in excitement. 'Forgive me,
sir. But I have never accepted the integrity of this IRA
ceasefire.'

'We are aware of your views, Geoffrey.'

'Yes, sir. But this escape is the perfect opportunity to wrongfoot the IRA before the world's media. Are they willing to
co-operate to maintain the peace? Or is this the shabby excuse
for resuming hostilities they have planned?'

'I strongly disagree with the IRA or Sinn Fein being in any
way involved in this matter, sir,' June Maybury said.

'Be that as it may,' Rawlings said coldly, 'the fact is that we
cannot afford to miss either the opportunity to wrongfoot
them, as Geoffrey says, or the chance to exploit their knowledge.'

'You mean that someone has already been summoned, sir?'

'Yes. He'll report to you in the morning. The liaison officer we have dealt with before. Stafford, I believe.'

'*Jody* Stafford, sir?'

'I believe so.'

June Maybury stiffened and pursed her lips. She said angrily then, 'May I put on record, sir, my absolute opposition –'

'But the men who sent McDaid last year,' Gilston cut back in impatiently, 'before the ceasefire was in place –'

Rawlings raised a hand, grateful for the distraction. 'The men who sent McDaid are dead themselves, Geoffrey. So we have been told. It appears that only McDaid knows when to hit the target and where the explosives are concealed.'

9

At one o'clock in the morning, Jennifer Crooks felt a little cold and stirred out of sleep.

She thought the bedclothes had slipped from her body. But when she reached to pull them back, her hand brushed against another's in the darkness.

A hot, sweating hand, thick with hair.

It was drawing the covers away from her breasts, its knuckles riding over the bare flesh of her stomach between the jacket and waistband of her silk pyjamas.

She might have screamed. Except that, again, her throat was dry.

For once her silence pleased her, though.

The police helicopter was still raking the marsh beyond with its searchlights. And local constables were still patrolling the streets outside.

The warm, wet palm came back from pulling the bedclothes aside to settle on her stomach, covering her belly-button, before working its way upwards, its fingers climbing over her ribs.

She opened her eyes.

All she could see was the man's shadow leaning over her. For the moment there was no light. The heavy curtains were pulled on the window and he'd closed the bedroom door behind him.

But then the circling helicopter hovered nearer and its searchlight arced across the window and sharpened everything.

It was Denis Reilly stooping there.

She made no sound, but her body stiffened against him.

He felt it, and growled slightly with frustration. His fingers curled and turned inwards to dig their nails into the soft flesh of her breast.

Jennifer Crooks felt sorry. Nervous and restless herself, she wouldn't really have minded sharing her bed for that long night.

But not with Reilly.

She found the boy disgusting. His lumpish face. His high colour and bad skin. His still adolescent awkwardness and dangerous sullenness.

She wondered what to do.

Reilly took his hand from her breast and trailed it downwards, across her stomach, under the waistband of her pyjamas. He laughed and breathed fast. His body trembled, a little out of control.

With both hands, he then unfastened his belt and lowered the jeans over his hips.

She knew, without looking, that he must be hard and already close to ejaculation. She thought if she reached out and took him in her hand she might bring him off quickly, without having to take him on top of her and inside her.

Before she could move, before Reilly could step from his jeans, they heard a noise outside. Footsteps on the floorboards. The click of a light switch. And then the unlocked door being roughly handled and thrown open, spilling light from the landing outside.

Sean McDaid, holding an automatic pistol in his right hand,

stood there in the doorway.

McDaid looked, but said nothing. With his free left hand he reached across to flick the light switch and flood the bedroom with harsh, naked light. But then thought better of indulging himself with that.

He walked across to the bed. His look downwards at Jennifer Crooks's naked breasts was so blackened with repulsion that she felt self-disgust, felt somehow to blame, and she scrambled to drag the covers back over her.

Reilly, though, his jeans around his ankles like manacles, still kept an almost defiant erection.

McDaid walked around the bed and put the cold muzzle of the automatic against Reilly's penis, until the flesh gave way to the steel and shrunk, smaller than what might've left Reilly with a trace of dignity.

'Now get out,' McDaid told him coldly.

Reilly bent to pull up his jeans, but his face came against McDaid's rising pistol and he straightened again.

'Out,' McDaid repeated.

So Reilly, simmering with hatred, with resentment, reversed from the bed with the jeans and underpants still restricting his legs. By the time he was clear enough to dress himself again, there were tears in his eyes.

Jennifer Crooks, not wanting to witness the boy's humiliation or McDaid's cruelty, kept her own eyes closed.

She heard McDaid ask icily, 'Why couldn't you lock your door tonight?'

He waited a moment and then said, 'Do it when I'm gone.' Before turning to leave.

Jennifer Crooks felt sick when she got up to do as he'd said. Physically sick. She felt as if she'd been abused. Twice.

10

There'd been silence for a while in the minister's office. Except for Rawlings's pencil tapping lightly on the surface of his desk.

'You mentioned a reliable source within the prison, sir,' Superintendent Gilston said then. 'Did you mean an inmate, sir? A paid informer?'

Rawlings nodded. 'Yes.'

'Was his information considered reliable at the time, three months ago?'

'Yes.'

'But there was no attempt to escape at that period?'

'No, none.'

'Who is running this man, sir?'

'I am,' June Maybury said.

Gilston swivelled, his eyes narrowing. 'Have you questioned him about McDaid's plans?'

'I can't.'

'Why not?'

'Because he's one of the four who escaped tonight. His name is William Barr.'

Gilston slapped his thigh with impatience, with exasperation.

Rawlings said coldly, dampening Gilston's irritation, 'As I mentioned earlier, Geoffrey, and you may recall the occasion, two of the prisoners should not have escaped. One of these was William Barr.'

'And the other is –'

'Denis Reilly, yes,' Rawlings confirmed. 'A very dangerous young man. Violent, resentful. Perhaps beyond McDaid's control. Apparently his commitment to the IRA's cause is no longer taken for granted. An extremely volatile group, as you can see.'

'And more dangerous because of it,' Gilston remarked gloomily.

Rawlings nodded. He said, 'There is, on the other hand, every possibility, since his escape was unplanned, that William Barr will contact us with information on the group's whereabouts at the earliest opportunity. Every possibility.'

'Also,' June Maybury went on, 'I don't quite agree that McDaid himself is the only one who knows of the explosives and the location for the target. I gather from previous conversations with Barr that McDaid is apprehensive about both his own brother, Dixie, and a former associate of his in Northern Ireland named Tommy Brennan.'

'Dixie McDaid?' Gilston repeated derisively. 'Living here in London?'

'Yes.'

Gilston shook his head. 'The man knows nothing of recent IRA operations. He was placed under surveillance by us after his brother's arrest last year. Nothing of any value was discovered.'

'Six months ago,' June Maybury said, 'he came to visit Sean in prison for the first time. Did you know that?'

'He was not under surveillance by us at the time.'

'Quite,' she agreed coldly. 'The visit must have been by some prior, long-standing arrangement. Sean was in hospital that week. Dixie spoke to Barr instead. The impression Barr got was that some plan was still operational, that nothing had changed. No details, of course.'

'A merely personal note,' Gilston dismissed it.

'Nevertheless,' June Maybury said, 'I would like to question Dixie McDaid. I would also like the RUC Special Branch to question this Tommy Brennan in Northern Ireland.'

Rawlings was nodding, but cautiously. He said, 'To avoid

37

precipitating supporting action from dissidents within the IRA, it has been decided not to release news of the prisoners' escape just yet.'

For once, Gilston and Maybury were in agreement, opposed to this. Both started to object.

'Or rather,' Rawlings hurried on, 'since we cannot possibly conceal or otherwise explain the manhunt in the area, it will shortly be announced that two non-IRA prisoners have escaped from the special secure unit. I need not remind you that this is rather a delicate gamble. Nor do I need to stress that we cannot be seen, even by our own constabulary, in the act of arresting or questioning someone like Sean McDaid's brother.'

Gilston had been the more restless. He said now, 'Personally, sir –'

'The question is,' Rawlings continued, 'can you do it discreetly, June. Have a chat with Dixie McDaid.'

'Yes, sir. But –'

'Personally, sir . . .' Gilston said again.

'And can you liaise with the RUC, Geoffrey? About this Brennan chap. Discreetly, too. Use a personal contact.'

'Yes, of course, but –'

'Good. Excellent.'

'But personally, sir,' Gilston persisted, 'I believe our superior chance of averting the danger lies in recapturing the escaped prisoners by committing all available resources to the continuing search.'

'But of course,' Rawlings soothed. 'Of course you must throw everything into the search. But I also have an interest in this Dixie McDaid and this Brennan chap. As . . . What shall I say? As *supplementary* chances. Can we see irreconcilable incompatibility there? Eh? June?'

'No, sir,' June Maybury agreed.

'Geoffrey?'

'No, sir.'

'Good,' Rawlings purred. 'Excellent. Recapturing the four terrorists and preventing them reaching their target are your only concerns. We must forget old rivalries, eh? Co-operation. Do I make myself clear?'

June Maybury nodded, but without looking at the Special Branch man. 'Yes, sir.'

Gilston frowned. But added, 'It would help, sir, if we had some clues to point us towards their target.'

Rawlings sniffed. He said, 'Ah!' Rather miserably.

'We know what McDaid's target is,' June Maybury said.

'We?' Gilston repeated. 'I presume you mean your section in MI5.'

'I'm no longer attached to the Irish desk, Superintendent.'

'Miss Maybury has been seconded, Geoffrey.'

'Then I presume your meaning is that you favour a certain theory.'

'I'm afraid we do know,' Rawlings put in quickly. 'Have done for more than six months, in fact. Since Dixie McDaid spoke to Barr in prison. Has no one told you, Geoffrey?'

Gilston bristled. 'No.'

'Ah!' Rawlings said again.

'Might I be permitted to ask what it is, sir?'

'Yes,' Rawlings said slowly. 'Yes. McDaid's objective, you see, is not really to challenge Her Majesty's Government, but rather to provoke Her Majesty's subjects. If he succeeds, no Irish person will be safe in England, no nationalist safe in Northern Ireland. We are talking, Geoffrey, about importing the conflict in Ulster into the mainland.'

'Yes, sir,' Gilston put in impatiently. 'But what is McDaid's target?'

Someone knocked just then, very lightly, on the office door. Rawlings coughed and sat back in his chair to call out, 'Come in!' Gilston sighed with irritation.

A tall young man, a thin smile on his plump, aristocratic face, opened the door and stepped in.

Rawlings said, 'Ah! Do you know David Bromley, Geoffrey? One of our bright young officers in, ah, T Branch. Ashby-Newcombe is on winter holidays, would you believe? Have you met before? David, this is Superintendent Gilston. Special Branch.'

'How d'you do,' Gilston said brusquely. He turned immediately to Rawlings again. He said, 'McDaid's target, sir. What is it?'

Rawlings glanced uneasily from Maybury to Bromley.

'It's the Queen, Geoffrey,' he said then. 'Her Majesty, the Queen. And as many others of the Royal Family as happen to be with her at the time.'

PART TWO

Wednesday

ONE

1

Five minutes out of his flat in the centre of Kilburn, Dixie McDaid knew that someone was tailing him.

He'd crossed the road after coming through the street door, picked up a paper from the news-stand opposite and hardly glanced at the well-dressed drunk slumped in the nearby doorway.

Drunks. He hated drunks.

Not even the dark-haired Irish girl in the flat next door to him, Mary Cassidy, who went on soup runs to the hostels and even fed the tramps and the beggars in her own home, could soften his disgust.

Because Dixie's old man had hocked the farm in Northern Ireland to stay on the juice and had driven his wife and kids into mean estates in West Belfast.

And in 1972, when Dixie was six years old and his brother Sean only twelve, their mother was killed by a loyalist gunman.

So Dixie glared at this soak only long enough to sneer. And then moved on, down Kilburn High Road, stopping at the greengrocer's stall before the tube station and looking over the neat rows of fruits and vegetables into the shop window.

And finding the same drunk's reflection in the glass right

behind his own.

Dixie had *moved* along those five hundred metres between stand and shop.

It was seven-fifteen on a dark winter morning and there was this sharp south-easterly keeping the air temperature close to freezing. You were talking about *effort* to keep yourself warm. You were talking about a walking pace of five miles an hour.

And yet the drunk, out on his feet a few minutes earlier, had matched him all the way, step for step, junction for junction.

The guy was young, Dixie noticed. Maybe twenty-five years old. No more than thirty. Big. Powerful.

The look he was after said he'd had too long and too rough a night in some classy night-club. The shirt collar open. The creases deep behind the knees of his grey suit's trousers. The woollen overcoat stained with booze at the hem.

Dixie wondered who had sent him.

He took a brown paper bag from the pile on the greengrocer's stall and started filling it with Gala apples, taking his time, checking the fruit for colour and shape and bruises, working on his options all the time.

He didn't know the greengrocer's name and would've put money on the Indian couple who owned the shop being just as ignorant of his. But they all did a little business together every morning. And they chewed the fat for a minute or two, bad-mouthing the weather in Belfast and the climate in Delhi.

If Dixie asked to use the shop's toilet and rear exit, they wouldn't turn him down.

But it wasn't his style, Dixie decided, turning his back on the trouble. Putting it off to another day.

The drunk knew where he lived, anyway. He'd just sit there, holding the advantage, waiting on his chance.

Just as the shopkeeper came from inside to stand beside him on the pathway, Dixie made up his mind. He tipped the apples from the paper bag back on to the stall again. Did it

44

carelessly, mixing the Galas with Granny Smiths and Pippins and Stark Crimsons. Not thinking of anything except keeping his fists free.

But the Indian put a hand on Dixie's arm to hold him. And then the Indian laughed and said, 'It is a soft day. This is what I am thinking. It is correct?'

Dixie looked coldly at the brown hand on his sleeve. He took it away with two fingers and pressed the crumpled paper bag into it.

'In Northern Ireland, son,' he said, 'it's only a soft day when it's been pissing for sixteen hours.'

He swung violently away, brushing past the startled shop-keeper.

Turning to cross the road again at Kilburn tube station, he looked back sharply to catch the drunk off guard. Easy, really. The guy still striding after him for a second, pumping the arms and legs, before lapsing back to a stagger.

While the drunk was down like that, Dixie suddenly upped his own pace and stretched the gap between them.

Ten years ago, he'd had a programme for dealing with tails like this. All right, he argued with himself. He'd been twenty years of age. And always armed. And always on his home patch in Belfast.

But still, he thought, the trick might serve another twist.

Dixie laughed. Remembering the trick.

Across the road from the tube station there was a narrow cul-de-sac called Coventry Close. Still laughing, Dixie hurried through and slipped away, into the darkness of the first doorway. Not making the running any more. Leaving the question with the hunter now. Was it a bluff? Or was there another way out?

Dixie waited, the entrance to the Close like a high and narrow screen to him, watching it for an image of the drunk's grey overcoat and suit in the early morning crowds out on

45

Kilburn High Road.

Except it was a sound that hit him first.

And when it came, it took him from behind.

A second before, Dixie had sensed a presence all right. Something back there the other side of his right shoulder. Something that'd moved stealthily and was now still.

A second. That was all.

Thinking it was an animal, a cat prowling around the rubbish bins and now stiff with fear, he hadn't turned to check it out immediately. Not wanting to take his eyes from the scene in front.

Until this rich Ulster voice, this voice used to being heard and heeded, summoned him quietly.

'Dixie McDaid!'

Dixie swivelled, his face flashing through a beam of orange light that shone from somewhere, surprise and fear and anger in his eyes.

Two men, both dressed in blue jeans and dark jackets, stood there on the pathway, a little out of his reach.

One had this sparse, carefully trimmed beard and was raising his pallid hands, the palms outwards, saying he wanted calm and reason and quietness.

The other guy, taller and clean-shaven, kept his right hand inside the breast of his black LA Raiders jacket, resting on the handle of the gun that was going to bring them the calm and the quiet and the reason.

'Dixie McDaid,' the guy with the beard said again.

It wasn't a question. It was a gloat.

Dixie moved a little, trying to line up the beard between himself and the gun.

Two of them, he thought. Maybe a third if the drunk joins in.

He raised his hands and settled back, hitting a defensive pose.

46

Just as a grey Volvo rolled around the corner from Kilburn High Road and eased up beside the little group.

'Have a bit of sense, Dixie,' the guy with the beard said. 'Don't even try anything. Just get in the car.'

'Go and fuck yourselves, lads,' Dixie invited.

'Nobody's going to hurt you, Dixie. You know who we are.'

'Never saw you before.'

'Just get in the car, Dixie. You'll be back home before lunch.'

'What if I don't?'

The guy with the beard sighed. He opened the rear door of the Volvo to his right. To his left, a little behind him, the one with the Raiders jacket showed the butt of the revolver inside.

Dixie shrugged.

Surrounded. Outnumbered. Outgunned.

He had to take his chances with that promise of safety, he decided. Because right now, here in the cul-de-sac, he didn't have any chance at all.

He stooped to get through the rear door of the Volvo and slid along its back seat, pushing up close against another of the gang who'd already been sitting there.

The guy with the gun came quickly after him, boxing him in.

The one with the sparse beard took the front passenger seat.

'Mind telling me what the story is, lads?' Dixie asked.

No one answered as the Volvo reversed into Kilburn High Road and drove north-west through Cricklewood and Willesden and headed out of London on the M1.

2

The drunk in the classy suit back on Kilburn High Road.

He was David Bromley, from MI5's Counter-Terrorism T Branch.

And things hadn't been flowing his way that morning.

He'd followed Dixie McDaid from the news-stand to the greengrocer's, making himself conspicuous all the way, just as he'd been ordered to by June Maybury.

Not much liking his own clownish role in the game. And not having a lot that was good to say about the overall plan it was a part of.

But it wasn't his call.

Today, he was just the bait on the hook.

Maybury had told him that Dixie would take a swing at him as soon as he tried to touch him for a couple of quid.

'Rather left myself without the taxi fare home, you see.'

That was Bromley's line.

Making Dixie lose the rag.

And then Bromley's support, two Special Branch officers dressed as constables in a nearby car, would simply arrest the drunk and the scrapping Irishman and bundle them both into the car and drive away, all to the amazement of absolutely no one who happened to be on Kilburn High Road at the time, and to the interest of even less.

Nice and neat, Maybury had promised. No raids. No fuss. No questions from worried neighbours who lived in the same house as Dixie McDaid. No attention. No publicity.

And totally up front as well, Rawlings had crowed. No mysterious disappearance. No nocturnal visits. Just picked up

48

being disorderly.

But Bromley hadn't even managed to get a cold paw from his pocket to shove it out for alms.

Instead, Dixie McDaid had wheeled away from him and raced down Kilburn High Road, forcing Bromley into a near sprint and his back-up in the car into a ludicrous pursuit in second gear through heavy traffic.

A comic routine.

Dropping quickly into farce as Dixie cut back across the road by the tube station and disappeared in a cul-de-sac, leaving Bromley wondering if he should follow him in, act the totally committed drunk in pursuit of a touch, or wait for his return, holding on to a kind of *laissez-faire* position in the practice of vagrancy.

Not wondering very long, though.

A minute more and this grey Volvo was in and out of the cul-de-sac and driving north-west, away from central London, with Dixie McDaid wedged on the back seat between two heavies.

They were lucky then, Bromley and his Special Branch detectives.

Because they'd had trouble changing direction in Kilburn. And if the Volvo had turned anywhere between that and Edgware, they would've lost it.

But it didn't. Stayed straight as the road itself. And they caught sight of it again, still on the A5, at Burnt Oak.

'Get Miss Maybury on the radio,' Bromley had ordered.

With relief.

3

One night of freedom, Sean McDaid thought bitterly, and they were already falling to bits.

Already four separate strains instead of a unit.

And all because of the woman again, McDaid decided.

For some reason, without offering them a signal, Jennifer Crooks had left for work that morning before making them their breakfast. She hadn't come to the attic. She hadn't brought them the portable radio.

So they were all edgy now. Reilly. And Woolly Barr. And Boyce. Even McDaid himself.

Edgy and dangerous. Not knowing whether it was safe to go down from the attic or not.

Some of them wondering a bit about Jennifer Crooks, whether to trust her, whether she was going to shop them or save them.

None of them wondering more than Danny Boyce.

Like all big men who were led by their hearts, McDaid thought, Boyce worried when things missed a beat.

Boyce had his own reasons for concern, though. Unknown to Sean McDaid.

By now, he reckoned, his wife would've heard of his escape. She'd be getting herself ready to travel to Dublin with their daughter.

But he knew that it might kill her, if things went badly for the three of them again.

Deirdre Boyce suffered darkly from depression and had already tried to take her own life while her husband was in prison.

50

'When was she put here, Sean?' Boyce asked anxiously now. 'Jennifer Crooks. I mean, it must've been long before the ceasefire was called, was it?'

McDaid, his dead blue eyes checking out his own reflection in a small mirror, waved the thought aside. 'Don't worry about it, Danny.'

'Was it, though?' Boyce persisted.

'Of course it was.'

'So how do we know whose side she's on now, Sean?'

Boyce hesitated, knowing that he was playing a delicate role. He had to be careful.

He said, 'How do we know she's not going to sell us out to the fuckers who won't even shit on the boots of a squaddy these days? How do we know she's with us?'

McDaid, too tense to argue, decided that he needed a shave, even though the water was cold and the growth of hair light on his face.

In the silence, Denis Reilly watched him gather lather from the soap bar on to his hands and then apply it to his cheeks.

Watched him bitterly.

Reilly himself wasn't shaving properly yet. The few times he'd tried it, the blades had cut and scorched his dry skin.

And besides, Reilly was thinking of the previous night, of another reason why Jennifer Crooks might want to betray them that morning.

He imagined he could see the same thought in McDaid's mocking blue eyes.

He said suddenly, 'I say we get out of here. Right now. Before they come looking for us. We're sitting ducks here. What do you say, Danny?'

Boyce shook his head. He knew that their only hope of escape lay with ditching Sean McDaid's meticulous plan at the right time. And he knew that this wasn't the time.

Above all, though, he knew that Reilly, wild and unreliable, wasn't the card to take a chance on.

He said, 'You're not in command here, Denis.'

Reilly turned away from him with disdain. 'What about you, Woolly?'

Woolly Barr had had a bad sleep the night before, dropping off into nightmares that jerked him awake again in the sweats.

And now the odours in the cramped space were getting to him. Reilly's bad breath. Boyce's heavy perspiration. And always something sweeter thrown in, aftershave or deodorant, from McDaid.

It sickened him, every time someone moved in the crowded attic.

He wanted away. And not only from the attic.

He said, 'We'd have to split up, wouldn't we?' Stuttering over the next bit, because he meant the opposite. 'I mean, it's the only way we're going to make it.'

McDaid drew the razor down his jaw, from earlobe to chin, and said quietly, 'We stay. Stay here. Stay with the plan.'

'Plan?' Reilly repeated derisively.

He put his hand on the .38 revolver in the pocket of his jacket. Feeling powerful again. Hoping McDaid might make the same move with his automatic that he'd made the night before.

With his left hand, he tossed a newspaper away from him, showing his disdain.

'Plan?' he said again. 'What fucking plan? You haven't told us what the plan is.'

'There's still a cordon around this area,' McDaid said.

Reilly snorted. 'I'll take my chances with that.'

'You wouldn't even reach it,' McDaid told him.

'What the fuck's that supposed to mean?'

'Sort it out yourself. One way or the other, you'll leave this attic when I say so. Not before.'

'Sean is in command here, Denis,' Boyce came in dutifully.

Making it sound like a touchstone to himself. The dumb loyalty giving him the right to ask again, 'But what about the woman, Sean? Jennifer Crooks. She was supposed to signal us this morning.'

McDaid carefully worked with the razor on his stretched upper lip. Thinking.

'Someone must've called her on the way to work,' he said.

'The buzzer didn't sound.'

'A neighbour, Danny. They knock on windows. She'll be back.'

'Who with?' Reilly asked with a sneer. 'Half the British Army? Or the other half of the IRA?'

Reilly went to answer his own question, but they heard the telephone then from the living-room, two floors below them. The sound was faint. But unmistakable.

McDaid held the razor poised over his left cheek and listened intently, counting the tones. When it passed five and kept on ringing, he put the blade back to his flesh, his muscles tense with disappointment, and nicked himself painfully.

Not Dixie, he realised.

He towelled his face and washed the razor, wondering where the hell his brother was, why the hell Dixie hadn't yet made contact.

He looked at Woolly Barr. And saw in Woolly's shifty eyes the same thought, but a different fear.

He said, 'The last time you saw Dixie, Woolly. When he came to visit. Did he mention anything about this house?'

4

All his adult life, Jody Stafford had had the same hairstyle. Cut fairly short and combed back off his forehead without a parting.

The way James Dean used to wear his.

Funny thing, Stafford thought. Sean McDaid had had the same hairstyle all his life too. Trimmed short and naturally curled.

Even as a twelve-year-old kid, when he'd come with Dixie to live at their aunt's house after their mother had been killed, and Stafford, twenty at the time and living in the same Belfast street, had taken him under his wing.

Stafford, suffering with a cold, maybe even the early aches of flu, put away the memories of twenty years and got up from the armchair he was sitting in. He stood in front of the fire to warm himself, deciding to put in the rest of the wait there.

Stafford was tired that morning.

He hadn't slept the night before, driving down from Manchester to Hertfordshire to get to this isolated farmhouse deep in the English countryside. And he'd already put in too many meetings and too much argument in too short a time. Activists in London who wanted the ceasefire to end. Sympathisers who prayed it would last.

He felt dangerously confused.

He didn't have to wait long now, though.

Nine o'clock, he heard the Volvo rolling over the frosted gravel in the driveway outside and then its doors opening and closing.

Stafford went to sit in the armchair again then, just as Junior

54

Doherty came in with Dixie McDaid, closing the living-room door behind them and standing there on guard.

Stafford gestured Dixie into the armchair opposite. He didn't get up himself.

He said, 'How've you been keeping, Dixie? Since the last time I saw you.'

Dixie didn't move, didn't say anything.

The fact was, Dixie could *smell* his own fear since coming through the door.

He'd crossed his arms, his hands clasping at where they'd been broken by Stafford three years before. Not even knowing he was doing it.

And now he was stuck like that, desperately trying to figure it out, what the hell Jody Stafford could want him for again.

The last guy on earth he'd expected to see that morning.

The last one he *wanted* to see.

'Sit down, Dixie,' Stafford said.

Just as Junior Doherty pushed from behind. *His* way of communicating the same invitation.

Dixie shuffled across and sat, tense and wary.

Stafford said, 'Has your hearing been damaged, Dixie? Since the last time I saw you.'

'What?' Dixie asked.

And sniggered nervously.

It was like a joke.

Has your hearing been damaged? What?

'I asked how you were feeling,' Stafford said.

'Oh, fine, you know. I'm feeling fine.'

'Seen any of the old comrades lately?'

Dixie shook his head. 'No, no one. Not from back home.'

'What about Martin Hughes?'

'Oh, Martin, right. Martin dropped in a few months back.'

'Expecting to see anyone?'

'Like who?'

55

'Anyone.'

'You mean someone from back home? Someone I know from Northern Ireland?'

'Could be. You want to tell me?'

Dixie didn't answer that one, *sensing* something now, something more than his own fear.

Because *Stafford* was nervous, too. Stafford was probing instead of threatening. He was questioning instead of ordering. He was just talking, not *doing* anything.

And the only thing Dixie had ever known to make Jody Stafford nervous . . .

Dixie tensed, guessing the answer.

He swallowed, his mouth suddenly full of saliva, and said faintly, 'It's Sean, isn't it?'

Wondering if his brother was out. If he was dead. What the hell was happening.

There was nothing on the news.

Every day the last six months, Dixie had caught the major bulletins. Waiting for news of a break.

'Sean?' Stafford was repeating. 'What makes you say that, Dixie?'

'I don't know. It just . . .'

Dixie laughed, but couldn't help glancing at his watch.

If Sean was out, Dixie should've made that phone call more than half an hour ago.

But he hadn't known. It wasn't on the news.

Why hadn't they publicised the break? If Sean was out.

Stafford was looking at him, wondering why he was silent.

He said, 'It's just, I mean, three years back, when you put me in the hospital, Sean came in to see me. He said you'd wanted me shot. Right?'

'Go on.'

'When I asked him why you didn't, I mean, do it, he told me it was because of him. So I thought, you know, this has to

56

be something to do with Sean. This now. That's all.'

Over by the doorway, Doherty shifted on his feet. Restless. Impatient.

Dixie glanced nervously across at him. He could tell what was on their minds.

Sweating now, stumbling a bit over the words, he said, 'I should've known it was you, Jody.'

'This is how it is, Dixie,' Stafford began.

'No, you see –'

'I won't bullshit you, Dixie. It won't be baseball bats this time. It won't be just broken arms. Junior over there spent his teens in a bakery, so he's had a lot of practice with burns. Okay?'

'Jesus, Jody –'

'So let's hear it, Dixie. All about Sean.'

'No, Jody, what I was saying, you see, I mean back there in Kilburn. You knew, didn't you, that I'd head for the dead end with the drunk tailing me? You were already waiting there.'

Stafford frowned.

'Drunk?' he wondered. 'Tailing you? You're dreaming, Dixie.'

'For Christ sake, Jody . . .'

So Stafford was shaking his head, blackly amused by this drunk, this idea of being tailed by a drunk, when someone hit the front doorbell from outside.

Someone who hadn't been expected.

Someone who'd taken care to kill the headlights on their car while approaching the isolated farmhouse.

Dixie whispered, 'Jody . . .'

'Shut up!' Stafford hissed.

'Jody –'

Over by the door, Junior Doherty whipped a flick-knife from his pocket and pressed the button to snap open the blade.

And after that everything was silent.

Until the front doorbell rang again.

57

5

The darkness had been slow to lift that winter morning.

Even at nine-fifteen, sitting in the car outside the farmhouse a couple of miles west of Radlett village, David Bromley had trouble following the movements of June Maybury through the heavy mist.

She'd joined him from London less than ten minutes before, asked for a briefing in the car itself, then left him again to walk across the damp footpath.

And now she was ringing the bell on the front door of the farmhouse.

Bromley peered at her anxiously through the mist, still not thinking much of the way this operation was going.

There were, he reckoned, at least four men inside that farmhouse. And probably all of them were armed.

Bromley himself still had only two others for support. And even they had separated. One to the rear of the house. One to the side, where a dirt track from a recent extension led through the fields to the main road.

More were on the way, of course.

But when would they get there, Bromley wondered.

Before or after Maybury got herself shot or captured?

Before or after the IRA men escaped again with Dixie McDaid?

6

Jody Stafford had come to the front room of the farmhouse, waiting for the doorbell to ring again.

Wondering who the hell was outside.

Hardly a raid, he thought. You never knew. But hardly. They wouldn't politely announce themselves.

The doorbell rang again.

This time it was longer, more impatient, the caller keeping a finger on the button for more than ten seconds, saying that they knew there was someone in there, they weren't leaving without being admitted.

'Open it,' Stafford ordered.

Crawley, one of the two IRA men guarding the front, pulled the bolt and let the opening door swing towards him, concealing him behind it.

Stafford, half expecting a rush of policemen, preparing himself for that, was caught off guard.

Only a woman stood there in the doorway.

But the image she made, framed by the door and with the dull light of the misty winter morning behind her, brought his mind hurtling backwards.

Four years ago.

An underground cell in an RUC station in Northern Ireland.

Stafford not knowing what time it was, whether it was day or night. Not knowing how long they'd held him for, how long they'd been questioning him, how long he'd gone without sleep. But a long, long time.

Every so often, in the middle of one of their questions, or

while one of them was shouting at him, threatening him, he'd drop off, still sitting upright at the table. They'd thrown icy water over him to keep him going. Or McIver, the worst of the RUC Special Branch men, had jerked his head backwards, tearing at his hair.

But Stafford hadn't broken. Hadn't even thought of it.

Until the door opened suddenly and this woman stood there, the light from the hallway bulb directly behind her.

The same woman who stood in front of him now.

She'd stayed in the doorway, flanked by two RUC police-women, while his interrogation continued.

'Your shoe prints were all over that hill, Stafford,' McIver had said again. It was this voice, sharp and superior and con-temptuous, that Stafford always recalled. 'We have the pair you wore.'

'There's no problem with identification.'

'Even the soil matches. The same soil we found on Sean McDaid's shoes.'

'McDaid is planning a split, by the way,' McIver whispered. 'Did you know that? The rest of you are not sectarian enough for him.'

'And Bill Enright's shoes. And Philip Ganley's.'

'They were all on the operation with you.'

'And now they're all in here.'

'With you.'

'And McDaid is hanging you, Stafford.'

'McDaid is talking. Can't stop talking.'

'Same as a certain tart you might recognise,' McIver had sneered.

'How else could we know so much? Enright was wounded, wasn't he? Nicked in the arm.'

Stafford had found himself thinking of objections then, instead of leaving his mind blank. The shoes he'd worn on the ambush were mass produced. They didn't have distinctive

60

markings. And the soil was common to many areas.

The woman's presence in the doorway was distracting him, eating away at his self-confidence.

If they'd brought her in to confront him, he might've cracked. But they didn't. And he'd survived.

They'd put him on trial after that interrogation. But the charges hadn't stuck and he was free again a couple of months later, long before he was needed to supervise the breaking of Dixie McDaid's arms and his expulsion from Northern Ireland.

Only Stafford himself had been tried. They'd never picked up the others, McDaid and Enright and Ganley. All bluff.

Ganley was dead a week later, though. Enright skipped to London and went underground. McDaid they put away for a short stretch on a minor charge about two years afterwards.

The best and most efficient active service unit in Northern Ireland just didn't exist any more.

Destroyed by a woman called June Maybury.

That same woman who stepped in through the open farmhouse door now and walked forward to stand in front of him.

She hadn't changed much, he noticed. Physically, anyway. Her hair was still jet-black and closely cropped, still looking a little punkish in style. Her clothes were as casual as ever.

Not what you'd expect from an MI5 agent.

How old was she now? Thirty-five? Thirty-six?

But he had to stop thinking of her like that, he told himself. As a woman.

7

Denis Reilly, smirking at the thought of another needle to toy with, finally made his play.

The thought of what had happened the night before was still eating him up. The thought that Jennifer Crooks might've ratted on them because she'd turned up her prim little English nose at him was like acid in his stomach as well. And her unexplained absence was just a constant reminder, just a constant taunt.

He had to do something, had to open the valves.

Sean McDaid had put away his shaving gear and was brushing imaginary dirt from the sleeve of his jacket.

The telephone had stopped ringing downstairs.

And Woolly Barr still hadn't answered McDaid's question about Dixie.

Reilly said to McDaid, 'Your brother. Dixie, right? I heard he was just a small-time punk with a big mouth that Jody Stafford shut for him. Maybe it runs in the family.'

Woolly Barr, sitting right between the pair in that terrible atmosphere, felt suddenly cold, suddenly exposed.

These two madmen either side of him had guns.

Reilly had his *hand* on his own revolver, Woolly saw. Right now.

McDaid's automatic was out of reach, lying on the floor to his right. But he was moving to it. Disguising the approach. Fiddling with the plastic pouch he'd put the shaving gear in.

Chances were, though, Woolly thought, that big Danny Boyce would throw his hat in the ring before the pistol was in McDaid's hands.

Boyce, lying on his sleeping bag behind Reilly, was getting ready to land his weight on the youngster's back.

But McDaid said quietly, 'Stay out of it, Danny.'

As Reilly's eyes flicked backwards to check on Boyce, McDaid's hand slipped closer to the automatic without being noticed.

McDaid said softly, drawing Reilly's attention back to his face, 'This is what prison does to you, Reilly. You think the routine is keeping you in shape. You think you're still a fighting soldier. But you're not. You've got to learn it all again.'

Reilly thought about it. But not too deeply. He knew that thinking could cost you your life.

He'd bought it all before, of course, when he was a kid, less than sixteen years old. The idea of all those certainties. A cause. An army. A unit. Comrades together.

He'd come from a slum, with holes in the soles of his sneakers and nothing to wear under his ragged jeans. They'd given him a gun. And a few basic orders. And people had looked up to him.

It was over, though.

Because now – and he didn't care what McDaid had to say, what McDaid's intentions were – the IRA wanted to give him back to the slum. They needed politicians these days, not gunmen any more.

And of course, as he thought about the past, the memory of the previous night came back to him too.

So he took the revolver from his jacket and pointed its muzzle at McDaid's groin and gave a cracked, edgy laugh.

McDaid's automatic was still slightly out of reach.

Woolly Barr was stiff with fear, knowing he'd be the first casualty in any cross-fire.

So when Danny Boyce moved suddenly behind Reilly, Woolly jerked uncontrollably and dived backwards out of the firing line.

He didn't see Boyce laying a hand on the barrel of Reilly's revolver and forcing it slowly downwards.

Although he heard him saying urgently, 'Listen!'

From somewhere below them, outside the house, there came the sounds of an engine in reverse and heavy tyres manoeuvring in a small space.

'Land Rover,' Boyce whispered. 'Some sort of four by four, anyway.'

Because he knew his vehicles.

'What do you think?' McDaid asked. 'Police?'

Reilly laughed at the thought.

Boyce prayed, forgetting to answer McDaid, and thinking only of his wife on a wasted journey through Dublin to France to have hope crushed in her.

8

Standing a little to the side of the open front door at the farm-house, Crawley looked in astonishment, his mouth hanging, at the bitterness on the faces of his commanding officer and the woman who had just walked in.

'I was told there wasn't going to be any interference from you,' Stafford snapped.

'Interference?' June Maybury repeated. 'You're in England, not Dublin.'

'I was told –'

'I wasn't told what you were told, nor by whom,' Maybury interrupted. 'You were allowed to re-enter the mainland on the understanding that you travel on a military flight accompanied by your liaison officer and that you report to me for orders.'

Stafford shook his head. 'I don't take orders from the British security forces. I don't report to them, either.'

'Then you're in breach of the agreement.'

'Tie me down,' Stafford invited contemptuously.

'Not for that.'

'What do I have to do to you?'

'Perhaps for the abduction of Dixie McDaid, however. Where is McDaid? Have you already questioned him? What information has he given you?'

'You couldn't get anything out of me four years ago in a –'

'That's a matter of opinion.'

'Name it! Say what you got!'

'Part of a successful technique is to leave your victim with the impression that nothing has been conceded.'

Stafford scoffed. 'You *got* nothing! And you're hardly going to manage it now.'

'Let's make something clear about our respective roles in this affair,' Maybury said. 'Since we both want Sean McDaid back in prison –'

Stafford was already shaking his head. 'You don't understand,' he said.

'Back in prison –' she repeated.

'Look,' he said. 'We have a long history back in Ireland.'

'I've lived part of it.'

'With your eyes closed.'

'On the contrary. I never close my eyes.'

'Don't fucking annoy me. When you have a few spare hours some time I'll sit down and explain the basics of our history to you in monosyllables.'

'Don't be childish!'

'But this will do for the moment.'

'Can't you understand –'

'We don't work to put our own people in English prisons,' he shouted above her. 'Because we don't accept your claim

65

to jurisdiction. We have our own courts.'

'And your own sentences,' Maybury put in angrily. 'Such as breaking limbs.'

Stafford ignored her again. 'I'll put this the way you'll understand it,' he said.

'You must have brought a baseball bat with you, then. Have you?'

'There are no native Indian scouts in Ireland any more,' he said. 'None that we haven't already dealt with, anyway.'

The telephone rang in the living-room where Junior Doherty was holding Dixie McDaid and keeping him quiet.

Crawley, who'd eventually closed the front door and been standing on guard there, now moved carefully past the pair to take the call.

Stafford was saying, 'Sean McDaid belongs to us when we find him. I've already told this to your superiors. There is no other situation in which we'll help you track him down.'

June Maybury dismissed the idea with a flick of the wrist. 'The answer is a categorical no.'

'It's not a request.'

'I'm afraid the position does not allow us time for such postures, Stafford.'

'It's not a posture, either.'

'You simply have no idea what you're dealing with here.'

'Jesus,' Stafford said. 'You'd have thought that after twenty-five years you wouldn't keep making the same mistake of underestimating our intelligence.'

'It's not your intelligence I have a low opinion of. It's your control of your own organisation.'

'Listen, lady. I know exactly what we're dealing with.'

'You always did, didn't you?'

'Sean McDaid came over here to assassinate your Queen,' Stafford said. 'He broke prison to finish the job.'

Crawley came back from the living-room, carrying a

folded note.

Stafford took the paper and opened it.

It said that Tommy Brennan in Belfast had discovered Sean McDaid's safe house. It didn't say how exactly, but it had Jennifer Crooks's address in the village close to the prison.

Stafford, still wondering how exactly he was going to play this game, but determined to play it alone, without the clumsy hand of MI5, went back to the living-room and tossed the crumpled note into the flames of the open fire.

Just as June Maybury was walking towards him with her hand outstretched.

9

Jody Stafford's melodramatic gesture was wasted, though.

Three minutes after it was made, David Bromley picked up the mouthpiece of the car radio in response to an excited summons from a listener in MI5 Headquarters.

'Is that you, David? Are you there?'

Bromley was already feeling cold, sitting without heat in the stationary car. And he was irritable.

'Use the proper procedures, Grant,' he snapped.

Karen Grant, he thought bitterly. One of Maybury's people.

'Sorry, yeah. Okay. Ah . . .'

The rustling of paper could be heard as she searched for the call sign.

'Oh, get on with it!' Bromley interrupted impatiently. 'What is it?'

'Incoming call to the target,' Grant told him.

'Already?'

'Connection at 9.32. Duration ninety-five seconds. Source

of origin, Belfast, Northern Ireland. Caller was a Mr Tommy
Brennan, who identified himself –'

'What did he *say*?' Bromley demanded.

'He said he'd got the address of the safe house McDaid and
the others are using near the prison.'

'What is it? Have you checked it out? Does it have a telephone number?'

Bromley glanced at his watch as he wrote the details. It was
almost nine-forty by then.

He wouldn't interrupt Maybury in the farmhouse with the
news, he decided. He'd wait for her return. Grant would pass
the information on to Superintendent Gilston in the meantime, of course, and let Special Branch take it from there.

Bromley waited more than eighty minutes afterwards, constantly on the radio, issuing and receiving instructions.

Although the temperature had stayed close to freezing, the
mist had lifted, and he had a perfect view of June Maybury as
she left the house. She came away from it quickly, blowing
furiously through puffed cheeks, and obviously irritated.

When she reached the car she yanked open the passenger
door and slammed it shut again after sitting in.

She said angrily, 'This is *not* getting us anywhere!'

Bromley held out his notepad. 'Excuse me, ma'am –'

'I *told* Rawlings not to involve the IRA or Sinn Fein. It gives
them delusions.'

'Ma'am –'

'Have the reinforcements arrived?'

'Yes, ma'am, but –'

'Good! A call came through to the farmhouse shortly after
I arrived. Was the telephone surveillance in place to receive it?'

'That's what I've been trying . . . Look.'

He handed her the notepad.

She placed it on her lap to read it and when she was finished gave a small cry of joy and clenched her fists in triumph.

68

She looked at Bromley with moist eyes, almost lovingly.

But then she saw the distaste in his face and lapsed to cool-ness again.

Not knowing precisely how to respond. That was June Maybury's current difficulty.

She said coldly to Bromley now, 'Why didn't you let me know earlier?'

Bromley gestured helplessly, shrugging his shoulders. 'I couldn't, ma'am, not without also allowing Stafford to –'

'Has Superintendent Gilston been informed?'

'Yes, of course, I –'

'Fine!'

Jesus, Bromley thought.

'The caller from Northern Ireland is not named here,' she noticed then. 'Did he not identify himself?'

'Oh, ah . . .' he wondered if he could bury the detail, just to irritate a little, but of course she'd talk to Grant and dis-cover that he knew. 'Brennan, I believe.'

'Brennan? *Tommy* Brennan?'

'I believe so, yes.'

'You *believe* so?'

'It was Tommy, yes.'

'Thank you. You'll need to organise some transport for me to Cambridgeshire.'

'There's a helicopter already on stand-by, ma'am.'

'Good. Now. The farmhouse has three rooms at ground level, the front door leading straight into the first, then a liv-ing-room beyond, a kitchen off that. Like this.'

She quickly sketched a rough floor plan on the notepad.

She said, 'Dixie McDaid is being held in the central room. Here. He's not yet harmed, but very frightened. No doubt expecting rough treatment. There are four others, all armed with hand-guns. I don't want a shoot-out. Do you under-stand?'

69

'Yes, ma'am.'

'Nor do I want Dixie McDaid harmed or any of the IRA men slipping away from here. If you have to, you must arrest them. But only as a last resort.'

'Yes, ma'am.'

June Maybury paused.

'How old are you, Bromley?' she asked then.

'Old? Twenty-nine.'

'And how old do you think I am?'

Bromley stiffened and looked at her uneasily again.

One of those impossible questions, he decided. Pitch too high and you pricked her vanity. Aim too low for flattery and you didn't do your own reputation as a judge of character any favours.

That was the problem with having a woman as a superior, he thought bitterly. You could never really read their intentions. They didn't keep them separate from their feelings.

Or was that her point, he wondered then. Complaining about being called ma'am.

'Never mind,' Maybury sighed wearily. 'Stafford, the IRA man in charge, is expecting me back. Try to get away with filling in for me without raking over his suspicions.'

'Yes . . . ma'am.'

10

It was early afternoon, a little after one o'clock, when June Maybury's helicopter landed at the temporary police headquarters close to Jennifer Crooks's house.

Superintendent Gilston, already over an hour at the scene, was waiting to brief her.

'Any developments?'

Gilston shook his head. 'None.'

'Do you know that it was Tommy Brennan who supplied this address? You maintained that McDaid's uneasiness about him was irrelevant.'

'I maintained –'

'Brennan should now be discreetly picked up and held for questioning in Northern Ireland. He clearly knows a great deal more.'

'I'll pass it on.'

'Which RUC Branch officer are you working with?'

'Terence McIver. You worked with him before, when you were over there. Do you remember him?'

'Yes. Quite.'

Irritated, Maybury looked backwards, over the marshy fields and towards the prison the four had escaped from the previous night, and then to her front again, at the neat row of red-brick houses on the outskirts of the village.

Jennifer Crooks's place, she knew, was beyond that row, the other side of the road.

The nearby dwellings and work places had already been evacuated, Gilston told her now.

Armed police had occupied the attics and rooftops of the adjacent houses to cut off possible escape routes.

An SAS unit held itself apart from the main body, out of sight in their own transport, waiting only for the order to go in. Officially, of course, the regiment wasn't used against terrorists on the mainland; but Rawlings must have been pulling strings again.

Maybury, trudging with Gilston through the soft earth away from the helicopter and towards the siege, asked, 'What about the woman? The one who owns the house.'

'Bit of a mystery, I'm afraid,' Gilston admitted. 'She arrived at work – representative with the local Co-op – at the usual

71

time this morning, but shortly afterwards left with samples for an unknown destination. She took her car, a rather old Land Rover. Bit of an odd car for a woman.'

'Why?' June Maybury asked.

'Sorry?'

'Why is a Land Rover an odd car for a *woman*?'

'I beg your pardon,' Gilston corrected himself. '*Statistically unusual*.'

And Maybury, having started it, had to live with the sarcasm.

She knew now precisely what was bugging her, though.

Certainly not Gilston's out-dated and blunted sexism. And not particularly her boy-friend's petulance at having their evening disrupted by her work the previous night. And perhaps not even being dragged back by George Rawlings into the dirty world of Irish terrorism.

It was seeing Jody Stafford again. Having the memories of their earlier meetings revived.

'The Land Rover is not now at the house,' Gilston was saying.

'I beg your pardon?'

'The Land Rover. It's not at the house. We don't quite know whether she's in there herself or not.'

'Did anyone see her coming back from work?'

'No. At least none we've interviewed so far.'

They came into the street, a little above Jennifer Crooks's house, through the heavy cordon of armed police.

Gilston kept moving towards the house itself, but Maybury laid a hand on his arm and held him still.

'How do you gain access to the rear of the house?'

'Rear?' Gilston repeated, again raising his eyebrows in exaggerated surprise. 'Around by the bottom house on the row.'

'We'll go that way, then.'

A narrow laneway, again full of armed police, ran along by

the rear gardens of the houses.

Maybury stopped by Jennifer Crooks's garden door, under the stone wall, estimating heights and distances.

There were partial footprints, she noticed, left in drying mud on the concrete lane, and visible by the door. A lot of them. Crowding each other.

She went cautiously into the neighbouring garden on the left, then into the one on the right. Finding the same in each place.

The view of Jennifer Crooks's garden was obscured on both sides by high, neatly trimmed hedges.

Her mind already made up, Maybury walked back to Gilston in the laneway. 'How often have you hailed them?'

'Ten minute intervals. Past hour or so. No response, of course.'

'When is the next due?'

Gilston briskly checked his wrist-watch. 'Three minutes.'

'I think we should consider going in instead.'

Gilston smiled unpleasantly. 'I beg your pardon?'

'No,' Maybury revised. 'Give them one final summons. Tell the SAS unit they're in on the next deadline after that.'

11

PC Roddy Wark and his partner had finally come off duty a little after one-thirty the previous night. But they hadn't rested much. At eight o'clock that morning they were back on the search for the escaped prisoners again.

Both of them were tired now. The older man, Peter Williams, much more than his young colleague.

And because they were tired they were making mistakes.

73

At one-forty-five that afternoon, as June Maybury and Superintendent Gilston were arguing the toss about storming the terrorists, the two constables were on a minor road linking the village to the A141.

But they were there only because their patrol car wouldn't restart.

Williams had just flicked breadcrumbs from the last of his lunch off his uniform trousers and sat back in the driver's seat to turn the ignition key.

There was no response. The battery was dead.

Roddy Wark came from a gap in the hedge, pulling at the zipper of his fly. He came back frowning, staring at the front of the car.

He said, 'You left the lights on, Pete.'

Williams opened the driver's door and stuck his head out. 'Eh?'

'When we stopped for lunch a while back. You left the lights on. Ran the battery down.'

Williams swore.

He said then, 'Here, Rod. Give her a push. She'll start soon enough.'

Wark looked over his shoulder at the poor surface on the stretch of flat road that lay ahead of the car.

Somewhere beyond the distant rise there was a road-block manned by local police backed up by officers from the armed response unit. Behind, on the A141, there was another one.

Help was only a few minutes away.

Wark shook his head. 'No, we'll radio in.'

Williams got out of the car, laughing uncomfortably. 'Come on, Rod. We don't want any of those Special Branch lads from London pulling up here laughing at us, do we?'

It wasn't the Special Branch, Wark knew. It was Williams's local colleagues, his local superiors.

Williams, five years away from retirement, had been

74

building a reputation for lapses recently and was getting worried about making it cleanly to his pension.

'Come on, Rod.'

He wound down the window, closed the driver's door and started pushing by himself, leaning in to pull at the steering wheel with his left hand.

Wark swore at him quietly. 'Jesus, Pete! Cut it out, will you!'

Williams made only three or four paces, the effort too much for him.

By then, the patrol car's bonnet had crossed the broken white line in the middle of the road and was partially blocking the other lane.

Williams was breathing hard now and didn't look too good.

Wark came around the car to support him. He opened the driver's door again.

He said gently, 'Sit in, Pete. No, over to the passenger side. We'll say I was driving. Okay?'

Williams looked at him with dumb gratitude and scrambled over the gear-lever into the passenger seat.

Wark, his left arm resting on the car's roof, was reaching in for the radio mouthpiece when he caught a glimpse of something coming over the rise in the distance.

He waited for its approach.

He thought at first it was a police or army vehicle. Because it had the shape of a jeep.

But as it cruised closer he saw with surprise, with pleasure, that it was Jennifer Crooks's abused old Land Rover.

12

When Jennifer Crooks was coming over the crest of the hill she was thinking that luck was with her. So far, anyway.

She'd reversed the Land Rover into the lane behind her house at nine-thirty that morning, opening the back to the garden door.

Fifteen minutes later, no one had seen the four fugitives racing through the garden under cover of the high hedges. No one had seen them slipping into the back of the Land Rover.

While Jennifer Crooks was stacking samples from the Co-op on the shelf that concealed the prisoners, a neighbour coming home from night shift had stopped to chat with her. Seeing nothing odd. Suspecting nothing.

The route away from the village was slow and tortuous, but safe. Through the lands and along the tractor lanes of some of the local farmers attached to the Co-op. Sometimes having to stop and talk. Once having to lay up on a farm for almost two hours because there were patrols out on the nearby roads. But always skirting the road-blocks.

Luck had been with her. Until now.

She wasn't worried at first. The police car looked stalled. More in trouble itself than forming a road-block. And the chances were the officers were local and knew her anyway.

When she saw it was Roddy Wark, though, her right foot came immediately off the accelerator and hit the brake pedal, jerking the Land Rover before she got her composure back.

She could hear the four in the rear grunting and cursing as they were thrown together.

Sean McDaid put his mouth to one of the small air holes

76

drilled in the cover and hissed at her, 'What's wrong?'

'Police on the road ahead.'

'Do you know them?'

'Yes. They're locals.'

'Is it a road-block?'

'No, I don't think so. Just two of them. No guns.'

'Just get through them.'

Wark was standing in the middle of the road now, flagging her down, a big smile on his young face.

She slowed abruptly, giving herself time before she reached him. She tried to go over the routine in her mind, the reasons why she was on that road. But it sounded forced. It sounded like something that couldn't have happened in their usual conversation.

Wark wasn't interested, however.

As she pulled up beside him and wound down the window, he leaned in to greet her and ask her to release the bonnet catch so that he could use a set of jump leads on her battery.

He said then, 'I rang you this morning. Only chance I got. You must've been out. Left early, did you?'

But instead of finishing the movement with the kiss he'd intended, he drew back a bit, into the fresh air again, as he was talking.

What he'd got was a strong smell of stale sweat.

He'd thought it was from her. And thought it strange.

But it wasn't hers. It was from Danny Boyce, and coming through the air vents in the cover at the back of the Land Rover.

It still sent troublesome messages to Wark's brain.

Instead of pleasure, he now felt distaste. Instead of welcomes and jokes, he now had questions in his mind.

He was a policeman again.

He asked, 'Where are you heading, Jenny?'

'Oh, down below with some produce. At the junction. Local

77

shops are thinking of stocking there.'

Her voice. It was strained. Her eyes weren't meeting his. Her hands were tightly gripping the steering wheel, even though the handbrake was on and the Land Rover going nowhere.

Wark, searching now for faults, for signs of trouble, wondered then why her collie dog, Princess, wasn't with her as usual on the front passenger seat. If you were carrying food, of course . . .

But it reminded him of when he'd called at her house the previous night. The oddity had lodged in his mind without his being aware of it. He'd had too much to worry about. But Princess hadn't been around then either. She hadn't barked when he'd rung the doorbell.

The thing was, he hated that stupid dog. It always barked incessantly when he was visiting.

He said, 'I'll get the leads, Jenny. Hang on.'

He felt uneasy about turning his back on the Land Rover but couldn't reverse away.

His legs were stiff and seemed to take a long time to get him across the five or six paces to the patrol car.

Peter Williams was still in the passenger seat, but slumped now, with his eyes closed. He looked limp and ashen-faced.

Wark said quietly, 'Pete.'

Williams opened his eyes.

Wark said, 'Pete, I think someone is holding her hostage. Jennifer Crooks. Someone in the back of her Land Rover.'

Williams obviously hadn't heard. Didn't understand.

He said faintly, 'You'd better get me a doctor, lad. I'm not so good.'

Wark made his mistake then. Because he was tired and nervous and his fear stopped him from figuring all the angles.

He called across to Jennifer Crooks, 'You go ahead, Jenny. Pete here is not feeling too well. I've got to call an ambulance for him.'

78

Calculate it. Even if you believed him.

How long would it take to make the call and get an ambulance out there and get Williams in the ambulance and the ambulance back to hospital? And how long would it take to jump-start the battery and drive into hospital with the siren on?

That was the sum Sean McDaid did in his head.

And said immediately to the others in the rear of the Land Rover, 'He knows!'

Wark was in the patrol car again and had the radio mouthpiece in his left palm when he caught from the corner of his eye the back door of the Land Rover being pushed open.

He knew he was in trouble.

But instead of opening the radio line to base, he hit the accelerator hard and desperately twisted the ignition key.

The battery didn't even cough.

And its silence seemed to heighten even more the blast from the .38 revolver fired almost point blank at Wark's head through the open car door.

In the passenger seat, Peter Williams opened his eyes again as Wark was flung backwards against him and Wark's brains and blood splattered into his face. He saw the stooped, red-faced youth with the blotched skin grinning from outside. And then he saw the Smith & Wesson in the boy's hand.

He felt certain they were going to murder him too. But he was wrong. He was already dead, from heart failure, a split second before Denis Reilly pulled the trigger.

Reilly twisted away from the patrol car and had to run after the Land Rover, because Jennifer Crooks had driven on about fifty metres before the shooting started. Not wanting to see the killings. Not wanting it all made real for herself.

Spots of rain hit Reilly's face as he sprinted and the light wind that was rising blew back his untidy black hair.

He kept the .38 in a firing positon, suspecting that the others might try to ditch him.

79

They waited, though.

When he was safely back in the Land Rover, Jennifer Crooks took off erratically, accelerating quickly and taking the first track through the fields that offered itself.

Half gagging, half sobbing, but all of her shivering, she scrambled wildly for the controls to get the wipers clearing the rain from her windscreen. She hit the lights and the indicators instead, suddenly illuminating the outside of the Land Rover as it rocked and bounced across the uneven ground.

TWO

1

Any other time, Dixie McDaid would've been tortured to share whatever he knew. Or to convince his captors that he was ignorant.

He was lucky now. The IRA and the British security services were cramping each other's styles.

Jody Stafford wouldn't demean the cause he served in front of its oldest enemy. Even funnier, he wouldn't allow the British to get at Dixie either. Any torturing of Irishmen that had to be done, the IRA had a moral monopoly on it.

That was the stalemate June Maybury walked into after flying back in worsening weather to the farmhouse near Radlett.

With the murders of the two police constables, there was no point to staying at the scene, winding down the siege of Jennifer Crooks's house.

It was a straightforward police operation now. Pursuit and capture.

She didn't allow herself much confidence, though. The cordon around the prison and the village had already proved useless. So perhaps the hunt would be just as futile. And perhaps the additional security measures to protect Her Majesty might also be inadequate.

McDaid, it was clear, was a man of no ordinary inteligence,

no ordinary cunning.

The situation at the farmhouse didn't really add to Maybury's hopes.

David Bromley and the Special Branch officers now occupied the front room. Jody Stafford and two of his IRA men skulked in the kitchen. But Dixie McDaid still sat by the open fire in the living-room, guarded on one side by Junior Doherty and on the other by a young detective.

Dixie now had a few recent cigarette burns on his face.

And Junior Doherty was the only one in the house whose fingers were brown with nicotine stains.

'It happened before we got here,' Bromley explained. 'While we were still –'

'How long did you take, for God's sake?'

'It happened while we were talking. In the car. We put a stop to it.'

'Did Stafford find out anything?' June Maybury asked.

Bromley shrugged. 'I don't know.'

'Are they still armed?'

'You asked us to avoid gunfire, ma'am.'

'Christ!'

Negotiation. That was the name of the new game with the IRA. But they were supposed to put away their guns before the talking started.

Maybury went to the living-room and sat in the armchair opposite Dixie McDaid.

He glanced at her furtively, maybe with a little desperate hope in his eyes. When he twisted away from her again he winced with pain from the burns on his cheeks. His hands, although they were locked together, were still shaking.

She said, 'You know your brother Sean escaped from prison last night, don't you?'

Dixie nodded.

'Where would he come to?' she asked. 'If he made it to

London.'

Dixie grimaced again, but didn't answer.

She took a folded sheet of A4 paper from the file she was carrying and offered it to him.

It was a photocopy of a slightly charred page one of the detectives had taken from Jennifer Crooks's attic after the house was taken over.

A strange piece. Something architectural about it, like the interior layout of a building, but with everything out of proportion, out of scale. Geometric shapes where there might be doors. Stick men where there might be walls.

Dixie McDaid kept himself from looking.

'What is it?' he asked.

'It's a diagram,' she told him.

His reaction was hungry. His right hand moved away from the other to snatch at it, but he controlled himself in time and brought his fingers upwards gently to touch the burns on his face.

'Have you got any cream or anything?' he asked. 'Something to put on these.'

He didn't look again at the folded paper.

Maybury raised a finger to summon the detective in the room.

While the Special Branch man walked towards the door to pass on the message, she said to Dixie, 'We'll try and get you something.'

'Thanks.'

'Would Sean come to you?' she asked him.

'I don't know.'

'Where do you live in London?'

He picked his way. Slowly. Carefully. Trying to figure out what angle she was coming from, how much she already knew.

He said, 'I live in Kilburn. It's just a one-bedroom flat, on the second floor of a house on Kilburn High Road.'

June Maybury opened the sheet of paper. Silently, she studied the drawing inside.

Dixie pretended to lose interest. He gazed into the fire, until the heat on his face made him pull back again.

'Where do you work, Dixie?' she asked him. 'One of the Irish communities? Camden, Islington, Willesden, Harlesden . . .?'

Harlesden! Harlesden!

It suddenly echoed in Dixie's mind. It found the same rhythm as the blood pounding in his ears. Blocking out everything else. So that he didn't know whether he'd reacted much or not, if the look in his eyes had changed, if his hands had twitched.

He let her run through a few more names.

'Maida Vale, Finchley, Cricklewood –'

Then he came in, not letting her finish the list. He knew they had ways of telling if something was bothering you, a tremor in your voice, a twitch in your muscles. And he was going to throw her the red herring of Cricklewood.

He cut in, 'I worked the building sites a lot. But all around. All over London.'

He only noticed then that he'd been staring at the floor since she'd mentioned Harlesden. He looked up. The woman was nodding at him, making a note that he had this thing about Cricklewood.

He wasn't going to show any satisfaction, though.

He touched his burns and said again, 'All over London.'

2

They were heading down the M11 on the approach to London when Sean McDaid finally said, 'We'll ditch the Land Rover around here. Take the next slip-road off. Danny?'

'Yeah?'

'You pick up two cars. One for –'

Just as Jennifer Crooks caught sight of the police Panda in her wing mirror.

'Better look behind,' she interrupted McDaid.

It was dusk by then, about ten to fifteen minutes away from total darkness. The rain was heavy and persistent, blown by swirling gale-force winds.

The glass inside the Land Rover had misted, making it even more difficult to see properly.

Danny Boyce, sitting with Reilly and Woolly Barr in the back, found some tissue in a crate from the Co-op and wiped the rear window dry.

The Panda was about a hundred metres behind them. Not pulling up. Not pulling out. Just sitting there.

'It's too fucking late,' Denis Reilly said. 'I told you we should've switched cars earlier.'

He had, too. Every five miles or so since they'd got through the cordon around the prison.

Reilly's intention was going it alone. Getting a car of his own and seeing how he'd make out after shaking off the dead weight of the other three.

Only he couldn't do it while the Land Rover was belting down the motorway at sixty miles an hour.

'All I'm saying is it's too late,' he persisted, driven by frustration. 'They're on to us. All I'm saying is I told you this was going to happen. That's all.'

McDaid, sitting in the front passenger seat, turned to glare at him. 'Shut up,' he growled.

'All I'm saying is –'

'Shut up!'

McDaid told Jennifer Crooks then, 'Take the next slip road anyway.'

It came to them quickly, signposting Abridge and Chigwell to their left.

'No,' McDaid ordered. 'Right. Go right. Cross the motorway. Over the bridge. See if they follow us.'

They were heading now for Theydon Bois and Epping Forest.

The light was fading. The heavier rain was making visibility difficult. Speed was impossible.

And still the Panda stayed behind them.

'Speed up,' McDaid said.

Jennifer Crooks shook her head. 'I can't go any faster in this weather.'

'Just do it, woman!'

'I told you I should've done the driving,' Reilly chimed in.

McDaid said, 'Do it gradually. You don't have to put your foot to the floor. A little at a time.'

The other side of Theydon Bois, the Panda was joined by a light-blue Vauxhall Cavalier.

The two of them now, their bonnets nosing around the previous bend just as the Land Rover was taking the next. Not gaining on the Land Rover. Not falling away. Just sitting there.

'It's no good,' McDaid said then. 'They're trying to box us in. They'll have road-blocks ahead of us.'

'What do we do, Sean?' Boyce asked calmly from the back.

Boyce had been calm since breaking through the cordon, feeling he was on the way.

He'd wanted to listen to the radio, to check on how the news might've broken to his wife Deirdre and to imagine her reactions. But the Land Rover had a blown fuse that kept its stereo and the interior light not working. They'd left the portable behind in Jennifer Crooks's house.

Otherwise he was content. And calm. Even now.

'What do we do, Sean?'

Darkness finally settled in the silence that followed. So that they could see only the headlights now of the cars behind them.

'Take the next bend,' McDaid said. 'Then put your foot down hard.'

Jennifer Crooks did.

But nothing offered itself right or left to escape down as they hurtled dangerously through the storm. No track. No driveway. Not even another bend.

'We're fucked,' Reilly said, looking back at the headlights of the police cars rounding the last corner.

He took his .38 revolver from his pocket and laughed.

Danny Boyce shifted anxiously beside him, peering through the back window, starting to feel the strain.

Woolly Barr was quiet. His eyes were closed.

They reached the outskirts of the forest. All they could see of it were the shadows of its trees flashing past in their headlights.

None of them knew the road or the area. McDaid struggled with a map for a while, but couldn't steady a torch on it in the violent movements of the Land Rover.

'So what are we going to do?' Reilly challenged him. 'You're in charge. What are we going to do?'

McDaid had no idea.

Until she offered herself to him, half-way down that long, straight stretch of road through the forest. A girl, standing in the rain beside an AA recovery truck, whose driver was hitching up her station wagon for towing.

'Pull up beside her,' McDaid ordered urgently.

Jennifer Crooks glanced across at him. 'What?'

'Do it! Do it! Pull in!'

They came in at speed and braked hard.

The AA man straightened to look behind him. The girl, in plastic rain gear, actually smiled at them. Her boy-friend, probably the cause of the breakdown, got sulkily out of the passenger seat of the station wagon to wave them away.

McDaid threw open the Land Rover door and pointed his Browning pistol at the girl.

'Get in!' he ordered.

She looked baffled.

Until the police cars behind hit their sirens and cleared up the doubts for her.

She tried to back away then, but McDaid grabbed her with his free left hand, his fingers tearing through the plastic coat she was wearing. He had to put a foot out on the road to give himself the leverage to lift and drag her in.

The AA man gaped.

The girl's boy-friend called forlornly in the wind. 'Becky! Becky!'

The Land Rover door was still open, his shoe still on the tarmacadam, when McDaid shouted at Jennifer Crooks, 'Go! Get going! Drive!'

From behind him, Danny Boyce, thinking sharply, reached quickly forward and plucked the screaming girl into the rear of the Land Rover.

And Reilly did what he was best at, sticking the barrel of another hand-gun in her face. 'Shut up!' he shouted. 'Shut the fuck up!'

Woolly Barr looked out the rear window to check on the police. The Panda's flashing blue light had stopped by the station wagon. The Vauxhall Cavalier was still in pursuit.

McDaid said to Jennifer Crooks, 'Turn into the forest.'

88

'What?' she asked. 'You mean the next road, the next junction?'

'No! Here! Now! Anywhere you can!'

'There's too much water on the ground,' she protested. 'The mud. The wheels might get stuck.'

'We'll manage it better than the thing behind us, anyway.'

'But –'

'Just turn!'

She pulled the steering wheel left, hitting a deep pool of water on the edge of the road, but holding her speed.

Ahead of them now there were only trees. There were gaps between the trunks wide enough to take the Land Rover, but you couldn't manoeuvre at anything more than a crawl.

'Now what?' Jennifer Crooks wondered.

'Get in among the trees.'

She did.

'Switch off the lights,' McDaid ordered.

'What?'

'Turn off the headlights.'

'We'll hit something.'

'Just turn them off! Now!'

And Jennifer Crooks did.

3

June Maybury walked alone to the kitchen of the farmhouse, where Jody Stafford was drinking coffee with his two aides, Sheehan and Crawley.

She sat at the pine table across from him. She took the photocopy from her file again and opened it to lay it on the table in front of him.

She asked, 'Do you know what this is?'

Stafford looked at her over the rim of the coffee mug as he drank, glancing down only once.

'It looks like the floor plan of a building done by a child.'

'What building?'

Stafford shrugged. 'What child?' he asked facetiously.

Maybury said, 'My information is that Sean McDaid is heading for Harlesden tonight. Is there anyone you know of there? Someone McDaid can trust?'

Stafford was silent for a while.

He still felt bitter. A bitterness too old and too ingrained to be tempered by anything less than self-destruction. Like the bitterness of Northern Ireland itself.

'You always invite us to co-operate,' he said then, 'and you always lock us up after we've made our contribution.'

Maybury sighed impatiently. 'Please.'

'You've always recognised only two types of articulate Irish nationalists,' Stafford added. 'The penitent and the super-grass.'

'How long have you spent thinking that one up?'

'Several hundred years, in fact.'

'I see. I've touched a sensitive spot again, have I?'

Maybury paused. 'What about Harlesden?' she asked then.

Stafford drank again.

He said, 'It's too simple for you, isn't it? It's always too simple when you're in control.'

He put the coffee mug away and picked up the diagram to study it.

'Let me deal with Sean McDaid first,' he suggested. 'Before you lot get to him.'

Maybury shook her head. 'Don't be ridiculous.'

'Well, I can't just *inform*, can I? You've got to offer something in exchange. Then it's negotiation, it's a deal.'

'No deal.'

90

'No deal,' Stafford repeated. 'In which case, I don't have the authority to take any decisions by myself.'

'Nonsense! Your own Army Council has issued an order threatening the sternest action – is that the euphemism? – against volunteers who use weapons without permission during the ceasefire.'

'The action doesn't include their betrayal to British forces.'

Maybury said slowly, through gritted teeth, 'I do not honestly see the difference.'

'That's your problem,' Stafford told her.

'But it's not!' Maybury exploded. 'It's not simply *my* problem. It's not simply an *English* problem at all. Are you still too blinkered after twenty-five years to see that all such things have a larger dimension, that they involve more than you and me shouting at each other across a room?'

'That's rich,' Stafford said sourly. 'Coming from you.'

But then he stood up from the table to pace, working out an idea that had just struck him, the hint of a possible plan.

He didn't want to betray it by seeming too eager.

As a gesture, he said to Crawley and Sheehan, who were still sitting at the other end of the table, 'Leave us alone for a few minutes, lads, would ye?'

When they were gone, he muttered, 'About Harlesden.'

Maybury turned to look at him. 'What about it?'

He paced again. He seemed restless with indecision.

And then he said, with apparent reluctance, 'I need two assurances first. Nothing to do with Sean McDaid.'

'What are they?'

'First, Junior Doherty and the two lads who were here should be released immediately and their part in all of this forgotten about. No ticking off. No heavy-handed escorts back to Northern Ireland. They still have a role to play in this peace process and there's no point undermining it. Let them go their own way. I'll vouch for them.'

'And you?'

'I won't be with them. I'll come to that in a minute. Soon as we get past this bit.'

'I can't see that it presents any great difficulties,' Maybury said. 'Provided they hand over their weapons. And the other assurance?'

'That's for me. I'll have to go with you to the house in Harlesden.'

Maybury was silent, thinking about it.

Stafford went on, trying to sound reasonable, trying not to force the pace too much. 'The old man who owns the house there . . . It's too complicated to explain.'

'To an Englishwoman?'

Stafford publicly ignored the barb. But he knew that it meant well for him. She was taking the line he was playing out.

He said, 'If you don't want a row scaring off Sean McDaid, you need someone to convince the old man.'

'And I take it you'll only lead us there, without giving us the address beforehand?'

'Do you think it's easy?' Stafford asked with obvious bitterness. 'Don't make it any worse.'

And was delighted when she answered acidly, 'Keeping the peace? I think it's easier than you seem to imagine. But then, perhaps I've had more practice at it than you.'

4

The floodlights illuminating the stalled Land Rover on the edge of Epping Forest were so arranged that they left two channels of darkness along the vehicle's blind spots.

They weren't perfect. There was some overspill from the

92

various arcs of light, particularly near the vehicle itself.

But to spot anything in either of the channels, one of the terrorists would have to lean from a door or a window and hold his stare for a lengthy period.

Even with a hostage, it was unlikely that any of them would risk making himself such an obvious target.

Into those channels of darkness the senior SAS officer at the scene, Captain Laytham, had just sent two of his men to reconnoitre.

But they were out less than five minutes, crawling through the mud that was now the forest floor after the heavy rains, when a single shot was fired from the Land Rover.

Laytham, behind the barrier of police cars on the road, couldn't establish from where inside the vehicle the bullet came. Nor could he even guess what the intended target had been.

He wondered if McDaid had been clever enough to figure out the purpose of the dark channels and was now firing blindly into them.

It seemed so.

Because after the next two shots, Laytham's sergeant said from beside him, 'Approximate intervals of four minutes, sir.'

Laytham nodded, shaking loose the rainwater that was drenching his balaclava.

And he waited anxiously for his men to return.

They both came back on schedule, however. And both had almost precisely the same reports.

'The woman sitting in the driver's seat is the hostage, sir. They seem to have someone covering her from beneath, on the floor. She keeps looking down there. The rest are out of sight.'

'What about the approach?'

'Plenty of cover right up to the target, sir. If we killed the lights, we could take it from there.'

'What about the back door? Is it blocked by trees?'

'No, sir. Wide open.'

Laytham pulled on an oilskin cape and went to search for the tall, old-fashioned man in charge of the police to pass on the information.

'It's your call, sir.'

Superintendent Gilston frowned, aware of his own instructions, the pressures to end this quickly before it became a political symbol, another rallying point for all those still opposed to the ceasefire.

'Can you save the hostage?' he asked.

Laytham nodded in the darkness. 'Yes, I believe so.'

'Then we mustn't let it linger, Captain, must we?'

'Is that an instruction to go in now, sir? Because another hour or so and they'll be even tireder than they are at the moment, less alert.'

5

Actually, it was only Jennifer Crooks who was tiring inside the Land Rover.

Her eyes were getting sore and heavy. Her legs were cramping from the awkward way she was sitting on the floor, with her back against the passenger door. Worst of all, she couldn't keep holding the revolver on the girl in the driver's seat any more. Mostly, she had to leave it resting on the floor.

The broken sleep from the night before was starting to tell on her.

She kicked the girl's legs with her right heel and said, 'Put your hands on your head.'

The girl tried to look across and down at Jennifer Crooks,

94

but the glare from the searchlights dazzled her.

She said faintly, 'What?'

'Put your hands on your head.'

'Why?'

'So they'll know the hostage is still alive and won't start shooting you.'

The girl shivered and raised her hands, locking them together over her head.

Jennifer Crooks looked at her watch. Almost eight o'clock.

But even as she was counting the minutes to the hour, her head dropped on her chest and she dozed.

Twice she forced herself awake again.

Once she reached upwards into the glove compartment and took out a sheet of paper with her left hand.

She fell back asleep, though, before deciding what to do with it.

And she dreamed of watching television.

The second time, she opened her eyes in terror.

Because the Land Rover and the surrounding area were now lost in darkness again.

That dream, she realised. The flickering television. They'd killed the searchlights while she'd slept.

She desperately patted the floor, searching for the revolver. But as she found it, as she looked upwards to aim it, she saw that the girl was no longer there, that the driver's door was slightly open.

Jennifer Crooks opened her mouth. But she never managed a sound.

A shape appeared at the driver's window. The rear doors of the Land Rover were blown open by two small explosions. And the gunfire, concentrated and prolonged, hit her simultaneously from both directions.

She died immediately, without getting off a shot herself.

In front of her, Captain Laytham stepped over the girl that one of his squad had just pulled down to safety.

Keeping his gun trained on Jennifer Crooks, he reached through the Land Rover's door and across the front seats and took the sheet of paper she was still clutching in her left hand.

He shone a torch and looked at the drawing on the paper.

It was like the floor plan of a building. But it was absurdly proportioned, ridiculously drawn, with hangmen for walls, eyes for doors, a row of dashes across its centre.

In the top left-hand corner, there was a small X. Marking a spot of some hidden significance.

His sergeant came from the rear of the Land Rover, shaking his head.

'It's empty, sir. There's no one there.'

The girl was being helped to her feet beside Laytham.

She said to him, 'They left. There was four of them. But they left. When they turned the lights off and we pulled in here, they climbed out the back and went through the forest. I saw them.'

Laytham cursed. And immediately apologised to the girl.

But then he pulled his right boot from the gluey muck around his feet and cursed again.

More than three hours they'd been gone. And nothing would survive of their trail in the dark and in the mud.

He could only hope that one of the road-blocks between London and the forest would pick them up.

6

At eight-thirty that evening, though, in a disused factory two miles north-east of Harlesden, the only threat to the escaped prisoners was themselves.

They'd slogged through Epping Forest in the rain, getting

out of it before the road-blocks were in place and the search parties out.

On the A104, at the first pub they'd come to, they'd hot-wired a Peugeot 405 and then driven across north London before cutting down to Golders Green.

With nothing but strife the whole journey.

Denis Reilly's plans had been soured by the weather.

He had nowhere to go for the night, apart from McDaid's safe house, and no one he could rely on to help him.

The way he was, without money or a change of clothes or secure shelter, he knew he was nothing. Helpless. Dependent on McDaid.

If only McDaid had switched cars earlier after breaking through the cordon . . .

Reilly seethed as he drove the Peugeot down towards London, the nape of his neck tingling with the awareness that McDaid sat right behind him.

Beside him in front, Danny Boyce switched on the car's radio to listen to the news. He ran back and forth across the bands for ten minutes, searching frantically, and when he finally settled couldn't understand what he heard.

' . . . have confirmed that the two convicts who escaped from Whitemoor prison last night are still at large. There is growing confidence, however, that both men are trapped within . . .'

Boyce swivelled to stare at McDaid. 'What are they talking about, Sean?'

McDaid shook his head. 'I don't know, Danny.'

'But they said –'

'We all heard what they fucking said,' Reilly interrupted. 'You don't have to tell us again.'

Boyce was wide-eyed. 'But why are they saying it, Sean? What are they doing it for?'

McDaid, thinking hard, muttered quietly, 'They've obviously decided to keep the break-out quiet. Pretend it was

97

something else. Not an IRA action.'

'Why?'

'I don't know. Not yet.'

Boyce sobbed suddenly and closed his eyes to hold the tears. 'They can't do that, Sean. They can't do it.'

The others looked at him, wondering if he was cracking.

Until Reilly shouted, 'What fucking difference does it make? They play their games. What does it matter? Just don't keep going on about it.'

Boyce knew that he was pushing it too far, that he was in danger of blowing everything.

But he was out of control for the moment. And couldn't let it alone.

His wife wouldn't know, he kept saying to himself.

He was finally free and Deirdre, still sitting in Belfast and listening to the news, just didn't know about it.

Behind him, McDaid watched and listened, and knew that he had a little thinking to do before committing himself to the next step.

So instead of heading straight on to the safe house, he ordered them to rest up a while in the old factory they came on in Golders Green. Making it sound as if he'd planned the stop. But they were wet and cold and hungry, with no change of clothes and nothing to dry themselves with, and they were inclined to argue.

'Just ten minutes,' McDaid told them. 'It's important. Something I have to collect here.'

He left Reilly and Boyce bickering in one section and took Woolly Barr to what had once been the Managing Director's office.

'You're shivering,' he said. 'It's the cold.'

Woolly said, 'Bit nervous too, I suppose.'

'Of what?'

'This place,' Woolly said. 'Not the place itself. I mean,

98

staying here. Someone might notice and report to the police. Or maybe a dosser's already using it and might be back.'

McDaid nodded. 'We'll be moving out in a little while. Get to proper quarters for the night.'

Woolly said, 'Right.'

And then made up his mind to get it off his chest.

He asked, 'Why didn't we go there first? To the quarters.'

'I'll tell you what the problem is, Woolly,' McDaid said softly. 'It's knowing who you can shut your eyes with these days. Who you can trust. Do you understand what I'm talking about?'

Woolly nodded.

Then, when he realised that the gesture mightn't be seen in the darkness, he grunted agreement as well.

He tried to think of something to clinch his support, but the words wouldn't come. It wasn't a topic he was too comfortable on. Trust. Loyalty.

In the silence that followed, Woolly listened to the sounds from outside. A cat wailing from somewhere close and a little traffic, a couple of cars on the wet streets.

But McDaid seemed lost in a world of his own. Talking more to himself than to Woolly.

McDaid said, 'Pearse, before he led the rising against the British in 1916, always felt let down by people around him. He knew they hadn't the courage to carry their ideas through. You can really only trust someone who's ready to die with you, can't you?'

'I suppose.'

'It's always the few who are ready to die that carry on the fight in every generation, Woolly. I don't mean just carry it on. I mean bring it further, advance it another bit. Pearse knew that. Do you think he imagined he could beat the British Army with his small force of Volunteers in 1916?'

'No.'

'He knew he was going to die, Woolly. He knew what effect his death would have. *Bloodshed is a cleansing thing.* He wrote that three years before his execution. *There are many things more horrible than bloodshed; and slavery is one of them.*'

Woolly shivered and was silent. Out of his depth. History not being one of his stronger points, either.

Sean McDaid's hand was on his elbow. He was saying, 'Do you know where we're heading, Woolly?'

'What do you mean?' Woolly asked. Confused for a moment. 'You mean the target? What we're going to hit?'

'No,' McDaid said. 'Tonight. Where we're going to be sleeping tonight.'

Woolly wondered if it was a trick. And not only because *everything* looked like a trick to him now.

McDaid had told him, months before. *If we ever get to London town, Woolly . . .*

Except it hadn't seemed significant then, the two of them stuck in prison, a world away from London.

Was McDaid trying to catch him out in a lie? Was he testing him?

Woolly said, 'Pa Daly. In Harlesden. You told me about him before. He's some distant relation of your mother's.'

McDaid nodded. And patted Woolly's elbow. 'That's right,' he confirmed. 'I told you before.'

7

Like a lot of Irish nicknames, it had no obvious relevance. Pa Daly had never fathered a child in his life.

It was just that he was the eldest boy and had been called Patrick like his old man, and then had it shortened to Pa to identify him as the son rather than the father.

Now he was fifty-five.

He'd worked in a London biscuit factory the last twenty-two years, without ever getting to know or like anyone who was English.

Up to tonight, he'd never invited a native Englishman to his home in Harlesden.

'Yeah, well,' Jody Stafford had told him, 'life is a bit more complicated since the ceasefire.'

But Daly didn't really buy that one. Just because you weren't shooting at the bastards any more didn't mean you had to have tea and sympathy with them instead.

Daly didn't entirely buy the ceasefire either, of course. Except as a tactic. Get the Brits on the wrong foot. Get the Yanks rowing in behind you. Show the world the Brits didn't really want the peace.

This caper tonight, though, it was confusing Daly.

Stafford had come to the door alone. He'd come in alone. And then he'd let it out there was a whole regiment of the British security forces waiting to follow him.

'A couple of the lads escaped from prison last night,' Stafford had said.

Daly scratched his head. 'I didn't hear anything about it.'

'It hasn't been publicised yet.'

'Hasn't it? Why not?'

'Anyway,' Stafford said quickly, 'the information is they're heading here. The break hasn't been sanctioned by the Army Council. We've got orders to meet them here, turn them back.'

'Turn them back? Back to prison?'

'That's right.'

'Sell them out to the Brits, you mean. I'll not have any part in that, Jody.'

'It's an order, Pa.'

'Orders or no orders, I'm not squealing on a comrade.'

101

'You're not being asked to *like* it.'

'Whose orders? Tell me whose orders.'

'Just do it, Pa!'

Daly walked angrily away, rejecting the idea with furious gestures. Then a sly look suddenly came on his face and he turned to face Stafford again.

He said, 'It wouldn't be Sean McDaid who's escaped, would it?'

Stafford nodded. 'With some others.'

Daly laughed, without humour. 'I thought you wouldn't go that far for anyone else, Jody. There's still bitterness between you, isn't there? Still an old score to settle. And now it's him or you as well, isn't it, left to fight it out which way the organisation is going. But you're going about it the wrong way, Jody. He's not after you, the same as you're after him. He's after the Brits, isn't he? He only ever had the one enemy, Sean had.'

'Things aren't that simple any more, Pa.'

'Ah, well,' Daly said sarcastically, 'maybe you'll manage to do what you haven't been able to do up to this and take him this time, what with half the British empire at your back now.'

Stafford sighed, feeling he was losing the argument.

Daly's sympathy was with Sean McDaid.

But what could you expect? It was the history of Ireland the last two hundred and fifty years. The heroic gesture always packed more of a kick than the banal process of politics.

The daring prison escaper. The young martyr. The freeddom fighter. The hunger striker. All the romantic figures.

It wasn't a tradition that Stafford himself had much of an appetite for arguing against.

So he said curtly, 'We're taking over the house, Pa. That's an order. Look on it as the first joint IRA-British Army operation. A historic occasion.'

They came in discreetly over the next few minutes, the British security forces. Dressed in civilian clothes. Mostly in pairs, like social callers. Not alarming or alerting any of the neighbours.

Afterwards they kept Daly in an upstairs bedroom, guarded by two officers. More or less a prisoner in his own house.

It didn't look like they were going to trust him when it came to opening the front door to Sean McDaid's knock.

It didn't matter.

Not to Stafford, anyway.

He had other plans.

Which were better served with Daly ignorant and out of the way.

8

Sean McDaid squatted on the floor beside Woolly Barr in the abandoned factory.

His left hand was resting on Woolly's arm. His eyes were gazing out through a gap in the hoarding on one of the windows.

But he was thinking of the dead.

He knew the Greeks had a saying. About not calling anyone happy until after their death. He liked the idea, but he preferred to put *trust* in for *happy*. You couldn't really *trust* anyone unless they were dead.

He thought of the Irishmen who'd died in all the risings against British rule, from 1798 to 1916. The men who'd died on hunger strike in Long Kesh in the Seventies. And all the volunteers who'd died on active service the last twenty-five years.

You knew where they stood, he decided. You knew they couldn't change their minds any more. You knew you could rely on them.

Everyone else, they let you down. One way or another. Sooner or later. They lost the faith. They buckled under the pressure and caved in.

Because of them, because of their weakness, one man, one *special* man, had to die in every generation to redeem all the rest.

All this, it was what he'd been hinting at to Woolly Barr the last few minutes.

'Who can you trust, Woolly?' he'd asked the little man. 'That's the big question these days. Who can you trust? I came over here a year ago to do this thing, and I was grassed on by someone. By one of my own. I was doing my time over here when they made this decision back in Ireland. Ceasefire. No more fighting. All the fighting we did, Woolly, you and I, it was all a waste of time. And who's up there at the head of this surrender? Who's leading the charge away from me? Jody Stafford. He brought me up, Woolly. He was a father to me. He showed me the way. And now he's telling me it was all a mistake. My mother wasn't really butchered by Prods. The British Army wasn't really occupying a part of Ireland the last twenty-five years. All mistakes, Jody says. So who can you trust, Woolly?'

Woolly hadn't answered, of course.

And not only because Woolly was uncomfortable with the topic. Not only because he'd been turned to work for MI5 and had grassed about everything he could ferret out, including the earlier plans for escape.

No.

Woolly hadn't answered because Woolly was already dead.

A couple of minutes before asking him who he could trust, McDaid had taken the pistol and silencer from the right-hand pocket of his overcoat and shot Woolly between the eyes from close range and then again through the temple.

104

Thinking it was an advance in their relationship. Because he'd never have to distrust Woolly again.

McDaid stood up now.

He took a handkerchief from his left pocket and wiped at the spots of Woolly's blood that had splattered against him.

He walked across to the window, even though at that angle, while he was standing, he couldn't see to the outside through the crack in the hoarding.

And he thought about the dead.

After a while he heard a noise behind him and turned.

Danny Boyce and Denis Reilly were standing in the door-way, looking down at Woolly's blood-soaked head.

McDaid said, 'He knew about Pa Daly's house in Harlesden. And if Woolly knew, the world and his mother knows as well.'

But it wasn't only that.

Woolly Barr had been sprung because McDaid wasn't sure how much Woolly had picked up from Dixie that time Dixie had come to visit the prison.

With the pistol aimed between his eyes, Woolly had finally answered the questions McDaid couldn't put to him in prison without having them repeated to the Governor and MI5.

Woolly was a grass.

Something McDaid had learned about him only long after that visit by Dixie.

Something he couldn't make Woolly pay for inside without jeopardising the escape.

The thing was, Woolly had known about the plans to assas-sinate the Queen of England. Dixie had told him. And surely, McDaid decided, the British security forces must also know by now.

'What are we going to do, Sean?' Boyce was asking.

Reilly looked from one to the other, then down again to Woolly's shattered head. Struggling a bit. Realising there was something going on that he hadn't been in on.

Right then, he didn't feel so sure about things any more.

'We're not going to Harlesden, anyway,' McDaid said.

'Isn't Bill Enright still over here?' Boyce suggested. 'Living under some other name. Dalton, isn't it?'

McDaid stared. Did *everyone* know *everything* in this organisation, he wondered. And had to change again.

He said, 'No, there's another place we can use. It's safer.'

Boyce raised his eyebrows, learning something himself for the first time. 'You didn't mention it before.'

'No,' McDaid said, 'I didn't.'

'You want to split up and leave at five minute intervals, Sean?' Boyce suggested helpfully. 'You can give us directions.'

The answer was a bit chilling.

'No. We stay together.'

'Are you going to tell them, though?' Boyce persisted.

'Tell who?' McDaid asked. 'What?'

'People. Everyone. Tell the media. Tell them it was us escaped. The IRA.'

'Why?' McDaid asked.

Knowing his own reason. But wanting to hear Boyce's.

But Boyce had thought it through as well. He said, 'Otherwise what's the point? It won't have any effect. It might as well be two ordinary criminals for all anyone knows.'

McDaid stared again. And ran his fingers through his short, curly hair.

The way he always did when he was crossed.

Something bothering him about Boyce.

The signs of an intelligence he hadn't noticed before.

He pushed his fingers through his wet hair again and said quietly, 'Let's go.'

9

A little after midnight, George Rawlings told his driver to take the black Mercedes past the opening to Fry Road in Harlesden and park down the next side-street.

Then he clambered from the rear of the car and walked back in heavy rain under a dark umbrella.

Stopping at Pa Daly's front door, he rapped with his cane on the wood, ignoring the electric doorbell.

The sound had an old-fashioned terror to it, he felt, and made a more efficient summons.

A tall man, stooping a little, cautiously opened the door. Early forties. Rugged face. Unshaven black stubble. And in the shadowy light, unpleasantly reminiscent of a Hollywood gangster.

Stafford, Rawlings remembered. Jody Stafford.

Their paths had crossed in the round of meetings between British officials and Republican negotiators in the months prior to the IRA ceasefire, at the height of the struggle to replace the more hawkish former Director-General of MI5, Sir Andrew Pinnington. They hadn't liked each other.

And now, as he blocked the doorway, the distrust flashed again in Stafford's moist eyes, which seemed to be streaming with a heavy cold. So that for a moment Rawlings wondered if his little joke had backfired, if the IRA had somehow diverted the security forces and occupied Daly's house themselves.

But then Stafford relaxed and shook his head at someone concealed in the hallway behind the opened door. He turned sharply and walked quickly away from Rawlings.

Rawlings stepped inside. He touched the tip of his hat with

107

the cane handle in a desultory salute to the armed detective behind the door and followed Stafford to the front living-room on the right.

Three other Special Branch detectives were stationed in there. Superintendent Gilston was sitting in the only armchair. David Bromley rested against the wall near a window. June Maybury stood with her back to the fireplace.

Rawlings stopped, leaning on his cane.

He looked from one to the other and said softly, 'Perhaps Mr Stafford might be kind enough to excuse us for a while.'

Stafford frowned. 'Sorry?'

Rawlings ignored him. He said, 'Superintendent?'

At a nod from Gilston, two of the armed detectives moved on either side of Stafford and took an elbow each to escort him. The third slipped in front to hold the door open and to close it behind them again.

When they were gone, Rawlings sat at the cheap circular table in the centre of the room and rested his cane against his legs, crooking the handle over his left knee.

He said to Gilston and Maybury, including Bromley with a wave in his direction, 'I'm afraid our friend Sean McDaid won't be obliging us with a visit here tonight. And I fear our previously limited chances of obtaining information from within the group have now disappeared completely. The body of William Barr was discovered by local police in a derelict factory a little over two miles from here. Shot twice through the head.'

There was a gloomy silence for a while.

'Bit of a mistake, really,' Rawlings muttered then.

'What, sir?' Gilston asked.

'Suppressing the details of the prisoners' escape,' Rawlings explained. 'Bit of a mistake. In retrospect. Of course, you had every reason to clamour for it, June.'

Maybury started.

108

She said, 'Could I remind you, sir, that I was the one –'

'What with your informant out with the prisoners and your hopes in McDaid's brother,' Rawlings interrupted. 'Perhaps we were all confident it might be over in twenty-four hours. Hasn't quite worked out for you, however.'

Maybury had waited. Impatiently.

She said now, 'I specifically asked for it to be put on the record, sir –'

'Well,' Rawlings sighed, 'I suppose we'll have to do it now, won't we? Come clean about the whole thing. Issue photos and descriptions of the three.'

'It will squeeze them, sir,' Gilston approved. 'Restrict their movements. Once they're under that sort of pressure, they'll make mistakes.'

'Of course, the media are bound to come back strongly at us,' Rawlings predicted sourly. 'You know what they'll ask, don't you? Why was the truth distorted? They're so damned faithful to the truth, aren't they? And so concerned about their beloved public. Why was the public misled? The thing is . . .'

Rawlings tailed off. Looking from one to the other again, but this time for inspiration.

'No doubt the subsequent disturbances in Whitemoor, sir,' Bromley offered then, 'were designed to distort the true situation and it was not until full order was restored in the prison that the real identities of the escaped prisoners were discovered.'

Rawlings thought about it.

'Yes,' he agreed then. 'No doubt. Well spotted, Bromley. Used to this sort of show, are we?'

'In a way, sir.'

'Good.'

Rawlings took his cane from its resting place and put his weight on it to rise from the table.

He said, 'Oh, and before I say good-night. Perhaps you might let Mr Stafford know, June, that two of his friends are still waiting for him at the corner.'

'Friends?' Maybury repeated.

'You might invite them in to dry off.'

'What friends?'

'Such a wretched night and we don't wish to appear inhospitable. Dreadful weather, really. Already reports of flooding in Devon, one hears, and some considerable threat of it here in London also . . .'

10

East through Hampstead and Islington and Bethnal Green and Plaistow, and then south across the Thames and into Woolwich, McDaid and Boyce and Reilly travelled in silence, not trusting each other.

Reilly drove. The others sat behind him in the rear.

On Plumstead Road, McDaid finally tapped Reilly on the shoulder and told him to pull over. Reilly eased the car against the right-hand kerb. He killed the lights and cut the engine and waited, not turning around, tense with anxiety and thinking about the bullet that had shattered Woolly Barr's head back in Golders Green.

But it was Boyce that McDaid addressed.

He said, 'Go and check out this house, Danny. Take the second turn on the right from here, then the third on the left. Number twenty-eight. You got that?'

The headlights of a passing truck glared through the rain on the car's windows and caught Boyce nodding miserably. 'Yeah. Second right, third left, twenty-eight.'

'The woman's name is Maisie Connolly,' McDaid told him. 'She lives alone. She's old. About fifty-five or sixty.'

Reilly shifted uneasily in front, reckoning that the description was for his benefit.

'Who is she?' Boyce asked.

McDaid didn't answer, uncomfortable with his own memories now. He thought of a big, tearful woman half smothering him with pity and grief when he was twelve, trying to lay claim to his dead mother's place in his life. He'd shrugged her off. And taken a gun instead from Jody Stafford.

'Can you trust her?' Boyce persisted.

'She was an old friend of my mother's in Belfast,' McDaid explained. 'She left after my mother was killed.'

'Is she one of ours, though?'

McDaid shook his head. 'No. No connection. Tell her it's for me. I need beds for the three of us for a few nights.'

'She won't know you're free,' Boyce objected then. 'Nobody knows we're out.'

'So?'

'She mightn't believe me.'

McDaid sighed. 'Just check that the place is clean then, Danny. No cops. No watchers. I'll ask her myself.'

When Boyce had left, stepping into the puddles on the roadway and rounding the front of the car, the others watched him through the rain on the windscreen until he'd hurried down a side-street and disappeared.

'Put your hands on the wheel,' McDaid ordered Reilly then.

Reilly hooked his thumbs around the bottom of the steering wheel and left his fists where they had been, resting in his lap.

'Higher,' McDaid said. 'Up where I can see them.'

Reilly snorted and slowly raised his hands, separating two fingers on each side and wagging abuse with them.

'Now listen,' McDaid told him. He took three sealed envelopes from the waterproof pouch holding his maps and offered them into the front. He said, 'I'm releasing a statement to the media. You'll have to organise a courier to collect

111

and deliver these. Not around here. Take the car. Dump it on the way back.'

Reilly glanced sideways at the envelopes and turned away again without taking them. When he heard them dropping to the passenger seat beside him, he asked, 'What about money?'

'There's enough left to cover it.'

Reilly sneered. 'I'm not talking about postage stamps. I'm talking about money. For the job. And afterwards. Is this old woman going to dig us out or something? Is that the idea?'

McDaid hesitated. Just a second. And then he said, 'Dixie has our money.'

'Yeah, but Dixie's been lifted, hasn't he? It's obvious. Otherwise you'd have been in touch with him, wouldn't you?'

'I know where he has it.'

'Yeah?' Reilly's hands tightened a little around the steering wheel. 'How much?'

Wrong question, McDaid thought to himself. Should've asked where. He shrugged and said casually, 'Forty, fifty thousand.'

'The fuck!' Reilly scoffed. 'Where would he get fifty thou? What I hear, he wasn't even working full time.'

'You know why he was run out of Northern Ireland three years ago?'

'Yeah, well. He had his fingers in the Brigade's funds, didn't he? But . . .'

'But what? You think he's spent it all?'

Reilly hesitated. 'I don't know, do I?'

McDaid rested a hand on Reilly's shoulder. Lightly. Without pressure. He said, 'You know who helped him lift all that cash? I did. Five years ago I could see this ceasefire coming. Stafford and the rest of the old men. Getting tired. Five years ago I knew we'd need another organisation if we couldn't get rid of the old men. Do you think Dixie stole that money for himself? That's what Stafford thought. What do you think?'

112

Reilly shrugged, easing his shoulder away from McDaid's grip with the gesture. 'Where is it, then?' he asked. 'The money.'

'At the flat.'

'Dixie's place? That's being watched by now.'

'That's why I need you to get that statement out,' McDaid said smoothly. 'And something else I need you to do.'

Reilly was silent. Thinking. Not certain about the chances. But knowing at least that the money would never be his until it had passed through McDaid's hands first. So he picked up the envelopes from the passenger seat and asked, 'What? What else?'

Danny Boyce, coming back on to Plumstead Road after checking out the house, noticed Reilly and McDaid laughing together in the car and wondered what they were planning, and whether the joke was on himself.

He didn't sit in when he reached the car. He tapped the side window at the rear and when McDaid lowered the glass he said, 'Everything's clear. No problems.'

McDaid got out and stood on the footpath beside Boyce.

Without waiting, without saying a word, Reilly drove off.

Boyce asked, 'Where's he going? Dumping the car?'

McDaid said, 'Yeah.' He turned and strode away. 'Let's go. Get cleaned up.'

Around the corner he slowed again, though, and probed gently, 'Danny?'

'Yeah?'

'Don't let Reilly in on any of our plans from here on. Okay?'

'Yeah, okay.'

'And let me know if he mentions anything about money to you. Dixie has some stashed away as funds. I'll be picking it up. Let me know.'

'I will, Sean.'

'I issued a statement to the media, Danny,' McDaid said

113

then. 'Telling them it was us who escaped. Reilly's gone with it.'

Boyce was too relieved to trust his speech. Instead, he put his arm around McDaid's shoulders and squeezed gratefully.

McDaid wriggled free after a while, pretending to hunch his shoulders against the driving rain. Intimacy, he thought sourly. It always came as a camouflage for betrayal. He thought again of the woman hugging him when he was twelve, trying to lure him into helplessness, away from revenge. And then he remembered another embrace, the first that Jody Stafford had inflicted on him. A couple of months before Stafford broke Dixie's arms. As false as Judas's lips on the cheek of Christ, he thought bitterly.

11

Jody Stafford came quietly down the stairs of Pa Daly's house and walked slowly into the living-room ahead of the three detectives, affecting a composure he didn't really feel.

'A joint IRA-British Army operation,' Daly had cackled sarcastically in the bedroom above. 'Was that it, Jody? It doesn't look much different to me than when the two of you were on opposite sides. You're still the one who ends up in jail.'

Stafford controlled himself now, though. He needed to make a play for information.

He saw that Rawlings and Gilston had left the house and realised that no one was waiting any more for McDaid to show up. There could only be two reasons, of course. Either McDaid was captured by now or he was already elsewhere. But which one was it?

Stafford said quietly, 'You want Sean McDaid. But you don't understand him enough to find him. I do.'

114

June Maybury, standing at the fireplace and staring moodily into the flames, didn't trouble herself to answer him. She
didn't even bother to turn.

She said, 'Take some men, Bromley, and escort Mr Stafford
here down to his two friends at the corner to inform them that
their vigil is pointless.'

Bromley lightly touched Stafford's arm with his left hand.
'Yes, ma'am. And then?'

'Keep them all safe for Mr Rawlings's attention in the morning,' Maybury told him curtly.

Stafford went silently, again suppressing the intense resentment he felt.

As he was walking down Fry Road with Bromley and the
three detectives, he tried to see what surveillance they'd had
in place for Sean McDaid's approach to Daly's house. But he
couldn't spot anyone.

Maybe they'd already gone home, he decided. Or maybe
they were still concealed in darkness. Behind hedges. In other
houses.

Junior Doherty and Sheehan and Crawley weren't standing at the corner as Maybury had said. But Stafford didn't
expect them there. The fact that she'd mentioned only two
meant that they'd split up as arranged, with Doherty and
Sheehan covering the approach from Longstone Avenue and
Crawley at the corner with Drayton Road, and that only the
first two had been spotted.

But how close was Crawley, Stafford wondered. And how
would he react if he saw the rest being lifted?

Stafford took a chance.

He stopped just before the bend and said to Bromley, 'Look,
there's four men, not just two. Two pairs. Covering each other.
If we approach one, it's only going to excite the other.'

Bromley sighed. 'Unless you can manage bi-location, you're
going to have to, aren't you?'

Stafford said angrily, 'Okay, it's your show.'

He threw up his hands and strode sharply away, turning left at the end of the road and putting five or six paces between himself and Bromley before the MI5 man could react.

Obscured for a moment by the bend, Stafford took off and ran up Longstone Road, calling to Doherty and Sheehan and hoping there were no more police stationed between them.

He gambled on Bromley not being certain enough of his brief to shoot at him; on the man's doubts about the consequences.

And he seemed to have called it correctly.

Bromley shouted at him to stop. But when there was no response, he only instructed the others to chase.

The detectives were all young and fit and well trained. Stafford was forty-three and a little out of condition, and not really dressed for flight. Already his breathing was harsh and his leather-soled shoes were slipping on the wet surface.

Without Doherty and Crawley to help him, he had only seconds of freedom.

And he still couldn't see the pair.

But then, just as he reached the bend into Roundwood Road, they suddenly emerged from the shadows on either side of him and fled with him.

If he'd had the breath, Stafford would've laughed at the irony.

Instead he managed to gasp, 'Go back! Block them! Behind! No guns! Give me space!'

He didn't see them turning and falling back, but a moment later he heard the grunts and shouts as the wave of pursuing cops broke against them and they all went down, grappling with each other.

Stafford ran on, expecting to hear the splash of pursuing feet in the puddles behind him again. But they never came. All he caught were the sounds of the struggle, growing

116

gradually fainter.

He tried to recall the geography of the area from the A–Z he'd studied earlier with the others.

The Avenue twisted around the perimeter of a sports ground, he remembered, and came back down towards Fry Road. He couldn't follow it. They'd have men coming up the opposite direction to cut him off.

His only hope, and a slim one, lay to his right, over the wall and through Willesden Cemetery.

He stopped and checked in front and behind. No one was in sight of him yet. No one to notice his route. He crouched then and sprang upwards, clinging to the top of the wall and dragging himself up with difficulty, cutting his left palm on a jagged stone.

When he landed on the other side the ground was like a bog beneath him. Waterlogged. Gluey. Every step seemed to end in a loud splash, advertising his new position. Every effort seemed to slow him further, like wading through a swimming pool.

In the darkness he lurched against a headstone, deadening the muscle in his right thigh. He limped on, not knowing where he was going, just guessing the direction and plagued by the fear that he'd traced a circle and was heading back into the chasing policemen.

It was only when he tripped over a fallen slab of marble and lifted his face from the water to peer at a name on the head-stone in front of him that he realised he'd made it to the Jewish section in the north-east of the cemetery. He remembered it being marked on the map. Jewish Cemetery. It was close to the wall that led out to the centre of Willesden.

Again he hurt himself clambering over the perimeter, graz-ing a knee this time.

If the police had guessed his route, he would've been easy to pick up as he fell into Tower Road. He was exhausted. And he was half crippled. But they obviously hadn't sussed it yet.

He hobbled away, down Clare Road, through – of all things – Maybury Gardens and into High Road, and cut from there to the tube station at Dollis Hill.

The few who were still out in the rain were as soaked and battered as himself and paid him little attention.

He took the first northbound train and travelled only one stop, getting off again at Neasden. He limped northwards, up Neasden Lane and into North Circular Road, knowing the number of the house that would offer him refuge for the night, but trying desperately to remember the alias Bill Enright had been using in London.

In the doorway, he ran his finger down the column of illuminated name cards beside the bells. Kidney, McCarvill, Teale, Tihabane, Levi . . . And rang the next one.

Dalton. That was it. Bob Dalton.

12

Denis Reilly came out of a telephone booth in Limehouse and walked towards Gill Street, back to the address he had just given to a courier company.

The wind had dropped to a light breeze by then, although the rain was still heavy. It wasn't possible to avoid the puddles on the streets and footpaths any more. There was water everywhere.

Reilly had parked the car in a tight space about half-way down Gill Street and he sat back inside it now to wait.

The courier, a youth driving a Renault van, took more than thirty minutes to reach him. Reilly let him hop from the van and sprint towards the house number he'd been given. Then he opened his own door and stepped out and shouted angrily, 'Hey! I thought you weren't going to come at all. I was just going to deliver them myself.'

The courier ran back. He looked at the rain dripping from Reilly's hair and said defensively, 'Sorry, mate. It's this bloody weather, isn't it? Has the traffic backed up.'

'Get on with it, then,' Reilly snapped.

'Yes, sir.'

So the exchange was hasty afterwards. Letters and payment on Reilly's side, receipts and excessive guarantees and even more apologies from the youth.

Reilly sat back in the car, pretending to collect something from the glove compartment, and waited for the courier to finish a three-point turn and take the Renault back out of Gill Street. Then he got out again and walked to the other end of Gill Street before turning from there on to Millwall Docks.

Huddled between two rusting containers there was a pale, bearded youth wrapped in a sodden blanket. He was sleeping, his arms wrapped around his knees, his chin resting on his forearms.

Without waking the man Reilly passed on.

Hearing voices from one of the abandoned warehouses past the north section of the dock, he stooped and crept through a gap in the side wall of the building.

Five or six down-and-outs sat around a dying fire of damp wood, arguing over the dregs of a bottle of cheap wine.

Again Reilly turned away. Getting a little irritated now. A little desperate. Wondering if he'd picked the wrong place.

Trudging on to the next warehouse, though, he heard someone else shuffling towards him. One person alone. Splashing through the pools of rain water.

Reilly stopped and took a quart of whiskey from the inside pocket of his jacket. Something came with it and dropped into the water by his feet. Reilly crouched. He patted the ground

119

through the puddle, feeling odd shapes, stones or small lumps of coal, but nothing that might be his.

The wino staggered into his view before he could search any further. Reilly stood up again. Coughing a little, he unscrewed the top of the whiskey bottle, put its neck to his lips and noisily sucked in the alcohol.

The wino trotted nearer, his bloodshot eyes widening with need.

He was an old guy, Reilly noticed. Bearded. His long hair was matted. He was a bit smaller than Reilly would've liked, but the clothes were loose and baggy on him. Two torn and ragged overcoats. Laceless shoes. A battered trilby. All steaming with rain and stinking of old grime and stale food and piss and sweat.

The man stopped in front of Reilly and kept nodding his head uncontrollably towards the whiskey.

Then he croaked, 'Any chance of an aul' sup, is there?'

So that Reilly realised, with disgust, that the wretch was Irish too.

Reilly held out the bottle. The wino whimpered with greed and grabbed at the whiskey. He threw his head back to pour it into his mouth.

He was on the point of turning away, intending to finish the bottle before letting it go, when Reilly put his hands around the scraggy, exposed neck and squeezed with his powerful fingers.

The wino made a slight choking sound. The empty bottle dropped from his hand and shattered on the dock by his feet. The whiskey that was still trapped in his mouth gurgled and spurted outwards, over his own and Reilly's clothes.

It was only then, when the booze was wasted, that he seemed to think of struggling. His filthy nails clawed outwards towards Reilly's face. Unable to reach, they came back to tear at the exposed hands around his neck.

Reilly cursed with pain. But his grip didn't loosen.

120

Outraged, he brought his right knee violently upwards, into the old guy's shrivelled groin. As the wino jerked forward, Reilly crashed his own forehead into the gasping face, breaking the nose. Blood spurted. Into the beard. Again on to Reilly's clothes.

The old man lost consciousness. With nothing to resist him any more, Reilly's momentum carried him off balance and he fell, still gripping his victim, into the pools of oily water at their feet.

The tramp's head cracked on the concrete. He must have been already dead, but Reilly, charged with adrenalin, straddled him and kept squeezing on the ragged windpipe, until he finally realised that the man was limp and lifeless.

He got up then and checked on his stinging hands. The cuts weren't deep, just surface wounds. He wiped them with a handkerchief, walking away to check that no one had heard or witnessed the fight.

When he came back he dragged the corpse into the darkness beside the warehouse and started undressing it. He took a collapsible plastic kitbag from his own jacket and opened it. Into it, with incongruous neatness, he folded the wino's clothes. The greatcoats. The jackets. The trousers. The lengths of string and old twine he wound carefully around his left hand before dropping them into the ruined trilby for packing.

When he was finished he carried the naked corpse to the side of the dock and lowered it in without too much noise.

He thought if he took the tunnel across the Thames and left the stolen car on the other side, he might make it back to McDaid in Woolwich in about an hour. Better if he walked the last stage, he decided, even in the rain. There was too much blood and booze on his clothes to take a taxi or a bus.

121

PART THREE

Thursday

ONE

1

Eight o'clock the next morning, June Maybury was resting in the bedroom of her apartment, half-listening to her boy-friend bitching about the Irish, when news of the IRA jailbreak finally broke on television.

She sat up in bed and raised a hand to quieten her lover, saying softly, 'Tim . . .'

Aston pretended not to notice her.

A small man, impeccably dressed in designer clothes, his dark good looks were ruined by the extra shadows that worry left permanently on his face.

He worried about his height. He worried about an early tendency towards baldness. He even worried that the clothes labels he patronised would suddenly become unfashionable.

Most of all, though, he worried these days about the threat of redundancy. The small merchant bank he worked for was being swallowed by some Irish institution. It was a fear he wouldn't let go of himself and wouldn't allow Maybury to forget.

More than three years she'd been living with him now, ever since coming back from Northern Ireland to a position as deputy section head in Counter-Subversion. She'd thought of it then as a new beginning in her life. A chance to bury the recent past. A chance to recover.

Aston had been prosperous and successful when they'd met, six months before, on one of her London holidays. An attractive change from the grey, pinched individuals she'd mingled with in Belfast. He was colourful and confident. Popular and witty. And indifferent to race.

The recent negative thing about the Irish was caused by corrosive self-doubt. And then sharpened by the late discovery that Maybury herself had been raised as a child by relatives in Dublin, in southern Ireland.

Lately, and particularly the last few weeks, she was tiring of his self-absorption.

She'd been up late, for instance, into the previous night. Hopelessly searching for Jody Stafford around London. And afterwards trying to find the threads between Stafford and the two McDaid brothers and Woolly Barr. Desperately struggling to wind up the case that had brought her reluctantly back to dealing with the violence and the impossible politics of Northern Ireland.

But Aston, having missed her the previous night, had woken her at seven to complain about some new slight at the office, some careless word or gesture that had fed his anxieties.

Now, fully dressed in a business suit, he was pacing in front of the noisy television he had switched on without wanting to watch.

'You quite understand exactly what this is, don't you, June?' he was saying. 'Properly read, it is, as we say, an indicator of just how low England has sunk as a player on the world stage. I mean, taken over by the *Irish*, for God's sake! One could almost predict borrowing from the Isle of Man to fund the budgetary deficit in the current year.'

The national news headlines on the television were just as bleak. But they had slightly wider appeal.

'Manchester United Football Club suspend Eric Cantona

126

for the remainder of the season,' the newsreader announced. 'Government admit escaped Whitemoor prisoners were IRA terrorists. And the risk of major flooding in London as weather continues to worsen.'

'Stay quiet a minute, Tim,' Maybury asked.

Aston stopped and swivelled. 'I beg your pardon?'

'I want to listen to this.'

'I see.' He turned to the television and watched as Eric Cantona once again cleared a barrier to reach a heckling spectator and he asked, 'Why?'

She didn't bother answering.

The newsreader said then, 'In a statement issued from the Home Office this morning, the Government has admitted that the four inmates who escaped from the special secure unit of Whitemoor Prison last Tuesday night and who shot dead two uniformed police constables yesterday morning are, in fact, convicted IRA terrorists. Pete Carter reports.'

The next shot was of Carter standing outside Whitemoor early that morning. Behind him riot police in full gear were filing through a side gate. The riot squad was a blind, Maybury knew. There was no trouble inside the prison after the escape.

Carter was saying, 'Following the restoration of order in Whitemoor late last night after the riots which started Tuesday, the Home Office has now confirmed that four and not two men escaped during the disturbances and that all are convicted IRA terrorists. The men, who haven't yet been named, wounded a prison officer with a hand-gun smuggled into the unit and then cut their way through . . .'

'IRA?' Aston interrupted suddenly. 'Is this the case you're currently dealing with?'

'We'll talk later, Tim.'

'I thought you were finished with Northern Ireland?'

'Later. After the news.'

The report got through the escape and its aftermath and

127

then switched to analyse the impact on Northern Ireland and to take interviews with Unionist politicians who claimed that the ceasefire was dead and that the peace process had already ended. One of them managed to make it sound as if a wish of his had just come true.

No one mentioned the deaths of Jennifer Crooks and Woolly Barr.

Barr's execution, Maybury knew now, meant that Sean McDaid had always been a step ahead of her. But why was Barr *taken out* of prison before being killed? Why not shoot him during the riot? It made no obvious sense.

The little man was on her conscience that morning. Because she had still been his handler when he was killed, and you always felt a sense of personal responsibility.

She'd recruited him the usual way, through information passed on by another tout she'd run in Northern Ireland, an IRA man named Philip Ganley who'd picked up a drugs habit along the way. It was Ganley who told her that Woolly Barr had been involved in the same ring, embezzling a little IRA money to keep himself happy with crack and hash. Easy, then, to put pressure on the terrified Barr, newly locked away in Whitemoor with twenty or more of his old comrades.

Or it would've been easy, if Maybury could've forgotten what had happened afterwards to Ganley himself.

It wasn't something she'd ever got round to dealing with. So when Aston grew restless again she was almost grateful for the interruption to her thoughts.

'I thought you'd finished with Northern Ireland,' he said impatiently.

'It's only temporary,' she told him.

'Temporary?' he scoffed. 'Good God! Have they *any* idea in what condition you came back to me from that god-for-saken place? Have they *any* understanding of how close you were to breakdown and ruining my career? Do you remem-

128

ber the dinner the Chief Executive –'

Aston was just warming to it, how she was born to adorn his life and came near to besmirching it instead, when the doorbell rang.

He fell silent. And looked at her accusingly.

She shrugged. Just as the doorbell rang again.

She was out of bed and already dressed before he finally moved to answer it. While she was opening the curtains in the bedroom and looking out over the Thames, she heard him release a surly invitation to the caller.

Her boss, George Rawlings, was installed in the best armchair by the time she reached the living-room.

'Morning, June,' he greeted breezily. 'Have a good sleep?'

'Not particularly, sir, no,' she admitted.

'Ah!'

Aston smiled nastily and stood in silence, looking from one to the other, as if awaiting an explanation for the disruption to his life.

'Wretched weather,' Rawlings remarked. He waved vaguely in the direction of the river. 'The Thames,' he said. 'I hear there's flooding up river, in Richmond.'

Aston grunted. He threw his hands in the air and searched for his overcoat and scarf.

'Doubt if I shall be home before late,' he threw back as he stormed out.

Rawlings rested his cane, a sign of more comfortable occupation.

He said, 'Bit of a mess last night, June.'

'In my report –'

'Yes, I read it.'

'Might I remind you, sir, that I was always opposed to Stafford's involvement. I consider that his behaviour since arriving here bears me out. Abducting Dixie McDaid to prevent us interrogating him. Concealing from us the address of

129

Jennifer Crooks's house. Bringing us to Harlesden last night to divert our attention while McDaid operated elsewhere.'

'Nevertheless,' Rawlings said, 'Stafford may lead us to McDaid. If not voluntarily then unwittingly.'

'We no longer know where Stafford is.'

'Not at the moment, no. But I'm sure he'll let you know.'

She tensed. She felt as if ice were travelling down her spine and around her waist and into her stomach. 'How do you mean, sir?'

Rawlings's right hand again described a meaningless pattern and then came back to settle on the handle of his cane.

Maybury let it go, storing it to worry about later. She said, 'I think it might be more fruitful to concentrate on Dixie McDaid at this end and Tommy Brennan in Northern Ireland. It's obvious that Sean McDaid and the others had a network outside the prison. Jennifer Crooks was a part of it. I believe Dixie is also.'

'Perhaps you're right,' Rawlings conceded. 'Have you seen their statement?'

'What statement, sir?'

With his left hand, Rawlings took a page from his inside pocket, released his cane to open the paper and read: 'If we are tricked again, there is a band in Ireland, and I am one of them, who will answer the English with violence and the edge of the sword. These words were delivered by the Irish Republican leader, Patrick Pearse, on 31 March 1912. Nothing has changed in more than eighty years. England continues to betray Ireland and her people by its occupation of the northern six counties. On behalf of the oppressed peoples of Ireland, we hereby declare war on England and on its lackeys, the tired old men of the IRA who recently surrendered to the imperial power. We have already struck the first blow in this new campaign. Contrary to the craven propaganda of England's rulers, three volunteers escaped from Whitemoor

130

Prison last night, wounding a prison officer and subsequently killing in open battle two of the Crown's forces. This is only the preparation, however, for a far more devastating blow against the oppressor.'

Rawlings paused and folded the paper before adding, 'One presumes he must mean the attempted assassination of Her Majesty, who continues to decline to alter her schedule. Have you any idea how many engagements the Royal Family perform in a week? Schools, charities, the Barbican, the Royal Albert Hall . . .' He sighed and shook the paper angrily. 'It is signed by the Commander-in-Chief, United Irish Army, by the way.'

'Who was it sent to, sir?'

'The BBC and two of the national newspapers. We managed to convince them to hold it back.'

Maybury frowned. She said, 'Surely, sir, it would have been better if it was publicised. The group would be seen as a small splinter, not the main body of the IRA, and the ceasefire would hold.'

Rawlings purred, like a stalking cat. 'Ah!'

Maybury stared at him.

Her mind raced. Trained in suspicion, she couldn't help the direction it took.

Was Rawlings deliberately trying to keep the IRA involved in the attempt on the Queen's life, she wondered. Was he going to blame *them* for the breakdown of the peace process before they blamed the British Government? Did he intend taking them on? Did he hope to crush them? Did he see his role in history as the man who finally subverted Republicanism in Northern Ireland?

In the latter stages of the peace talks, he'd been brought in to replace Sir Andrew Pinnington, an anti-IRA hawk, as Director-General. Had he since become infected with the Service's oldest delusions?

131

And what had he meant by predicting that Stafford would contact her again? What did he know? How could he be so confident of Stafford's intentions? Or was that merely a casual guess?

She was so deep in thought that she started when Rawlings said, 'I've asked young Bromley to play a more active role in the whole affair.'

'What?'

'Young Bromley. David Bromley.'

'Bromley, yes. But what did you mean, a more active role?'

Rawlings coughed and sought the comfort of his cane. 'Yes. Well, we all know how reluctant you were to return to duties directly relating to Northern Ireland.'

'In the circumstances, sir –'

'No, no, I only mean that perhaps you . . . How long is it now since you returned from serving in Northern Ireland? 1992, was it?'

'1991.'

'It was unfair to expect you to be fully up to speed on recent developments. Of course, there was the fact that you were still handling Woolly Barr. By his own request, of course. Not something I would normally approve, an officer in one section handling a source from another. But we all have our oddities, and Sir Andrew must have been no different. Eh? However . . . Do you wish to interrogate him again, by the way?'

'Interrogate? Who, sir?'

'Dixie McDaid.'

'I'd like to search his flat first, but –'

'By all means.'

As Rawlings returned the folded photocopy to his pocket and brushed his coat, Maybury found her enthusiasm for searching Dixie McDaid's flat slipping a little. The trouble was, if Rawlings was playing a mad game to crush the ceasefire, anything he agreed to so readily couldn't be a threat to him.

But *was* he playing a game?

132

Or was *she* just overtired, overwrought, too confused, too nervous . . .?

'By the way,' Rawlings said quietly as he put his weight on the cane to stand up. 'Nothing to Special Branch about McDaid's statement just yet, eh? Just between ourselves.'

2

Nightmares don't have dates. But this one came from a damp early morning, way back in November, 1991.

Not yet dawn. A heavy mist. The grass wet with dew.

The location, a few miles outside Belfast, Northern Ireland.

The action, four men running up a hillside in single file. Each armed with a Kalashnikov assault rifle. Each wearing a balaclava and army boots and fatigues.

Four men. Jody Stafford. And Sean McDaid. Philip Ganley. And Bill Enright.

And now, this morning in January, more than three years later, Jody Stafford was reliving that episode in a dream.

Mid-way through it, a hand shook his right shoulder, waking him. When he opened his eyes, the image was confusing. Enright's long, blond hair and boyish face.

'Trap!' Stafford whispered urgently, struggling to get up. 'Trap!'

Enright laughed. 'Wake up, Jody,' he said. He shook Stafford's shoulder again. 'Wake up. You're in my place. Not back home. You're in London.'

And Stafford remembered. Of course. It was where he'd limped for refuge the previous night, to Bill Enright's two-room flat in Neasden. Only Bill wasn't known as Enright any more. Dalton. Bob Dalton. Ever since he'd started working undercover in London.

Enright hadn't asked any questions yet. The night before, he'd poured some whiskey and boiled the water for coffee while Stafford cleaned his cut hand and checked the damage to his thigh muscle.

Afterwards they'd reminisced, and mostly about that incident back in 1991, the last time they'd fought together and one of the last times they'd seen each other.

Was it a mobile platoon of a Parachute Regiment that was due along the road at the base of that hill? No, nothing as definite as that. Remember? They'd take the first army or police patrol that came their way.

The Kalashnikovs would be used to finish off survivors. But the real weapon was a 500-pound bomb buried under the road and fitted with a remote control.

The others left Ganley, more nervous than usual, at the approach to the hillside, partly as look-out, partly to cover their own retreat if necessary. Then they climbed to the summit.

On the way, Stafford stumbled over a large stone. He cursed and briefly shone his torch to investigate. A worm was still wriggling in the dead grass where the stone had lain.

Stafford didn't think it out until the unit had settled down and McDaid had primed the remote control. But then it struck him. He hadn't moved that stone himself. And how long does a worm stay above ground after being exposed? It could only mean that someone else had disturbed the stone a matter of minutes before Stafford stumbled on it.

He remembered Ganley's edginess going out on the mission that morning. The others had worried about it, too. And now he understood it. Not the nervousness of a man who feared too much, but the jumpiness of someone who already *knew* too much.

He whispered to the others, 'It's a trap! They're waiting for us!'

Despite the cold, Stafford started sweating. He reckoned the army would close in on them from behind, past Ganley, cutting off their retreat. They'd open fire from there, as well as from one side of the hill. A killing area, they called it. Maybe there were some patrols further below as well, but out of the cross-fire.

He whispered again, 'Detonate the bomb, Sean!'

'There's nothing there,' McDaid complained. 'Nothing to hit.'

'Detonate! It'll catch them off guard. Then get down that fucking hill as fast as you can. Not the way we came.'

And the blast had the right effect. The hidden soldiers seemed confused by the premature explosion and held their fire too long.

Enright picked up a flesh wound at the bottom of the hill. It was Stafford who helped him away, while McDaid covered their retreat with automatic fire.

All three made it back to freedom.

With Enright muttering through his pain, 'How the fuck did they know? How did they know?'

'Ganley,' Stafford said. 'That's how they knew. But how did they turn him? What makes him so vulnerable all of a sudden?'

'I'll find out,' McDaid had promised.

Neither was mentioning the word as they sat opposite each other four years on from that firefight, but betrayal was again on the minds of Stafford and Enright.

'The story was on the news,' Enright said. 'About an hour ago.'

'What story?'

'About the four lads breaking out of Whitemoor. Did you know about it?'

'Yes.'

'Was Sean with them?'

135

Stafford nodded. 'Yeah. And I need to contact him.'

Enright didn't ask why. He just drank his coffee.

Stafford said, 'You probably know his London haunts better than anyone. Better than me, anyway.'

'Try Pa Daly,' Enright said immediately. 'You know him? Fry Road there, over in Harlesden.'

'I'll give it a go,' Stafford promised. 'Anywhere else?'

Enright shrugged. 'There's a lot of others won't run with him now, will they? What with the ceasefire and everything. I'll ask around, though.'

'What about yourself?' Stafford suggested. 'Would he come here?'

'The trouble is', Enright said, 'knowing which side who's on any more, isn't it? For or against the ceasefire.'

'Yes.'

'So I wouldn't think he'd come here, no. Bit too much of a gamble.'

'Is it?' Stafford asked.

'Has to be, hasn't it? Anywhere. Bit of a gamble.'

'Right,' Stafford said. 'Why don't you ask around, then. We'll meet back here for lunch. Say, one-thirty. That okay?'

Stafford stood up, but his right leg gave as he put his weight on it. So he sat again.

He said, 'I need to take this slowly. Stretch it a bit before I go. Get rid of the stiffness. Don't bother waiting for me. Deadened it on a gravestone, of all things.'

Enright was still laughing as he pulled on a denim jacket and left the flat, descended the stairs and went out the street door, past the pay phone in the hall.

Outside, the wind had risen again, but the rain had eased.

Enright stuffed his hands in his pockets and kept his head down as he walked two hundred metres to a telephone booth, well out of sight of the flat. The number he dialled, written on a note he kept in his wallet, had been given to him late the previous night, before Stafford had limped back into his life.

The phone on the other side rang engaged the first time he tried it. After that an old woman's thin voice answered him nervously.

'Yes? Hello?'

'Mrs Connolly?' Enright asked.

'Yes. What is it?'

'Put Sean on to me. Tell him it's Enny.'

In the hallway of her house in Woolwich Mrs Connolly lowered the receiver but still held it tightly in her right hand, wondering what to do. She wasn't happy. She wasn't really certain in her mind.

Her relatives and old neighbours, they all thought she'd left Northern Ireland because the loyalists had killed her friends. But it wasn't only that. It was also because of what she was experiencing again now. The confusion. The ambivalence. Wanting to stop the IRA, but not wanting to do anything about it. She knew it wasn't merely fear. It was a code of silence born out of closeness. For the most part, IRA men were relatives and neighbours too. She herself, for instance, still remembered the curly-haired orphan Sean McDaid had once been.

While she was debating, of course, McDaid came from the living-room and took the receiver from her. He put his palm over the mouthpiece and asked, 'For me?'

She said nothing, but the answer was obvious in her eyes.

'Enny?' McDaid asked into the receiver.

Because only Enright, another part of the small network that included Jennifer Crooks and Pa Daly, now knew where he was. McDaid himself had contacted him the previous night.

'Stafford turned up, Mac,' Enright said.

'Where?'

'My place. Late last night. I couldn't get out to ring you. He's looking for you.'

'Is he still there?'

137

'No, we're meeting back there about one-thirty.'

'You'll have to deal with it yourself, Enny.'

Enright paused. 'How do you mean?' he asked then.

'You know what I mean,' McDaid told him. 'Get rid of him.'

'Are you coming over?' Enright asked uncertainly.

'No,' McDaid said.

'Why not?'

'For the same reason I didn't go there last night. Too many old comrades know where you are. Including Stafford.'

'That was because –'

'Besides, I've got to get into Dixie's flat. Something I have to pick up there. Have you got your own gear ready, by the way?'

'Not here. It's going to be the weekend at the earliest.'

'Tomorrow,' McDaid ordered.

'I don't think I can –'

'Tomorrow, midday. Bring them over here. Okay?'

'All right, all right. Look, stay away from Dixie's flat, Sean. I told you last night. It's crawling with cops.'

'I know, but I've got to get there.'

'What for?'

'Dixie never told me where the junction box was located.'

Enright exploded. 'What?'

'Look,' McDaid said, 'it's not the sort of information you send through the post or over a telephone line to Northern Ireland or pass on during a prison visit. Too many ears. The bomb's in place. I just don't know where the junction box is.'

'Why the fuck didn't Dixie tell *me*?' Enright demanded.

'It was more than a year ago, Enny. No one knew how things were going to fall, or how people would be after the fall.'

'He didn't fucking trust me!'

'He didn't trust anyone,' McDaid said. 'And he was right. Have you written down the address or the telephone number here?'

138

'Yeah. Why? I'll remember them. I'll make it there on Friday.'

'Exactly,' McDaid said coldly. 'So destroy the notes.'

3

There was a Special Branch man named Spencer standing at the newsagents on Kilburn High Road and another detective, John Fowler, patrolling the corridor outside Dixie McDaid's flat.

No need for concealment any more. No need for the neighbours to be kept in the dark.

Had there ever been any *honest* point to it all, June Maybury wondered as she stepped through the street door that Spencer unlocked for her, into a damp, grimy hallway. Any point to not immediately organising a routine man-hunt? To not alerting the public with descriptions and photographs?

'Start questioning the need for secrecy, June,' her old boss in MI5, Sir Andrew Pinnington, had once warned her, 'and you deny us all the necessary protection.'

Protection for *what*, though? Another question, of course. And one that hadn't occurred to her until recently.

Standing in the hallway, surrounded by peeling floral wallpaper and unwashed ochre paint, she looked distastefully up the stairway without seeing any promise of improvement. Instead of a pile, the carpet had hardened discs of chewing gum and cigarette burns. And the wooden rail was so caked with grease and dust that it was the last place you would've willingly put your hand.

She knew from the Special Branch reports that Dixie McDaid hadn't made much of an effort to keep his own flat against the grain of the house. She also knew that nothing of any interest had been found there by people a lot more skilled and a lot more practised in turning a place over than she was.

But what she hoped for now was more an insight into Dixie's character than any miraculous lead.

She was already familiar with his history from the file. How he'd arrived in London in 1992 with both his arms in plaster after a punishment beating. Hard to imagine him making a living in the construction industry after that. But that's what he'd done.

He still didn't mix much with the rest of the Irish community. And he hadn't bothered with Republicans at all.

Disillusionment? Or cunning?

John Fowler, the Special Branch man outside Dixie's door, was middle-aged and balding, a little fat and a little short of breath.

Maybury showed her ID and took the key from him, then put on a pair of plastic gloves before opening up.

The first thing that hit her *was* the untidiness. Unwashed clothes were scattered over floor and furniture. Plates with congealed fat had been left on seats and carpet. And there were other plates with unfinished dinners, chop bones, potatoes, carrots, turnip. The smell, stale now in the sealed flat, was of over-cooked vegetables.

Dixie's brother, Sean McDaid, had always been neurotic about cleanliness, even while in prison. She'd seen him only once. And even then, she'd watched him impatiently brush dirt from his sleeves.

Like a lot of younger siblings, though, Dixie seemed to assume that order would be restored by someone else after he left a room.

He obviously didn't read. There were no books about. He didn't listen to music, either, because there was no CD player or tape deck. So what *did* he do with his time, apart from watching the small television stuck away in a corner?

The answer was in the other room, where he usually slept. Past an awkwardly placed upright lamp that stood like a sentinel, guarding the doorway.

Dixie McDaid was a modeller.

On the wooden shelves that he'd mounted around the wall, there were scale models done in mixed materials of public buildings in England and in Northern and southern Ireland.

Ironically, the first one she recognised was Queen's University in Belfast, where she herself had taken a postgraduate degree in 1986 and worked as a junior lecturer a year later.

The second was the old Stormont building, the Northern Ireland parliament, where successive Unionist governments had sat in power before the imposition of direct rule from England.

The thought struck her that the models might be bombing targets for the IRA. But only for an instant. The one beside Stormont was of Arbour Hill Cemetery in Dublin, where the leaders of the 1916 Rebellion were honoured. As for the rest, they included the Barbican, the Thames Barrier and St Paul's in London, Christ Church Cathedral in Dublin, and the Guild Hall in Londonderry.

Tell Sean the hobby still keeps me interested, she remembered then. The only instruction Dixie had given Woolly Barr when he'd visited Whitemoor Prison six months before. She'd thought then that it might have been a coded message.

But the impression she got now was of a melancholy loner, expelled from his tribe and his land, not able to start a new life elsewhere, obsessively turning to his hobby to kill both the time and the pain.

And yet, the feeling that there was something she was missing just wouldn't leave her.

For all the disorder, there was a sense of something prepared about the place. And something else, something that

141

clashed with the character of the terrified but superior man she'd met the previous day.

Only she couldn't get a hold on it. Couldn't put a word to it.

Outside in the corridor again she peeled off the plastic gloves after locking the door and handing back the keys.

She wanted to talk to the balding detective on duty, wanted to cover her disappointment. But she couldn't think of anything easy to say.

Instead, she watched a tramp shuffling furtively past them to knock on a neighbour's door. And it gave her a topic.

But even that came out sharply, almost as a grilling.

'Have you spoken to him?' she asked.

'Yes, ma'am.'

She gestured impatiently. 'And?'

'The woman next door,' Fowler explained nervously. 'Her name is Mary Cassidy. She seems . . . She's a charity worker. She seems to have a regular group of, ah, homeless callers. There were three yesterday. And one other this morning. I can't think how the neighbours –'

'Yes,' Maybury interrupted.

She didn't *really* want to gossip after all, she discovered. She wanted to be alone, to think.

She said, 'Well, I'll leave him to you, then.'

And she hurried away without waiting for a response, down the stairs, through the hall and back into the relative freshness of Kilburn High Road.

As well as the stench of boiled vegetables, the house had that cloying, sweetish odour of dampness. Both smells always reminded her of Northern Ireland, of another damp flat, in another damp building, where she had watched Sean McDaid put a bullet into a man's stomach and then, an eternal five minutes later, finally put a second bullet into his temple to finish him off.

4

Superintendent Geoffrey Gilston also smelt something disturbing that morning. Except that, at first, he thought it was agreeable. And it wasn't just a physical odour. More a feeling in the air. An atmosphere that unsettled his copper's nose.

Gilston was a blunt man. Sitting down to a briefing in George Rawlings's office at MI5 Headquarters, he looked pointedly around and saw only the Director-General and Rawlings's effeminate private secretary, the long-haired, fleshy young man named Nicholas Orrinsmith.

So he asked outright, 'Where's Miss Maybury this morning? I thought she was joining us.'

While Orrinsmith bowed from the office, Rawlings played on the sympathy for his dead leg, wincing as he manoeuvred round the desk and sat down. He smiled apologetically and said faintly, 'I beg your pardon?'

'Maybury,' Gilston repeated. 'Where is she?'

'Ah!' Rawlings said. 'Hasn't she been in touch with you?'

'No.'

'Your office, perhaps?'

'No.'

Rawlings raised his eyebrows in surprise and glanced at his watch. 'Well. Let's start without her, then, shall we?'

Gilston shrugged. And would've left it at that. Because it was nothing to him. No skin off his nose. And he'd never been all that comfortable with the woman anyway.

But Rawlings overplayed it, killing off suspicions that hadn't even been expressed. 'Bit of a fiasco last night, as you know. And someone has to carry the can, eh?'

143

Gilston nodded, but only as camouflage. He knew from his own men that Jody Stafford had escaped while in David Bromley's custody. So either Bromley had fed lies to Rawlings, or Rawlings was now feeding rubbish to Gilston himself.

They were entitled to their family squabbles, of course, but not at the expense of the truth. Because if someone was lying about one thing, as Gilston knew from long experience, the chances were they were spreading the muck more thickly somewhere else as well.

Gilston didn't pursue it, though. As a tool, bluntness only had limited uses.

He shrugged again and said, 'Might as well start, then.'

'Yes,' Rawlings agreed. 'Quite.'

Gilston opened the folder he'd already placed on the desk. He said, 'Analysis of the drawings found in both Jennifer Crooks's house and vehicle has not yet yielded any definite results. We're in the process of collecting architectural plans for the buildings on Her Majesty's itinerary for the sake of comparison. It's a tedious procedure, particularly if we include other members of the Royal Family. Personally, I'm not hopeful. Some of your own people are.'

'Why the pessimism, Geoffrey?'

'I feel the drawings may be cleverly distorted, done in some sort of visual code which must be broken before they can be translated.'

'But it is a building, is it?' Rawlings probed.

'They could equally well be sketches of a park, couldn't they?'

'And what do you think it all means, Geoffrey? The bomb? Or a bullet?'

'Well, they brought out two explosives experts, Boyce and McDaid himself.'

'Yes,' Rawlings agreed. His eyes brightened and he leaned forward on his desk to make the point. 'But Sean McDaid was

144

a crack marksman. Still is, no doubt. Did you know that?'

'No.'

'When he first joined the IRA, he was used as a sniper in Belfast. Perhaps this is where we should all be looking.'

'Maybe,' Gilston conceded uneasily. 'But for political gestures the IRA has always preferred the bomb.'

'Perhaps we're dealing with a new phase of the struggle, a new organisation. Jennifer Crooks, for instance. She's English, isn't she? What else have we got on her?'

'English born. Her mother was Irish. She grew up in Bury, Lancashire. Her older brother joined the army and was one of the early fatalities in Northern Ireland. It's believed she became embittered and convinced that we should withdraw from the province.'

'One of our own, eh?' Rawlings lamented. He eased back in his chair and searched for his cane. 'Not quite one of *ours*, of course. Not like Philby and the others who defected eastwards. Have you ever wondered, Geoffrey, precisely what circumstances would convert one of ours to work as a double agent for the IRA?'

'The thought never crossed my mind,' Gilston lied.

'Perhaps it should, Geoffrey. Perhaps it should.'

Someone – with a lousy sense of timing, as Gilston remarked to himself – knocked on the office door just then.

Actually Gilston didn't have to guess who it was or wait for the entrance. He already knew. He'd heard the same knock on the same office door the night before last and decided then that there was something too deferential and, at the same time, something too assured about it. It was a servant's knock. It didn't request admission. It announced an arrival.

'Come in!' Rawlings called. And then, as the door opened, 'Ah, David! You know the Superintendent.'

Gilston turned and stared at Bromley. For almost ten seconds he held the look, not saying anything. 'What happened

145

last night, lad?' he demanded then.

Bromley raised his eyebrows, but didn't otherwise register any reaction. 'Sir?'

'Jody Stafford slipped away from you.'

'Yes, sir. Your men tried to chase him down, but he managed to elude them. I don't understand how. Stafford is forty-three.'

Something had changed overnight in Bromley's attitude, Gilston observed. An added certainty. A new insolence.

Not hard to see where it came from, of course. Maybury out of favour. A leg up and the ear of the Director-General for young Bromley. That smirk of his came from sharing too many whispers with the powerful.

Gilston stood up and said brusquely, 'I'm off.'

'Keep in touch, Geoffrey,' Rawlings advised.

Bromley held the door open for the Superintendent. Whether as courtesy or irony, though, Gilston couldn't tell. And couldn't care, either.

5

Down Kilburn High Road, past Quex Road and into West End Lane where she'd parked the car, June Maybury thought about the execution she'd witnessed in Northern Ireland.

The victim's name was Philip Ganley, the small-time pusher she'd come across while he was a student in Queen's. Peddling dope to feed his own crack habit. As it turned out, he was an IRA volunteer as well and claimed to be part of an active service unit that had notched up more killings than most.

Ganley.

146

She would always remember his face the way it had been when they'd first sweated him in an interrogation cell. It was drenched with his tears. His skin was blotched. His eyes were scrunched in pain. His mouth was open in a scream.

He'd been crushed between his craving for a fix and his terror at being tossed back to the IRA as a pusher. So he'd come over, to act as a mole within the IRA, with Maybury as his only handler.

She would always remember that face. Just as she'd always remember the first titbit he'd given her.

'I'll tell you things,' Ganley had rambled. 'Sure I'll tell you things. Like, someone else. He was in on this, too. In on drugs. Woolly Barr. You have him yourselves in Whitemoor. In prison. Over there.'

Two weeks before he'd died, in November 1991, Ganley had given her the plans for an ambush on the security forces by Jody Stafford and Sean McDaid and Bill Enright. But the SAS had fouled up the kill. And Ganley's chances of survival.

He'd been shot in a basement flat that smelled of rising damp and boiled turnips.

Maybury had the key in the driver's door of her red BMW and was trying to shake off the memories when she glanced up and saw the Special Branch man, Superintendent Gilston, coming down West End Lane towards her. One of the last persons she would've picked to bump into.

She intended nodding before slipping through the door she'd opened, but Gilston put his big, awkward frame in the way. On a dull English morning, the greyness of his English clothes irritated her all the more. A dark suit that had never been respected and that had no self-esteem left.

'Any luck?' he enquired.

'At what?' she asked sharply.

'I was coming here anyway, but the chaps rang me to keep me up to date. Who else can I rely on for information?'

147

'Not me, Superintendent. My report goes directly to the Director-General.'

'Directly Director,' Gilston echoed. 'I wouldn't rush back, though. Your Director is currently closeted with Mr Bromley and it looks as if they're going to take some time allocating the blame for last night's escape. I was there earlier myself. In Rawlings's office. Thought you might be, too.'

Maybury tensed, sensing greater shifts in allegiances and faster manoeuvring than she'd allowed for.

Gilston noticed. And smiled. One of those annoying paternal grins that came from knowing you were older and thinking you had a wiser head. A sparkle in the eyes that insisted you'd seen it all before.

What was he getting at, she wondered. What was he implying? Was he offering her a deal? Some sort of co-operation? Against what? Or was he setting her up?

She took a chance. Because he'd never pretended to like her and she believed in his rudeness. But even at that, only a small chance.

She said, 'I found nothing in Dixie McDaid's flat. Apart from the feeling that I'm missing something.'

'I think we're all missing something,' Gilston suggested. 'Don't you?'

'What do you mean?'

Gilston used his fingers to number the evidence. 'The terrorists leave Jennifer Crooks's house just before we get there. The terrorists slip through the cordon around the prison. The terrorists never show at Daly's house in Harlesden where they're expected. Maybe we're all missing different somethings and if we shared what we have, we might get a fuller picture.'

He paused and leaned on the roof of the car. Towering over her, he had to stoop to bring his face closer to hers. And then he said, 'Denis Reilly was seen last night.'

148

'Reilly?' she repeated. 'Where?'

'Millwall Docks.'

'Seen by whom? What was he doing in Millwall Docks?'

'The Metropolitan Police fished the dead body of a wino from one of the docks last night. Beaten and strangled. This morning they picked up a broken piece of a cheap key-ring at the scene. A bit of plastic with a printed design inside. Two lions and a hand. The O'Reilly clan coat of arms. Some of the other down-and-outs recognised Reilly's photo.'

'Are you saying that he killed the wino?'

'Probably.'

'Why?'

'You tell me. The chap was Irish, so maybe because he was a disgrace to the tribe. He was naked when they fished him out, so maybe Reilly wanted a change of clothes. I don't know. I only just got the news.'

Gilston nodded curtly as he pushed himself away from the car and turned back down West End Lane. 'Your Director-General doesn't know about it yet, by the way. Keep in touch.'

Maybury watched him turning the corner, distracted by the hints he'd dropped, by doubts about Rawlings's game, by fears and worries. Where could you move if your own superiors weren't playing it straight?

So it was only when she was sitting again in the car, settling the gear-lever into neutral and turning the key in the ignition, that it finally struck her. Maybe Reilly *had* killed the man for his clothes! That down-and-out in the corridor outside Dixie McDaid's flat, keeping his head down as he passed the cops, knocking on a neighbour's door . . .

But tramps were frequent callers to the woman's flat.

Which was exactly the sort of commonplace familiarity that McDaid would exploit.

Slapping the steering wheel with frustration, she yanked the key from the ignition and threw open the driver's door, right in front of a passing pedestrian. She didn't wait to hear the curses or offer an apology. She ran to Kilburn High Road and turned right, sprinting back towards Dixie McDaid's flat.

She couldn't see Superintendent Gilston. And Spencer, the other Special Branch man, wasn't on duty any more outside the newsagents opposite the house. Maybe the two of them had gone for a coffee. Maybe they'd climbed to the flat.

She stood on the footpath, the doubts racing in her mind. Should she go up to Dixie McDaid's flat? Should she notify Rawlings? Should she act alone, exposing herself to mistakes, to suspicion, if things went wrong? Should she risk being ordered to return to base?

Settling on a compromise, she ran back to the car and passed the information on to MI5 Headquarters in Millbank without waiting for a direct connection to Rawlings.

Then she hurried back towards Dixie McDaid's house again, troubled by yet another problem now. Without Spencer to open the street door for her, she'd have to rouse one of the other occupants by ringing the electric bells.

6

Mary Cassidy knew that she was just a soft touch. But she couldn't help it.

At the local Shelter branch, she put in twice as many hours and twice as much work as any other volunteer. Sometimes she spent her own money on food for the destitute. Sometimes she fell behind with her rent and worried about being made homeless herself. Sometimes she bent as far as asking her mother to dig her out.

But that's where the sometimes ended. Her mother, the rich

Managing Director of a grocery chain in Dublin, invariably wrote a curt, disapproving note. And never put a stamp on the envelope.

This morning Mary Cassidy had fallen out of bed at ten o'clock. Working the evening shift at a sweet factory down in Harlesden messed around with her schedule. Finish at midnight. Home after one in the morning. Not sleeping until well past two.

When someone knocked on her door she was still wearing only a cotton nightshirt. She thought it might be the cops again. Two of them had questioned her before she left for work the previous day, asking about the guy who lived next door, the easygoing, blue-eyed character from Belfast that she liked a lot. She was Irish, too. But from the south. Watergrasshill, way down in County Cork.

She took a dressing-gown from the wardrobe and pulled it on. When she left the bedroom she walked quietly, in bare feet, across to the front door, not making noise in case she wanted to pretend she wasn't there.

Once she'd looked through the spyhole that was set in the centre of the door she was hooked, though. The guy outside was holding a copy of *The Big Issue* up for her to view. She couldn't see his face, or any other part of him. The magazine cover filled the whole space.

It didn't matter that she already had the magazine. Sometimes she bought five or six copies of the same run from different sellers.

If the homeless guys who sold them had asked for a handout, she'd have given it. But they didn't ask any more. They held up the magazine for sale. The only help you could offer without insult was to buy another copy.

Without thinking much, she drew the bolts and opened the door. The guy lowered the magazine he was holding. Behind, she could see his pale-blue eyes, clear and hard and oddly

151

familiar. And she knew immediately that he was no down-and-out.

The rags were authentic. Their look, their smell. The clear, healthy eyes weren't, even though he'd filthied his face to conceal them. They weren't bloodshot, or raw, or clogged with mucus.

It was already too late. The man shuffled forward a couple of paces, still in a tramp's character, and then clasped his left palm over her mouth and spun her round. She got a faint smell of aftershave or perfumed soap from the hand. She heard the door closing quietly behind them and then a flurry of rustling as he dropped the magazine to the floor.

On the right side of her neck she felt a cold shock of steel, from what she guessed must be the barrel of a gun. And then, as her head filled with the smell from his hand and she started to lose consciousness, it suddenly came back to her. Where she'd seen those pale-blue eyes before. They were the same type as the ones she'd half fallen in love with, the ones that belonged to the guy next door, Dixie . . . Dixie . . .

While the woman was folding then in his arms, Sean McDaid was cursing his own lack of foresight.

Nothing to do with her. He hadn't wasted a thought on her yet. And nothing to do with the Special Branch man in the corridor or the black-haired woman talking to him, although he'd wondered for a moment who she was. He'd seen her turn away and head for the stairs, and he'd watched the Special Branch man follow and stare after her before he'd knocked on the door and slipped in.

What bothered him was that he should've brought a change of clothes.

Get in dressed as the bum Reilly had killed the previous night, he thought. That was fine. Dixie had always been moaning about the dossers hanging around, some of them flogging *The Big Issue* as an excuse for begging. But get out as someone else. Maybe even pretend to be living in the woman's flat.

Too late now. He'd have to live in the stinking rags for another few hours.

McDaid took his hand from the woman's mouth and let her slide to the floor, wondering if he should kill her or not.

Probably not, he decided. It didn't matter that she might've recognised him. And to snuff her quietly, he'd have to choke or smother her; and there was something too personal, too *intimate*, about finishing a woman like that.

He stooped to cover her naked thighs with the dressing-gown that had fallen open. Then he lifted her and carried her to the bedroom.

Her wrists and ankles he tied together with her own tights, securing them to the bed afterwards. He stuffed a sock into her mouth as a gag and was just rummaging in a drawer for a third pair of tights to hold it in place when the woman's door-bell rang.

The noise startled him.

Breathing heavily, half from exertion, half from surprise, he took the automatic pistol from where he'd left it on the bed-side cabinet and went quietly back to the other room and across to the front door to look through the spyhole.

There was no one in the corridor. No one visible, anyway.

For a moment he thought there might be police either side of the door, flattened against the wall; but then it occurred to him that there was no bell-push, no button, mounted on the door or the frame out there. He'd had to knock himself. So whoever was ringing was doing it from the street.

McDaid waited until the caller had given up and gone away. He put the pistol in a pocket then and went back to the bed-room.

The woman was breathing evenly, but hadn't woken yet. A red scarf lying on the floor by the open wardrobe caught his eye and he used that to secure the gag.

He sat on the bed afterwards and tried to remember everything his brother Dixie had ever told him about this building, tried to figure a way from where he was into Dixie's flat without exciting the cop in the corridor.

7

A tall, skinny youth, sticky-eyed and hung-over and dressed only in black denim jeans, finally opened the street door for June Maybury.

He shaded his eyes against the daylight with a grubby hand and squinted outwards. Not recognising her, he muttered irritably, 'Rang wrong fucking bell, missus.'

When he turned and slouched away, padding down the damp hallway in his bare feet, he left the door open.

She didn't bother closing it behind her. She took the greasy stairs without caution, three at a time, and swung into the corridor on the second floor. Then she stopped, still holding on to the splintered wooden upright of the stairway.

The Special Branch detective, John Fowler, wasn't outside Dixie McDaid's door any more.

He wasn't anywhere in the corridor.

She listened. And heard only the sound of her own breathing.

Chances were, she thought, that he was inside McDaid's flat, sweeping it clean after her own visit, checking that she hadn't disturbed or taken anything, trying to figure out what she was interested in. Acting on Gilston's orders. Maybe Gilston and the other detective, Spencer, were in there, too. Looking for clues.

It sounded plausible. But she didn't go and knock on Dixie's door. Because something was urging her that it wasn't true.

She went instead to the next door, number seven, where she'd seen the tramp calling, and knocked there. She noticed the spyhole set in the wood and stepped aside, out of its range.

No one answered.

She reached across without showing herself and knocked again, louder and longer. And again with the feeling that something was happening on the other side.

She reckoned that it might be safer to hold on and wait for the back-up to come; but she also reckoned that speed was vital and that there was no time to dwell on safety.

She slipped back to Dixie McDaid's flat and pressed her ear against the door. Nothing.

She went back downstairs, into the damp hallway, along the dirty tiles, to the flat the skinny youth had disappeared into. When he finally opened the door to her hammering, he was having trouble with the zip of his jeans and even more trouble trying to open his right eye. His left eye was raw and bloodshot.

She asked, 'Have you a caretaker here? Someone with keys.'

'Huh?'

'Is there someone around with keys to all the flats?'

The youth shook his head.

She flashed her ID at him, but doubted that he even registered the *movement*, let alone took in the details. 'Number seven upstairs,' she said. 'Who lives there?'

'Seven? Jesus! Em . . . Dixie, is it? They were here yesterday, asking about him.'

'Next door to Dixie.'

'Next door? Jesus! Em . . .'

Maybury shifted impatiently. 'Is it someone alone? A man or a woman? A couple?'

'Em . . . A woman. Yeah.'

'Is there a fire escape?'

155

The youth scratched his head. 'Fire escape? Yeah. Out the back door there. It's in the garden.'

The bolt on the base of the back door was stiff and slightly rusted. The garden obviously wasn't a place much visited by the tenants.

While working on the bolt, Maybury thought of the youth's long, skinny arms, more bone than flesh, more skin than muscle. There wasn't much point going back for him, she decided, even if she could manage to wake him again. She was stronger herself.

Still, she gashed a finger on the thing pulling it across and had to wind a paper handkerchief around the cut before she turned the knob to open the back door.

The garden was wildly overgrown. More like unclaimed countryside than the rear of an urban house.

Across to her left, the base of the rusting fire escape had been swallowed in thick blackberry brambles. If someone came rushing down in darkness to get to safety, chances were they'd end up in the casualty ward of the nearest hospital anyway with multiple abrasions.

Protecting her bleeding finger, she gripped a step a little above her head and pulled herself upwards, over the bushes. She didn't need to take her shoes off to reduce the noise while climbing the metal stairs. She was already wearing sneakers.

The house had two flats on each floor, both of them served by the same platform of the fire escape.

On the second floor, the stairs brought her first to the flat beside Dixie McDaid's.

The window there was already open, the lower sash raised a little from the sill. The tail of a white lace curtain was being sucked outwards through the gap. A door or another window inside was also open, creating a draught.

She put her hands under the window's lower sash, trapping the curtain between her fingers and the wood. She pulled

156

upwards. The window was stiff and resisted her. And it creaked loudly.

She parted the lace curtains and then the green drapes behind them. Directly inside, there was a small bedroom. A young woman, bound and gagged, but fully conscious and struggling, was lying on the single bed. Otherwise the room seemed empty.

Maybury stared at the woman, hoping for a sign, either of danger or safety. She pointed to the areas of the bedroom she couldn't see, to the walls and to the corners on either side of the window itself. The woman only stared back with bulging, terrified eyes.

Maybury climbed in, unbalanced for a moment by the bigger drop to the floor on the other side, and still half expecting an attack while she was vulnerable. It never came. There was no one else in the bedroom.

Passing the frightened woman, she stepped through the open door into the living-room and kitchen outside. There was no one there, either.

Coming back, she found a pair of scissors on the living-room sideboard and used that to cut the knotted tights and release the woman's hands and feet.

She put her own fingers to her lips for silence before taking off the gag. And then she whispered, 'Was it the tramp? A man dressed as a tramp?'

The woman had clamped her right palm over her mouth, stifling the sobs. She shivered and nodded quickly. She said, 'I –'

Maybury put a hand on the woman's arm to calm and restrain her.

'Don't call out,' she whispered. 'Just indicate.'

She thought she heard sounds as she spoke. A bump. A dull thud. Like someone moving furniture. Apparently from the flat next door.

157

'Where did he go?' she asked. 'To the flat next door?'

The woman stared. And then shrugged.

'Which way, then?' Maybury demanded urgently. 'Did he leave by the front door? No? The fire escape?'

The woman was nodding again, jerking her head towards the window and beyond, when the sound of a telephone ringing, muffled but unmistakable, came to them suddenly through the walls from Dixie McDaid's flat next door.

8

Sean McDaid was inside the bedroom of his brother's flat when the telephone rang.

It was the second time he'd been interrupted in the same position.

Coming in through the window from the fire escape five minutes earlier, he'd intended quietly collecting what he wanted and then leaving by the same route. Not that he fancied hacking through the overgrown back garden, though. He thought he'd hop from the metal stairs to the boundary wall and from there down into the neighbour's model English garden, maybe trampling a little wistaria on the way to freedom.

It hadn't worked out quite as simply as that.

He was thinking scathingly about the British. Thinking that, with all their obsession with order, they only managed to keep their dull clothes and their back gardens in good shape. Thinking that they wasted their affections on animals. So that, when it came to humans, they hadn't either structure or feelings left.

Between that and picking his way distastefully through the mess his brother had left behind, his attention was divided.

This was something about his *own* people that he despised. Their slovenliness. Their *disregard* for patterns.

Distracted by disgust, he stepped a little carelessly into Dixie's bedroom. The trailing hem of his tramp's coat flicked against the unsteady lamp that was outside the doorway. Before he could swivel to save it, the thing had crashed against the wall and then to the ground, shattering the bulb and knocking the metal shade across the length of the flat.

When that racket ended, McDaid heard another inevitable noise. Someone in the corridor outside had just inserted a key in the lock on the front door.

McDaid stayed calm. And for the moment, he stayed still also.

He tried to think himself into the cop's reaction. The entry was too immediate, he reckoned, too unprepared, to be prompted by anything more than annoyance. The foolish man hadn't waited for assistance. Chances were, he thought the lamp had been left unstable by the woman who'd come from the flat.

McDaid slipped into the bedroom then, leaving himself a narrow gap between the hinged side of the door and the frame. He almost laughed aloud when he saw the squat, balding detective come in alone and close the front door behind him.

The man stood and studied the fallen lamp and shade and then walked across and stooped, groaning noisily, to pick them up and put them together again. McDaid thought that he'd also close the bedroom door, now that he was in the swing of housekeeping, and that afterwards he'd go quietly back to his post in the corridor outside.

He didn't.

He wandered into the bedroom itself. Not warily. Not at all suspicious. Out of idle curiosity, maybe. Or just to pass the time. But too relaxed to think of trouble.

But he went straight to Dixie's model of the Barbican and

159

stood there, his hands clasped behind his back, studying the detail.

And it was only then that McDaid decided to kill him, before he kept looking and looking and saw too much.

McDaid had no knife and no gun that was fitted with a silencer. He had a strong cord tied around his waist, holding the tramp's rags together, but wondered if he could manage to loosen it without being heard.

The detective stooped a little more and laughed softly to himself, finding a door to open on the model of the Barbican. McDaid slipped the knot and moved, tightening the cord between his clenched hands.

The cop was too absorbed, and too slow when his senses finally signalled danger. The cord was around his neck and McDaid's knee was crashing into the base of his spine before he could turn.

But then he went *with* McDaid's pressure, as his training had taught him. Instead of struggling to escape the cord, he snapped his head backwards, into McDaid's face.

He was too low, and McDaid too tall, to cause serious damage. The back of his head smashed into McDaid's chin, forcing the lower jaw upwards and driving the teeth into the tensed upper lip.

McDaid groaned with pain and staggered back a pace or two, the strength and the concentration gone from his arms for a moment. The detective too lost balance and fell to the floor, where he sat, dizzy and choking from lack of air.

McDaid dropped the cord. He didn't have the expertise, he knew now, to use it effectively. He reached into his pocket for the pistol, intending at first to use the butt as a club while the cop was still dazed and struggling to his feet.

But a sharp pain seared across his own upper lip. Blood and spittle dripped from his mouth to the floor at his feet. It distracted him. It delayed him a vital second.

160

The detective was on his feet again. Still weak and groggy, but determined to attack. Stooped, he charged at McDaid, who had only one arm free to ward him off.

As they grappled, McDaid's right arm became trapped in the coat pocket and he suffered from the restriction. His hand closed around the butt of the automatic. While his fingers searched for the safety catch, then frantically tried to release it, he took blows to his chest and his face.

He didn't wait for the best moment to fire. Weakened from the punishment, knowing the cop would use his own handgun as soon as possible, he couldn't risk delay. As soon as they closed again, he forced the pistol as deeply as he could into the detective's body and fired.

The sound was muffled. But the blast burnt through the ragged clothes along his own stomach, making him cry out with pain, slightly louder than the grunt the detective gave.

The man wasn't yet dead as he slipped downwards, over McDaid's agonising burn, along his right leg, and to the floor. But he had lost consciousness again. And was silent.

It was then, as McDaid stooped a little to free himself from the detective and was straightening again, breathing heavily and holding his stomach, that the telephone rang in the other room.

He thought at first it was only a heightening of the clamorous ringing in his own ears. But it didn't subside with his heartbeat. It kept on and on, as insistent as if the caller was *certain* that there was someone in the flat.

Who knew that he was there, McDaid wondered. Reilly? Boyce? Bill Enright?

Only Enright, occasionally in touch with Dixie in London over the last few years, would also have known the telephone number.

McDaid hurried from the bedroom. Everything was frantic now. Everything quickened. The buzz from the fight had sent the adrenalin racing. The pain of his injuries drove him even more.

The black, old-fashioned telephone was sitting unevenly on a small mahogany table near the front door, next to a bowl of rotting fruit. A pulpy kiwi had burst its skin and seeped green, sticky juice on to the receiver.

McDaid wiped the instrument with part of the tramp's coat before picking it up. He held his breath. He said nothing.

He didn't have to.

Immediately he put the receiver to his ear, a voice summoned him with irritating authority. 'McDaid?'

An English voice. Educated. Plummy. Totally assured.

'McDaid?' it said again.

McDaid cleared his dry throat and controlled his breathing. 'Yes?'

And the voice, disembodied, unknown, but apparently omniscient, spoke to him again. 'If I were you, old chap, I'd get the hell out of there before the police arrive in numbers. They're already on their way.'

The line went dead on the final word, leaving McDaid with the strange, unwelcome feeling of having unwillingly served someone who was playing at God.

9

Until that phone rang next door and was answered, June Maybury had intended waiting in Mary Cassidy's flat for the back-up to arrive. But not afterwards.

She sensed something suspicious, something more than co-incidence. And she guessed then that whoever was in the dead tramp's disguise wouldn't be hanging around much longer.

She tried to think from the tramp's perspective, to settle on the best escape route. Not through the corridor and down the stairs, anyway, she decided. There were too many traps to negotiate. The narrow stairway itself. The front hallway. The street door.

Out the back and through the neighbours' gardens offered the better option.

She was climbing again through Mary Cassidy's window, one foot already on the fire escape, when she saw for an instant a filthy, unrecognisable face popping out the open window next door. She was too surprised to call out immediately. And then too late when she recovered. The tramp had vanished again.

She thought for a moment of doubling back herself and heading for the corridor. But if she didn't see him there, she wouldn't know exactly where he'd gone, front or back. Or whether he was sitting it out in the flat itself.

Better to drive him down the narrow channels, she reckoned. Deny him the open spaces at the rear. Hope that Gilston or one of his men was back on surveillance on the street.

She walked carefully along the fire-escape platform and went on all fours to keep under the window of Dixie McDaid's flat. She didn't think the terrorist was still inside, with a gun aimed at the opening, waiting for her head to appear. He wouldn't be certain she was alone and wouldn't take a chance on a guess.

Still, her mouth was dry and her hands were shaking as she raised her eyes above the level of the sill and peered in.

She couldn't see the floor at that angle. She saw that the unsteady lamp by the bedroom door had fallen. She saw the same mess of food and clothes on the furniture. And, at the other end of the room, the telephone receiver dangling by its cord on the low table beside the open front door.

There was some chance that the man was hiding in the bedroom to her right, lying in ambush. But not much, she thought.

163

So she risked it.

Nothing happened as she raised herself and climbed in. She quickened her pace, reckoning that he'd already gained ground on her.

She'd intended just a cursory check on the bedroom, but the figure lying on the ground in there delayed her more. John Fowler, she saw, although his face was away from her. Around his midriff, a pool of his blood had formed on the carpet.

She didn't linger after confirming that he was dead, killed by the bullet that had entered his left breast and hit something vital inside.

She raced through the front door into the empty corridor and again took the stairs carelessly, three at a time. Too carelessly. Immediately after the first-floor landing, her sole hit a frayed section of the carpet on the edge of a step and lost its grip.

She almost went over on the ankle, but then pushed herself away from the banister with her left hand and built up enough pace to get out of the skid, reaching the downstairs hallway still a little out of control, and only coming to a stop against the tensed shape of Superintendent Gilston.

Spencer, the other Special Branch detective, was standing by Gilston's side.

'Tramp!' she gasped.

Gilston held her at arm's length and considered her with raised eyebrows. Making a humorous point. Women! Always overwrought!

But it wasn't the time to exercise his new and undeveloped ease with a woman.

'Tramp!' Maybury repeated. 'Dirty face. Battered trilby. Dirty navy overcoat flapping open. Did he pass you?'

Gilston frowned. 'Coming in the front door just now. Why?'

'It was Reilly. Or McDaid. I couldn't see which. Up in Dixie McDaid's flat. He killed Fowler.'

'Christ!' Gilston swore. As he swivelled, he barked at

Spencer. 'Get some men into this area. You've got a description. Look after Fowler.'

Men, Maybury thought irrelevantly as she followed Gilston to the front door and into the street. *Get some men.*

Gilston turned right outside, without hesitation and without explanation. She figured that he must've seen the tramp leave and take that direction.

But it was lunch-time now and Kilburn High Road was crowded again. And it wasn't something she was experienced at, spotting a fugitive on a city street.

Gilston seemed to sense her lack of confidence. 'Look for a disturbance in the crowd,' he told her. 'Not for him. He'll be running, scattering people. Look up ahead and down the side streets. I'm taking the other side. You stay on this.'

She watched him as he cut away from her and across the road, and she saw immediately what he'd meant by disturbance. As soon as he hit the footpath on the other side, his progress through the crowd was as obvious as the hull of a ship through water.

When he stopped dead at a side-road and signalled back to her, she saw in retrospect that he'd followed the tramp's reasoning more accurately than herself. Obviously, the man had also crossed Kilburn High Road after leaving the house and then taken an early turning, hoping to lose his pursuers in the smaller streets.

The name-plate at the corner said Buckley Road and Gilston had already dived into it by the time Maybury got to the opening. After that she gained on him. Twenty years older than her, he was already tiring, already losing control of his breathing.

He pointed ahead, not able to explain.

She couldn't see anything.

They turned left and crossed Willesden Lane and then right and right again to recross Willesden Lane, so that they seemed to be circling crazily without a purpose.

Until she finally saw it, a ragged, hunched figure outside a disused school building ahead of them, shuffling through the broken entrance into the playground beyond the fencing.

'It's him!' she cried triumphantly. 'I see him!'

Gilston was shaking his head. 'No, no . . .'

She was going to swear at him, to leave him behind, cursing his age and infirmities, when she witnessed what seemed like a rerun of the same scene. A tramp, ragged and hunched, shuffling through the school entrance into its yard. And then another. And a fourth. A fifth.

'Soup run,' Gilston gasped, slowing as they neared the school. 'Lunch-time. Soup run. He's in among them.'

'Shit!' she swore. 'It's like looking for a needle in a haystack.'

'No. Particular piece of straw in a haystack.'

'How did he know?'

'Didn't. The bastard's lucky, that's what.'

In the centre of the yard, which was teeming with homeless and beggars and winos, two cheerful women volunteers were working behind a meal trolley, ladling soup into big disposable cups and hacking chunks of bread off a loaf.

It wasn't likely that the fugitive would've lingered. Still, Gilston and Maybury did the rounds, checking the queue that was waiting for food, and the others who were standing apart, gulping what they'd been given.

It was a world June Maybury wasn't familiar with. The men's docility, their indifference to inspection, irritated her.

After a while Gilston walked around the back of the trolley and showed his ID. 'Did anyone pass you ladies the last few minutes without taking any food?'

The older of the pair, a rosy-cheeked, middle-aged woman, looked indulgently at him and pointed with her ladle to the left, where there was a public swimming pool. 'Very many people thankfully have no use for our small service,' she

166

explained sweetly. 'They take a short cut through here.'

Gilston gritted his teeth. He tried to hold his patience while searching for a description that wouldn't provoke only a political correction.

'A homeless man,' he said. 'Did any homeless men pass without accepting food?'

'That new chap,' the younger woman put in. 'We never saw him before. He went past without even looking at us. I said to Margery – didn't I, Marge? – that he seemed ashamed, but he'd be back.'

'Which way?' Gilston demanded.

'I beg your pardon?'

'Which way did he go?'

Again the ladle rose, once more to indicate the swimming pool.

As Gilston and Maybury turned, they saw a group of uniformed constables, up from the police station on Harvist Road, filing into the yard. Gilston took a pair with him and ordered the others to seal the exits.

Inside the swimming pool, there didn't seem to be anyone on duty at reception. Gilston was passing, on his way to the dressing-rooms, when he heard a low groaning from behind the hatch, under the level of the glass.

A young man in track suit and sneakers, with a whistle on a cord around his neck, was lying on the floor. He was still groggy. His lips were badly cut where they'd been smashed back against his teeth and his nose was bleeding heavily.

'Police,' Gilston introduced himself abruptly. 'Where did he go?'

The man pointed limply and mumbled through his damaged teeth, 'Dressing-rooms.'

In his eagerness, though, Gilston got it a little wrong after that.

'Take that one,' he ordered, pointing to the right. 'I'll do the other.'

Maybury, with a uniformed constable at her back, hit the swing door to what she saw, too late, was the men's dressing-room and was hit in turn by heavy steam coming from the shower inside. She couldn't see clearly through the mist. Elsewhere, it was obvious that there was no one in any of the cubicles.

She was about to call out when the door swung open again behind. Gilston came in, muttering something about the women's changing room, and at the same time the shower was turned off and a small, fat man, with lather from his body gel still clinging to his pubic hairs, stepped out, rubbing his closed eyes.

Beyond him, Gilston and Maybury saw through the dispersing steam that the cubicle in the corner had had its lock forced. Inside it, on the seat, lay a battered trilby and two ragged overcoats.

Back at reception, the young man in the track suit had a small mirror to his face and was gingerly touching his swollen lip and nose, and worrying about the future.

'Ask your male customers to step out of the pool, please, and check their clothing,' Gilston told him.

They waited at reception while the young man, using only one side of his mouth, whistled the swimmers to silence and made his announcement.

'Why did you go back to the flat?' Gilston asked then. 'How did you know he was there?'

'I saw the tramp in the corridor when I was in earlier,' Maybury told him. 'When you said Reilly had killed a down-and-out in Millwall last night . . .'

They were silent again for a moment.

And then she said, 'The phone rang while he was in Dixie McDaid's flat. He answered it.'

Gilston frowned. 'I don't get you.'

They watched the swimmers flapping in. That forward

stoop people have when walking in bare feet on wet tiles. Heels raised, arms slightly out for balance. Like ageing penguins.

'Someone rang him,' Maybury said. 'Someone warned him that he was in danger. I don't think he hurried until the phone rang.'

Gilston stared at her. He said uneasily, 'It could have been one of his own. An arranged call. Not necessarily what you're thinking.'

'Maybe.'

There was another silence.

'What was he doing in there?' Gilston wondered then. 'Did you notice anything?'

'No.'

'We'll have to go back, check the contents against the inventory.'

A forlorn young man, tall and athletic, came miserably from the dressing-room, holding the trilby in one hand and the smaller of the overcoats in the other.

'The bastard,' he was muttering. 'The bastard.'

Gilston nodded sympathetically. 'What were you wearing, sir?'

Knowing that it was only a formality, that the man, Reilly or McDaid, whichever it was, had slipped away from them and was already safely on his way back to his unknown den.

'I mean,' the swimmer said miserably, 'we're talking about a valuable briefcase and an expensive suit here –'

'What type, sir?'

'Type?'

'The suit.'

'Three-piece. Narrow pin-stripe. Grey . . .'

10

The living-room of the large Victorian house owned by Sir Andrew Pinnington, the previous Director-General of MI5, had the feel and look of an old-fashioned gentleman's club, David Bromley always thought. All dark and heavy mahogany. All creaking leather upholstery. All hunting prints and murky lighting.

Pinnington, a small, ailing old man sitting in the armchair nearest the open fire and wrapped in a heavy rug, was lost against the imposing background.

Bromley, an enthusiastic supporter of the former Director-General, always remembered Pinnington as wiry and restless, and still couldn't quite reconcile himself to the decline.

It was said that the old man had been forced out of MI5 the summer before during talks with the IRA, that his replacement had been headhunted from outside the Service to see the ceasefire smoothly through, and that Pinnington's ill health had hit him afterwards.

Bromley didn't buy it. Sir Andrew had overseen the recent resurgence of MI5 in the early nineties, putting it centre stage in the war against the IRA and nudging it ahead of its rivals in MI6 and Special Branch and Scotland Yard in the affections of the Home Office and the Prime Minister. He was too powerful, too influential, too *well-connected*, to be merely cast aside.

Even his successor, George Rawlings, accepted the truth of *that*.

'Sir Andrew,' Rawlings had probed at their meeting earlier. 'Did you find him, ah, congenial at all, David?'

Leaving Bromley with a delicate problem. Which he'd

170

dodged. 'I believe his assessments of my work were always positive, sir.'

'Quite so. Quite so. But it might be helpful if you had, you know. Been rather close to him.'

'Sir?'

'It's this damn Maybury business, you see . . .'

Pinnington's nurse, or housekeeper – a stout woman who was dressed in white without managing to make the clothes into a uniform – served the two men whisky and soda and left the room.

They drank in silence for a few moments afterwards.

Until Pinnington asked abruptly, 'Rawlings send you then, David?'

Bromley started and nodded. 'Yes, sir.'

Pinnington sighed and settled the heavy woollen rug over his legs. 'Is Sean McDaid still free?' he asked.

Bromley nodded again. 'Yes, sir. But as I've said, he was almost captured this morning.'

'Almost,' Pinnington repeated thoughtfully. 'Almost. And now Rawlings regrets his hasty appointment of June Maybury to head the case and has sent you here to find confirmation of his fears about her. Eh? How changeable they all are now, David. How terribly uncertain.'

Bromley grunted. But without committing himself to anything other than appreciation of the whisky.

'Ah!' Pinnington sighed. He smiled faintly, lost in memories for the moment. And then he said, 'It's because I recruited her myself, you see. Personally. Did you know that?'

'No, sir.'

'Yes,' Pinnington mused. 'She was living in Dublin then. Just beginning her studies in Trinity College. She must have been nineteen, perhaps twenty years old. Reared by a brace of maiden aunts, I believe. Her mother had died in childbirth. English father. Banker. Old school friend of an old friend of mine. He hasn't seen the girl since she was a child. Always considered herself English, you know. June did. And yet had to conceal it. In Dublin, you see.'

Pinnington sipped his whisky, and then his eyes suddenly flashed with a new life.

'Imagine it, David,' he said. 'Attractive young woman. Already familiar with student politics in southern Ireland. Accepted on the periphery of the Sinn Fein group in University. Falling into my lap like that. By the time she'd moved to Queen's University in Belfast to take a postgraduate degree, of course, she had already penetrated deeply into Sinn Fein. Quite extraordinary. By far the most reliable, the most prolific single source of high-grade information in the late Eighties and early Nineties. Don't exaggerate when I say her contribution was decisive in allowing us to refocus the service and assume responsibility for all counter-terrorism on the mainland.'

It was all new to Bromley. Maybury's standard file was clearly a fiction written by Sir Andrew himself. And it was all fascinating. But it was hardly the sweetener he needed for Rawlings.

'Why was she withdrawn, sir?' he asked. 'From Northern Ireland.'

'Her cover was blown,' Pinnington explained. 'Far too dangerous. She worked as a junior lecturer in Queens then and mixed with some of these people as a sympathiser. But the SAS cocked up an intended kill in south Down. Bagged none of the targets June had marked for them. And then, of course, the RUC Special Branch quite insisted on playing their own game in the follow-up operation. They dragged her in for interrogation and dropped her like a hot potato when they were told who she was. Plain as daylight, of course, why she alone was released so quickly. Her informer was killed a few days later. We had to pull Maybury out. No choice. Showed our

172

appreciation afterwards, of course.'

Pinnington emptied his glass and waved towards the whisky decanter. 'Another, David.'

It was half a question, and half a command.

So Bromley stood and poured for both of them.

Although he muttered, 'Must be getting back soon, sir.'

11

Jody Stafford took a taxi back to Bill Enright's flat on the North Circular Road in Neasden. The driver, an overweight man in an Arsenal jacket, talked only about Eric Cantona's recent attack on a spectator at Selhurst Park. He seemed unaware of the break from Whitemoor Prison.

Apart from thinking, again, how small an impression the IRA made on the ordinary Londoner, Stafford didn't have to listen or respond. He passed the journey hoping that Enright had dug up something on Sean McDaid's plans and whereabouts. Because Stafford himself had drawn a blank that morning.

He knew of only two other IRA men living undetected in London. Neither had heard so much as a whisper about the escaped prisoners. But then, they were no allies of Sean McDaid. They didn't share his morbid romanticism. A romanticism, of course, Stafford himself had given birth to and nurtured.

One of the IRA men had redirected him to Barra Timmons, an old lag who'd spent time with Danny Boyce in Parkhurst Prison before Boyce was transferred to Whitemoor.

'Danny'll not be escaping to blow up anyone, mind,' Timmons had claimed. 'Danny'll be meeting up with his own

173

wee family. You don't know Danny. Nobody knows Danny.'

Except yourself, Stafford was tempted to cut in. But he was wary of the sarcasm putting the old man in a sulk.

Timmons went on, 'He put himself down as an old lag, you know, Danny did. A wee bit of muscle. So he got himself a part in every escape plan in every prison he was ever in. But all Danny cared about was getting away with his family. Australia, I hear. Or America. He has more brains than the lot of you put together, sure.'

Stafford found it hard to believe. Any of it. The weakness of Boyce's loyalties. The strength of Boyce's brains. But it was hard to believe anything anybody said these days.

Time was, crones like the old lag wouldn't have risked fudging anything with Stafford. But times had changed.

Now it was Stafford himself who constantly felt in the dark. Stuck on the sidelines.

He was supposed to be the official representative of his own organisation, but this show went skating on without him, run by the security forces and a couple of maverick gunmen.

So he felt what a lot of volunteers back in Northern Ireland were feeling. That they were falling behind. That they weren't driving events any more, the way they did when the campaign was in full swing. That they were just trying to keep up with things.

'When we put down the guns they'll start ignoring us,' Sean McDaid had told him a few years back. 'We're not fighting to win this war, Jody. We're fighting to let them know we're always going to be here.'

Stafford had taken a spare key to Enright's flat with him that morning. When he got back, after paying off the taxi outside, it was one-fifteen, a quarter of an hour earlier than he was expected.

All the way from the street and up the stairs and on to the third-floor landing, he thought about Danny Boyce.

174

But outside Enright's door, with the key already raised to the lock, he hesitated.

The long years on the run had tuned him to danger and he sensed trouble now.

But not from the police, he reckoned. They would've taken him at the street entrance or on the stairs.

Then what? McDaid himself? Calling on Enright?

He pressed the key into the lock and turned it. He pushed the door open on the single, cluttered room that was used for lounging and cooking and eating.

Bill Enright was sitting at the rickety table in the centre, rolling a cigarette. He looked up sharply, and stared, and took a moment before asking, 'Is the rain still holding off?'

Stafford stepped in and closed the door without turning his back on Enright. 'It's fine at the moment, anyway.'

'The forecast is bad again, though.'

Stafford shrugged. He wondered why Enright wasn't curious about the search for McDaid. But he was also tired of paranoia. And tired of the grey little world it made you live in. So he made the mistake of giving Enright the benefit of his weariness.

Enright got up, putting a lighted match to his rolled cigarette. 'Do you want some lunch? I'll put the kettle on, will I?'

Stafford sat, shifting his chair a little so that he had a broader view of the room and still kept the front door in his sights. He looked around. Nothing seemed out of the ordinary. Against the wall on his right there was a long wooden chest, probably once used for the tennis rackets and cricket bats in some old mansion and now converted to a bench seat. It looked big enough to conceal a man, but neither its cushions nor its lock had been disturbed.

The bedroom door was open. Stafford couldn't see all of the interior from where he sat, but there was a light switched on that would've thrown a visible shadow if someone was hiding behind the door.

175

Coming back to the table with a pot of strong tea and a plate with brown bread and cheddar cheese on it, Enright finally got round to business. 'So what's the story?' he asked. 'How did it go?'

Stafford took the knife and started cutting bread. 'Nothing. Not a sausage. How about you?'

Enright already had cheese in his mouth. He mumbled and gestured for Stafford to wait. When he'd swallowed he stood up again, putting his mug of tea on the table. 'I've got something for you. Hang on.'

He turned and went to the bedroom, out of view.

Stafford watched his shadow. Enright seemed to stoop and pick up something. As he turned again the shadow of his outstretched right hand flitted across the floor and seemed to be pointing with an elongated index finger.

Too late to escape, too late even to shift position, Stafford realised that the other was carrying a gun. And then Enright was in the bedroom doorway again, covering him with a Beretta 9mm automatic.

Shit, Stafford thought.

And understood it at last. That Enright was one of McDaid's men now.

Useless to argue or reason with him, he decided quickly. In the history of Republicanism, every splinter group was always convinced that they were the true inheritors of the pure tradition and that the real traitors were the parents who begot them. Their only weakness was the need to justify themselves. And the only chance Stafford had now was playing on that weakess.

He said, 'You haven't been in Belfast in years, Bill, have you? You don't know what the thinking is over there now.'

Enright didn't answer.

Stafford said, 'That thing in your hand has brought us as far as it can go. Take it into a house in West Belfast these days

176

and they won't put it under the floorboards for you any more.'

All the time thinking.

Enright intended killing him and would do so without hesitation if Stafford made a sudden, foolish move. But he had no silencer on the gun. For preference, he wouldn't fire here, in the flat. So what was his plan? If he had one.

In the quietness, they listened to the sound of footsteps pacing slowly along their landing, until they passed Enright's front door and started receding as their owner descended the bare wooden stairs.

Enright smiled.

12

Two streets short of Maisie Connolly's house in Woolwich, Sean McDaid, wearing a grey three-piece suit that might've been just about a size too big for him and carrying a black leather briefcase, got off the bus near Woolwich Arsenal railway station and walked the long way round, checking for trouble.

Because you never blundered back to a hide-out assuming it was still safe, even in a changed disguise.

Because you never knew who might've turned during the morning, while you were away. Maisie Connolly, who hadn't given him as warm a welcome as he'd hoped. Or Denis Reilly, who needed only cash before eliminating McDaid and who might remember, if only he cooled off long enough to think about it, that informers were well paid.

And Danny Boyce?

McDaid knew the dangers of Reilly and Maisie Connolly, but he worried about Boyce. He'd had the big man marked down as loyal muscle. But there was something more to him. Except that McDaid didn't know what it was and the uncertainty made him uneasy.

Just as worrying about it distracted his concentration. Instead of scouting around Maisie Connolly's house, he found himself in a cul-de-sac off Burrage Road after taking a wrong turn.

A blonde woman, holding a grease-stained wooden spatula in her right hand, was standing at her front door, watching for her child's return from school. Not noticing McDaid's cut and swollen lip, she smiled at him.

McDaid nodded and struggled to remember why she looked familiar. And then he realised that it was the same woman who, five hours earlier, when he was dressed as a tramp, had grasped her daughter's hand and given him a wide berth on the same footpath, with her nose in the air. Now, of course, he had his face newly washed and was wearing someone else's grey, three-piece suit.

He didn't really blame her. He would've felt the same distaste and the same acceptance. But the experience still made him resentful. He felt Irish in the rags, and English in the suit. And he didn't like either sensation.

There didn't seem to be any police near Maisie Connolly's place, but McDaid never relied only on appearances. From the phone booth at the corner of the road, he rang the house. Maisie Connolly answered and quickly passed it on to Reilly.

Reilly was excited. 'Did you get it?'

'Was there any trouble?' McDaid demanded. 'Is the coast clear?'

'No trouble. Did you get it?'

'I'll be there in two minutes.'

Reilly was waiting alone in the front room of the house, pacing by the fireplace. He didn't even notice McDaid's peculiar clothes. He was too preoccupied for that, too busy staring at the black leather briefcase and then congratulating himself on figuring out its function. He had his revolver ready, bulging in the pocket of the jacket he was wearing.

What was he going to do, McDaid wondered. Shoot him right there if he told him that he had the money he was supposed to collect from Dixie's flat?

McDaid took out his own automatic. Not sharply. Not as an obvious threat. Casually. So that it seemed just a necessary preliminary to pulling up his jacket and shirt and exposing the raw burn across his stomach. But he kept the gun in his left hand.

'Get me some ointment and bandages for this,' he ordered. He glanced at the clock as it chimed the half-hour. It was two-thirty by then. He said, 'We'll have a briefing at three-fifteen. In this room. Tell Danny. But get the medicine first.'

Reilly hesitated, fingering the gun, but then turned and left.

He was too confused to make decisions, McDaid knew. Sometimes he let his hatred slip. Sometimes he pretended loyalty. Sometimes he worried about which was more convincing. Too confused, McDaid thought again. And too volatile.

It was Boyce, tracked by Maisie Connolly's ginger cat, who brought the cream and bandages. And Boyce who helped clean and dress McDaid's wounds.

The attentive disciple, McDaid thought. Washing the feet. *Before the cock crows, you'll have denied me three times . . .*

Reilly slouched in a couple of minutes late for the meeting and leaned against the wall after closing the door behind him.

Boyce sat in one of the armchairs, cradling the dozing cat in his lap.

McDaid spoke without moving from the table over the front window, where he'd been working on papers. 'I said in the press statement that the jailbreak –'

'They haven't released it,' Reilly cut in insolently. 'I listened to the news all day. They never put it out.'

179

'They had our names on at lunch-time, Sean,' Boyce pointed out. As if *that* was some sort of compensation.

'It doesn't matter,' McDaid said coldly, the irritation still held just below the surface. 'They'll release it. Sooner or later.' He looked around, discouraging interruptions, before continuing. 'I said that the jailbreak was only the start. You all know by now that our first objective is the Crown itself and the Commander-in-Chief of the Crown forces. This is the last time any of us will refer to it openly. In future you will talk of it only as the target. You will *think* of it only as the target. We're too close now to have idle talk, even in this house, deflect us from our purpose.'

'How close, Sean?' Boyce asked.

'Perhaps the day after tomorrow,' McDaid said. 'Saturday evening.'

He wondered if he should mention anything about the money he was supposed to have collected from Dixie's place. But he thought not. Reilly had already made the connection between loot and the black leather suitcase. So why not leave him to go on thinking how clever and devious he was?

He took the briefcase from the table and stood up, placing it between his legs as he gathered his papers together and put them in the waterproof pouch. As he stooped to lift the briefcase again he said, 'Stand down until tomorrow morning at eleven-thirty. So let's take it easy until then.'

Except for the sleeping cat, Danny Boyce sat alone by the fire after the others had gone upstairs to rest.

He thought he could see light ahead of him now. Their names had been on the news from midday onwards. His wife was preparing to leave Dublin with their daughter about now. And McDaid had the money he himself needed to get away.

But Boyce was melancholy as well.

And because freedom, and sanity, were only a couple of moves away, he was also full of dread. Nothing specific.

180

Nothing he could argue himself out of. A vague feeling, fed by too much time for thought and worry and useless sentiment.

All the previous night, lying awake in yet another strange bed, he'd dwelt on Jennifer Crooks, abandoned in a forest and surrounded by police. Neither of the others had mentioned her since. But the image of her sad eyes, watching them leave her to her fate without thanks, haunted him.

And one scene of mourning evoked another.

He imagined his wife, Deirdre. He imagined their daughter, their only child. He imagined them dead. Mutilated. Captured. Tortured. Imprisoned. Widowed. Fatherless. Insane.

He couldn't help it, couldn't stop the flood of horrific images to his mind.

Their safety depended entirely on his own actions.

So when he wondered what his best move was now, he couldn't settle with confidence on an option.

Should he go up alone against McDaid?

Should he strike up an alliance with Reilly? They could take McDaid together and split the money between them.

But what if Reilly and McDaid were really allies?

What if *Reilly* was intent on going it alone and having all the loot?

Right now, all Boyce had were doubts and fears and questions. And no answers.

13

In MI5 Headquarters at Thames House in Millbank, David Bromley hung around the approaches to June Maybury's office, waiting for her return and trying not to be obvious about it.

It was well past three in the afternoon before she made it.

He fell in beside her as she walked along the corridor and asked quietly, 'Could I have a word with you, please?'

She still didn't enjoy the sight of the man, but noted that at least he'd stopped addressing her as ma'am.

Her secretary was flapping a handwritten message at her in the outer office. She took it, carried it into her own office and read it as she slumped into the seat behind her desk.

Bromley stood awkwardly opposite her, until he was told to sit down as well.

'Make it quick,' she told him irritably. 'The Director-General is waiting for me.'

'That's what I want to talk to you about,' Bromley admitted. He wet his lips and plucked at a hair that was straddling the crease of his right trouser leg. 'You see, the fact is . . . Actually, the Director-General asked me this morning . . .'

'Asked you what?' she demanded irritably.

He coughed and took a leap at it. 'Essentially, he wants an excuse to remove you immediately from the present case and he requested me to provide it by re-examining your record, including an, ah, interview with Sir Andrew.'

'He doesn't need an excuse, Bromley,' she pointed out. 'He can simply issue an order.'

'I realise that, yes.'

'Then what's the point?'

'I'm only repeating what he implied.'

'Why?'

'I beg your pardon?'

'Why', she asked slowly, 'are you telling me what the Director-General instructed you to do in private?'

Bromley blushed, a habit she found annoying in men of his age.

He said, stumbling over the words, 'The Director-General, as you know, *is* rather new to us, having come across from MI6 –'

182

The telephone buzzed, interrupting Bromley and summoning Maybury to Rawlings's office.

'In a sentence, Bromley,' she requested. 'Give me your reason in a sentence, if that is possible.'

He sweated, but finally managed it. 'Essentially,' he said once more, a concept he was attracted to, 'I'm not altogether convinced that our current Director-General has the very best interests of the Service at heart.'

She grunted, but without commitment. Not able to reassure him on the point, but not willing openly to share his reservations either, she merely acknowledged the opinion.

She said, 'We'll talk again later. After I see him.'

'I would be grateful, you understand, if what I've just expressed in confidence were not to become –'

She cut him off with a sharp gesture. 'I have no intention of *adding* to the intrigue.'

George Rawlings was sitting behind his desk, his cane clenched in his right hand, and obviously in no mood for courtesies.

His dandyish private secretary, the plump-lipped Nicholas Orrinsmith, hovered expectantly until he was dismissed. Like a vulture armed with advance notice of a death.

Rawlings's lips were pursed. He offered Maybury no greeting, no explanation, no invitation to make herself comfortable.

She sat anyway.

She said, 'I'm sorry, sir, but I didn't yet have time to prepare a written report on this morning's –'

'I heard the news,' he told her curtly. 'Apparently, despite your earlier opinion, we don't even know now who it was in Dixie McDaid's flat, whether it was Reilly or Sean McDaid?'

'No, sir.'

'Nor what purpose they were there for?'

'Not yet, sir.'

'And whoever it was escaped us yet again?'

'I know I'm getting quite close to something –'

'Close?' Rawlings picked up caustically. 'Less than ten metres away, I believe?'

She bristled a little, despite her resolve not to mix it with him. 'If you would agree to release McDaid's statement –'

'Apart from anything else,' Rawlings interrupted, 'do you realise how foolishly inept we are beginning to look, how wet behind the ears I must seem in my new position?'

Maybury, too practised in reading signs, went for the crucial part of his outburst and ignored the camouflage. 'What do you mean, apart from anything else?' she asked.

Rawlings waved the question aside with a flick of his cane. 'They slip away from us near Whitemoor, even though we know where they are. They lead us on a wild-goose chase around Harlesden. And now they examine sealed evidence under our noses.'

'What do you mean, apart from anything else?' she repeated.

'Precisely this,' Rawlings returned. 'On each of these occasions, it was you who proffered the reasonable explanation for failure. But I'm beginning to find both the failures themselves and the explanations unacceptable. Excuses for Whitemoor. Excuses for Harlesden. Excuses now. The plain fact is that the common denominator of these increasingly lame excuses is yourself.'

She guessed that he was probing, trying to draw her out, trying to elicit what *she* thought the reasons for the failures were. But she no longer trusted his motives.

She wondered if Gilston had mentioned anything about the phone call the tramp had received in Dixie McDaid's flat. She doubted it. Rawlings would've worked over that too. In the circumstances, she was going to keep it to herself, a small advantage over him.

Even though she knew that silence probably meant suspension and leaving the field to Rawlings's total control, she said nothing.

Rawlings let the silence hang there a couple of minutes. Then he leaned forward, tapping a pencil on the desk.

He said, 'I myself am assuming direct command of the present case. For the moment you are temporarily relieved of all duties, including those pertinent to your official position in F2, where I believe your deputy is already covering you while you are on secondment. You are instructed to leave your office as it presently is and report to the Personnel Director in the morning.'

'For what purpose, sir?' she asked.

He checked a note. 'Your official file says that you spent six years in the field in Northern Ireland, from 1985 to 1991, and it lists some of your undeniable achievements. What it lacks is a precise account of your, ah, social life during this period. It will be your responsibility, with the aid of Personnel, to fill in these gaps for us.'

It was, she thought, one of the cheapest, and yet still one of the most effective ways of deflecting blame and suspicion away from yourself. By off-loading them on to someone else.

She half expected to be tailed back to her own office and supervised while gathering her belongings. As it turned out, she was grateful that Rawlings hadn't pushed things that far yet. Her secretary was waiting for her impatiently.

'Ma'am? There was a rather garbled call on the reserved line while you were in conference. I . . .'

Maybury stopped and turned to stare harshly. The line was exclusive to the IRA liaison officer in the current crisis. To Jody Stafford, in other words.

'Why didn't you interrupt me?' she demanded angrily.

'I thought as you were with the Director-General –'

'What was the message?'

'I've logged the details and –'

'What *was* it?'

'The person sounded in pain,' the secretary explained. 'It

185

wasn't at all clear. I *think* he said to tell you that he was in trouble. The address he gave afterwards was quite distinct, however. He said that he was in a flat at a house on the North Circular Road in Neasden. I've written the numbers down. After that he said nothing else, although the line remained open for some time.'

Maybury collected her coat and her briefcase and took the log-book of phone calls from her desk.

'I'm taking lunch,' she said.

Unable to control herself, the secretary glanced at her wristwatch. It was four o'clock.

'Yes, ma'am,' she muttered.

14

Superintendent Gilston kept his hand on the telephone after replacing the receiver. He stayed like that, immobile, brooding, shifting from frowns to scowls and back again, until a constable came to his office with something inconsequential for him to sign.

'Here!' he ordered then. 'Get me a line to the RUC Special Branch Headquarters in Belfast. Detective Inspector Terence McIver.'

He glanced at his watch while waiting, hoping that McIver wasn't outside his office on a case. It was a little after four-thirty.

When his phone buzzed, he lifted the receiver immediately, to hear McIver anticipating their conversation in that lax, familiar manner that Gilston found irritating in the Irish.

'You'll be enquiring about Tommy Brennan again, Superintendent.' An impossible tone to capture. Part question, part apology, part statement and part complaint. 'But he's gone to ground. We've linked him to an armed bank robbery from last week, but he's just vanished off the face of the earth. Don't think we haven't saturated the places he might be. But things are a wee bit delicate over here at the moment. You can't issue a parking fine without being accused of deliberately jeopardising the ceasefire.'

'When we spoke yesterday,' Gilston said brusquely, 'you asked me to give your regards to June Maybury. Did you know her personally while she was in Northern Ireland? Did you work with her?'

'No.' McIver's voice wavered a little now. 'I hardly knew her at all. It was a joke, Superintendent.'

'I'm not a very witty man, Inspector,' Gilston told him coldly. 'What was the joke?'

McIver drew a breath. 'Four years ago, I was the officer in charge of the investigation into the active service unit commanded by Jody Stafford and Sean McDaid. I was also the officer who arrested June Maybury. When I discovered who she was, I made a mistake. I released her immediately. I was responsible for blowing her cover.'

'You have a bloody peculiar sense of humour, Inspector,' Gilston observed.

'Maybe. But I suffered for the mistake. I was demoted to Sergeant. So the joke is more on myself.'

'Did Maybury interview Stafford at the time?' Gilston asked.

'Not officially, no.'

'What do you mean, *not officially*?'

There was a long silence.

Until McIver finally said, 'You know how I climbed my way back to the rank of Inspector, Superintendent?'

'I'm not interested in how you salvaged your bloody career,' Gilston told him sharply. 'I *am* in saving the lives of people still threatened by Stafford and McDaid.'

'I took it on the chin,' McIver persisted. 'I didn't whine. I didn't try to point the finger somewhere else. I kept my head down and my mouth shut.'

'About what?' Gilston asked bluntly.

'I wasn't even on the investigating team any more, not to mention in charge of it.'

'Come out with it, man! I don't have the time. We're looking at a bloody time bomb ticking away in our faces and you're dwelling on the sensitivites of four years ago.'

'I arrested June Maybury in her apartment,' McIver said. 'There was a forensics team searching for evidence of explosives. I instructed them also to take samples of hair, skin and fibres and traces of semen and other fluids from her bed sheets. Someone else had been sleeping there. But the analysis was never done. There's no record of the samples being received or processed by the laboratory. These are the only facts, Superintendent. And you're welcome to them.'

Again Gilston left his hand on the telephone after replacing the receiver.

He played the conversation back in his mind. *Did Maybury interview Stafford at the time? Not officially, no. Samples of hair . . . traces of semen . . . her bed sheets.*

Lovers, Gilston realised. That was what McIver was saying. June Maybury and Jody Stafford. They were bloody lovers!

15

June Maybury went alone to Neasden.

Nobody but her own side, she thought, would now want to lure her into a trap. She wasn't a strong enough threat to anyone. Not any more. Except, perhaps, to the joker who had

188

phoned Sean McDaid in his brother's flat.

The house on North Circular Road was red-brick Victorian, big and ugly, and let out in flats and bed-sitters.

The flat she'd been directed to was number seven. According to the card under the bell on the street door, it was supposed to be occupied by a tenant named Dalton.

She didn't buzz. She rang another tenant instead, on the ground floor, wanting only access to the building. The story she'd prepared wasn't needed. An apology for ringing the wrong bell was enough to leave her alone inside the downstairs hallway.

A pay phone had been mounted on the wall just inside the street door. There was fresh blood on its coin box and on the carpet underneath.

It was easy to follow the trail, up the stairs and along the landing to number seven. She knocked on the bright-green door. Unlocked, it swung gently away under the pressure from her knuckles.

A table and chairs were visible in the centre of a cluttered room. Beyond them there was an opened door to a second room, its detail lost in darkness. A kitchen area lay to the right. The left was still obscured.

The surface of part of the table was again covered with blood, as was the chair drawn up to it and the floor underneath.

She coughed and muttered tentatively, 'Hello?'

There was no answer.

She stepped in. She looked anxiously behind the door and along the wall to her left, where a long wooden chest somehow suggested a coffin to her troubled mind.

The place was empty.

A sound, a bed or a chair creaking, came through the stillness then from the other room.

She moved cautiously over, into its open doorway. Inside,

189

the heavy curtains had been closed across the window. The only light came from behind her.

When she stepped further in and then to one side, a slanting ray of the light hit the bed in front of her and caught the pale, pained face of Jody Stafford on a blue pillow.

Stafford groaned and opened his eyes as she moved again to stand more comfortably. Not fully awake yet, he snarled at her viciously while searching desperately under the blue pillow with his right hand. Obviously, he could see a shape in front of him. But he couldn't distinguish her face in the darkness.

'It's me,' she said.

'Eh?'

'June.'

'Ah!'

'What happened?' she asked.

He was silent for a while, gathering himself.

'The good news?' he asked ironically then. 'I've shaken off my cold.'

He laughed softly. He brought his left hand upwards into the beam of light. It was bandaged in blood-soaked strips from the bed sheets.

'That's the bad news,' he explained. 'I need a doctor. I can't ring for one myself. I'll end up in jail. And I can't risk one from the Republican community. He might be a friend of McDaid's and give me a lethal injection.'

'What happened?' she asked again.

He didn't answer this time.

She moved a little closer and stooped to look at him and realised only then that he'd actually fainted once more.

She searched the flat for alcohol and found a half-full bottle of whisky and a drinking glass in a kitchen cupboard.

Stafford came to as she lifted his head and raised the glass to his lips.

She said, 'I'll get you a doctor.'

190

'No police?' he groaned.

'No, no police.'

When he nodded weakly, she left the flat and went back downstairs to the pay phone and tried to divide the Service's doctors between Rawlings's people and the rest. While she struggled to pick one from the right bunch, it struck her that Stafford had had the same problem with his own medical people.

Hessel, she decided then. Arthur Hessel. He owed her a little more than a free consultation, but that would do to even the score.

Stafford was awake again, sweating heavily, when she went back after making the call.

'Something for you,' he said weakly. 'Danny Boyce has no intention of staying with McDaid. Danny escaped only to get away somewhere foreign with his wife and daughter. They're in Dublin, I think.'

She frowned. 'Is Boyce still with McDaid?'

Stafford, unable to shrug, simply closed his eyes for a moment. 'I don't know. But I imagine so. He has to get money, hasn't he? And new papers. A passport and that. He can't do it all by himself.'

She watched him wince with pain and close his eyes again, and she felt useless, unable to ease his suffering. She had no resentment left for him. No anger any more. But neither could she help him.

And yet she owed him that, as much as Hessel owed herself a favour.

March 1991, she remembered.

Two days after she'd been introduced to Stafford by her newest tout, Philip Ganley.

She was aching with flu, tossing feverishly in a bed that was soaked with her sweat, too weak to care for herself, when the doorbell of her apartment rang about seven in the evening. She crawled out of bed and in her confusion pressed the wrong

191

button, releasing the lock on the street door instead of using the intercom. When he knocked, she opened the apartment door, intending to rid herself quickly of the caller.

But he said himself, 'Sorry. Bad time. You're not well.'

'How did you get my address?' she asked.

'Ganley. One of your students, isn't he? Don't blame him, though. I pestered him.'

'Why?'

'Why?' he repeated. 'I don't know. I thought you were kind of nice, you know. Two days ago, anyway. And I'm sure you will be again when you're over your, ah . . .'

'Flu.'

He nodded, still standing in the hallway, still staring at her with an amused expression on his face that he was trying to contain.

She looked awful. Her short, black hair was jutting at odd angles from her head. Her lips were white and crusted. Her eyes were raw and streaming. And she was stooped and shivering in cotton pyjamas that her sweat had made damp and stale.

He said, 'You know, I was going to suggest a drink or a meal or something. But not tonight, eh?'

She knew the risks he'd run by coming to her apartment to arrange a date. Like the vast majority of IRA volunteers, his identity was known to the security forces from informers. The danger wasn't arrest. There was no evidence for a conviction. It was being spotted and tailed.

She opened the door a little wider.

'Come in,' she invited. 'If you want to.'

She shuffled past him after he'd entered, back to her bedroom. He followed her, taking in the untidiness, the neglect, the poor condition of her bedclothes.

'Don't you have anyone to look after you?' he asked.

The question almost broke her down. Because she didn't have to think to find the answer. She had touts that she handled. She had Sir Andrew Pinnington as her sole link to the official world of intelligence agencies. She had students that she taught and academics who were colleagues. But she couldn't name one who cared a damn whether she was healthy or ill, dead or alive.

'You're from Dublin, aren't you?' Stafford asked.

She sat up in bed, shivering violently, the bedclothes pulled around her shoulders. She nodded.

'Two aunts,' she said. 'My parents are dead.'

'Don't you have any *friends* here? In Belfast.'

She didn't. She had no friends *anywhere*, in fact.

'Look,' Stafford said decisively, 'you need to change your bedclothes. At least the sheets and pillowcase. Where do you keep them?'

'In the hot press.'

'Right.' He rubbed his hands together, anticipating work. He said, 'You also need to shower and change those pyjamas. And you need to eat something. Have you eaten today?'

'No.'

'Something light,' he said. 'Clear soup and hot buttered toast, my mother always made when I had flu. You shower. I'll put the food on. I haven't eaten either.'

And looking down on him now, almost four years on, with the positions reversed, he wounded and she the carer, that's what she said when he opened his eyes and looked at her.

'Clear soup and hot buttered toast.'

Stafford smiled at the memory. And something like tenderness replaced the pain in his eyes for a moment or two.

'We've a lot to catch up on, June,' he said.

She answered softly, 'Yeah.' Remarking to herself again how odd it was that she'd never managed to address him by his first name.

'I've asked myself the same questions a thousand times since,' he said. 'If she felt anything at all, why did she set us

193

Armed and Dangerous

up to be ambushed and killed by the SAS? If she never felt anything, why did she wait eight months, from March to November, before betraying us? We carried out four operations in that period. And you knew about them, didn't you? Ganley told you.'

'Yes,' she confirmed.

'But you let some of your own people be killed. Why?'

'Because it was quite simply you or them, wasn't it? You make the same choice in the field. You or them.'

'But why change after eight months?'

She hesitated. And then finally said it. His name. 'Because the price was too high, Jody. Because you can't keep feeding a relationship that lives on death. It becomes a monster, constantly demanding a sacrifice of blood.'

Stafford groaned and shifted painfully in the bed. 'You know the worst part, June?' he asked.

'What?'

'Still thinking, after seeing you in the police station, that they were grilling you too, that they were putting you through the same rough treatment I was getting. All through the time I was held in custody, until Sean McDaid told me you were a spy. It was McDaid found out. He tortured Ganley.'

She nodded. 'I know.'

Two days after her sudden release from RUC custody. A damp basement flat in a Belfast slum, smelling of mould and boiled vegetables. She crouched, cramped, stiff with terror, in a wardrobe, peering through a slit in the wood into the room beyond the bedroom. McDaid's short, curly hair. His incongruous cherubic face. His gun barrel pressed into Ganley's stomach and the bread knife in his other hand tearing at Ganley's flesh.

'Ganley told him everything,' she said. 'Everything except the fact that you and I were lovers. I always thought that odd. He was willing to sell you to me, but not to Sean McDaid.'

194

'Ganley,' Stafford said. 'Poor bastard.'

'He was a drug addict.'

'So I've heard.'

'And Enright,' she said. 'Bill Enright. I wanted to ask you –'

A crisp knocking on the flat's front door interrupted her.

Stafford slipped his right hand under the blue pillow and came out with a 9mm automatic. But he held it by the barrel, offering her the hand grip.

She shook her head. 'It's probably the doctor.'

Stafford grinned and said, 'I probably wouldn't be alive any more if I relied on probabilities.'

It *was* the doctor, though. A small, rotund man, with glasses and a bustling manner, who asked questions with his eyebrows and acknowledged the answers with grunts.

She led him to the bedroom. He sniffed as he passed the blood-stained table and sniffed again at the sight of Stafford. He worked without introductions, without chatter, without even a running commentary on what he was doing.

Maybury left him to it and went back to the other room to think. Not about the past any more, though. About her present job.

Already she could see a use for the information about Danny Boyce. If it was true, of course. And if Boyce was still with McDaid. And if she herself hadn't been suspended.

Ironically, the last now seemed the biggest obstacle.

Leaving the door unlocked again, she followed the trail of blood backwards from the table, into the hallway and down the stairs. It stopped at the pay phone below. There was no blood on the street door and none on the steps outside, or on any of the footpaths leading to the house.

The injury to Stafford had happened in the flat itself. But how? When? And who had inflicted it?

The doctor was finished when she went back upstairs. He stood at the sink in the kitchen area, washing his hands. He

195

half turned as she came in, nodded brusquely, but said nothing. He seemed to be one of those practitioners you had to prise opinions out of. Maybe it happened to all professionals who worked for the Service, she thought.

In the silence she couldn't think of anything better than the conventional, 'How is he?'

'Sleeping,' the doctor said curtly. 'I've given him a sedative.'

'How bad is the wound?'

The doctor briskly dried his hands on paper from a toilet roll after discarding the two soiled towels hanging over the sink.

'The wound itself is not a problem,' he said. 'The bullet passed cleanly through the lower arm without shattering anything essential. The loss of blood is worrying. He really needs a transfusion, but as he refuses to admit himself to hospital I can't do anything more for him. I'll try and organise something and call again tomorrow morning, shall I?'

She gestured helplessly. 'I don't know, really. It depends. I'll call you.'

'Your show,' the doctor conceded airily, and gathered his bags and left.

She stood uncertainly for a while, struggling with separate temptations, but then turned and walked back to the darkened bedroom. And in there, sealed from the noise of the outside world, with Stafford sleeping heavily in the bed, she was tempted again by doubt. As she knew she would be.

Her life since coming back to England seemed unnatural by comparison with her past. Uncharacteristic. Not quite her own. The monotony of useless paperwork in the Service. The predictable jostling of career moves. Living the sensible affair with Tim Aston.

What was missing . . .

As a child, she'd been reared by those maiden aunts in Dublin's middle-class Donnybrook. They were Catholic.

196

Respectable. Fussy and over-attentive and too restrictive. Still stuck in the grey conventions of the Forties and Fifties.

She was born in 1960. And grew up with the decade. And her temperament was exactly the opposite of theirs.

So her pleasures were always stolen. Her excitements were always born from secrecy. Her games were always serious. Setting up elaborate façades to use as cover for running with a wilder pack.

She could draw a straight line from that. Through her recruitment by Andrew Pinnington as an MI5 agent. Through her undercover work in Northern Ireland while studying and lecturing at Queen's.

And through her affection for Jody Stafford as well, she wondered?

That was the question. Had it been real? Was she capable of love? Or had it merely offered an almost unbearable twist by suddenly transforming spying itself into the façade?

A question that brought her back to where she sat now, alone again with Stafford, and with the prospect of renewal.

Stafford was naked under the bedclothes, his torso visible from the waist upwards since he'd thrown off the blankets for coolness.

His muscles had slackened a little, she noticed, since the last time she'd made love with him.

The last time. That night he'd come back from the ambush that should've killed him, to stand again outside the door of her Belfast apartment like a silent ghost, not making it clear whether the agony on his face was need or fury, whether he'd called for comfort or revenge.

All that night she'd lain with the fear of being killed by him.

But the night had passed. Into a dawn that had separated them.

Stafford was picked up on his way back home and held for interrogation. A few days later she herself was arrested by

197

Inspector McIver and brought to the same interrogation centre.

The last they'd seen of each other was through an open doorway. Until a jailbreak by Sean McDaid brought them together, almost four years later.

She sat now and moved the chair closer to his bed.

He stirred and moaned softly in his sleep.

She was about to reach out to him, to lay her fingers on his forehead and perhaps run them gently across his strong features, when she heard a low sound, possibly from the room outside.

She tensed and listened.

Who was living in this place, she wondered.

She hadn't asked.

Were they expected back?

She hadn't asked.

She carefully shifted Stafford's head to one side and searched under the pillow for his automatic. Releasing the safety catch on the pistol, she stood up and opened the bedroom door.

Just as the sound came towards her again. Heavier now, and more insistent.

There wasn't anyone in the outer room, though.

It was someone in the corridor beyond, knocking on the front door.

But who?

Someone who had come for Stafford? By arrangement? A friend? An enemy? McDaid or Reilly, even?

She couldn't afford to ignore it. And she had the advantage, she reckoned. No one knew that she was there.

She walked silently across and stood to the left of the door, out of the path of its swing if it was kicked inwards. From that position, she released the catch on the lock. The door drifted slowly open.

But no one came in.

She stepped backwards, covering the opening with the gun,

until she could see into the hallway.

Outside, with an irritated look on his stolid face and his hands deep in the pockets of his dark overcoat, stood Superintendent Geoffrey Gilston.

She almost dropped the gun.

Her first thought was that the whole affair had been some-how set up by Rawlings. Her second, less absurd, was that the betrayed wasn't herself, but Jody Stafford. Someone who had known he was hiding here had sold him out.

Either way, she decided, her own position was now impossible.

But Gilston stepped inside, unbuttoned his overcoat and walked slowly past her, and was obviously alone. He took in the blood-stained table and the rest of the room, but didn't stop. He went on, into the darkened bedroom, and stayed there, silent and immobile, for two or three minutes, getting accustomed to the gloom and checking on the sleeping figure in the bed.

When he came back, his face was still set in that same expression of annoyance. He gestured her to close the door.

He said, 'My information is that you've been suspended, both from the present case and from your position as section head of F2.'

'Your information seems to extend beyond that,' she observed drily.

Because it obviously wasn't Stafford who'd been fingered, she realised. Gilston wouldn't have come alone in that case. It was *she*.

Gilston grunted and asked, 'Is it accurate? The information.'

'I've been instructed to report to Personnel in the morning, yes. Vetting.'

'What if you don't?' Gilston asked.

'Then I'll miss a positive vetting.'

'Yes,' Gilston said impatiently. 'But what if you came and

199

talked to me instead? At nine o'clock. At my office in New Scotland Yard.'

She raised her eyebrows.

But if he was going to accommodate her that much, she decided, she might as well push it a little further.

'If I do', she said, 'come and talk with you in the morning, I'd like another interview with Dixie McDaid. I have a number of new questions for him.'

'We'll see. After we've talked.' He jerked his thumb over his shoulder, back towards the bedroom. 'What do you want to do about Stafford?'

'I don't know. Put a couple of men outside to keep an eye on his movements, I suppose. But I doubt if he's going anywhere. Certainly not before morning.'

Gilston nodded. 'Are you staying here?'

She'd already made up her mind about that and answered quickly. 'No. I'll wait until your men show up, then leave.'

Gilston buttoned his overcoat. 'They're already out there,' he said. 'They've been out there since shortly before you arrived yourself.'

He strode past her to open the door.

'Until the morning, then,' he threw back. 'Nine o'clock.'

16

It was six when Jody Stafford finally woke.

For a long time, still groggy from the drugs and weak from loss of blood, he lay without moving on the bed, trying to work forwards, step by step, from the moment he'd got back to Enright's flat the previous day.

Lunch-time. A taxi. The driver berating Eric Cantona . . .

It took him fifteen minutes before he was satisfied that there was only one real danger to his plans.

By then his eyes were well adapted to the dark and he could see that he was alone in the bedroom. By then he'd checked under his pillow several times to confirm that the Beretta was still there.

He lifted back the covers and swung his legs on to the floor, but immediately felt a little light-headed and had to rest, sitting on the edge of the bed.

He found one of his shoes and tossed it at the door to make a racket.

No one stirred in the outer room.

He stood up and moved unsteadily to the door and opened it. He hit the light switch outside and immediately saw the note on the table, held down by an empty glass. He didn't dwell on it. Still supported by the frame of the bedroom doorway, he looked beyond the table, to the long wooden chest against the far wall.

The chest was still locked. It hadn't been tampered with. Even the cushions on top still held the same precise arrangement he himself had organised.

And that, he reckoned, was the major danger nicely out of the way.

Because inside that chest, his legs slightly bent for a better fit, lay the corpse of Bill Enright.

The blood that was staining the table, the chair and the floor underneath wasn't all Stafford's.

It had happened quickly within a minute of Enright coming back from the bedroom the day before.

The next-door neighbour had passed their front door and descended the stairs and left the house, and Enright, standing over Stafford at the table, had waved the Beretta a little and smiled. More confident now. The house was probably empty and he didn't feel so nervous about letting off a shot.

'Have you seen him yet?' Stafford asked. 'Sean, I mean.'

Enright was still smiling. 'I'll see him tomorrow.'

'So what time has he pencilled *you* in for? Morning? Afternoon? Maybe later?'

'I'll see him at noon. Why? What do you mean?'

'Noon? That's two hours after I see him.'

'Fuck off, Jody.'

'So where is he setting you up to be the fall guy?'

'Just shut up, Jody. Okay? Just shut up.'

Stafford shrugged.

He sliced brown bread with the black-handled knife and calculated the distance between himself and Enright. Still beyond his reach.

He speared the slice of bread with the point of the knife and dropped it on Enright's side of the table. Enright foolishly reached for it before the knife was fully withdrawn, his leering face hovering for a few seconds above the table.

Stafford struck sharply upwards, forcing the knife through Enright's neck.

Enright got off a shot. But it was involuntary, the same as his strangled cry. The bullet hit Stafford's left arm, which he'd raised for balance while attacking.

The amount of blood afterwards was terrifying. Left with only one effective hand, Stafford pulled a black plastic bag over Enright's head and upper body at least to contain the flow.

Before dragging him across and lifting him into the trunk, he searched his pockets and found nothing but rubbish, apart from the keys of the flat.

He didn't know much, Stafford thought afterwards, while clearing up the worst of the blood and bandaging his own hand. He didn't know where McDaid was staying. He didn't know what his target was. All he knew was that McDaid intended meeting Enright somewhere at noon the next day.

A day Stafford himself wouldn't stay on his feet for unless he got medical attention. And unless he found it outside a hospital, from a GP who wouldn't call in the police.

And then he remembered it. The card that Hanrahan, the MI5 agent in Belfast, had given him with the contact number for June Maybury on it.

So the way Stafford saw it now, his gamble had paid off. June hadn't turned him in. She'd organised help and even left him the automatic.

Why, he wondered.

Because, from her point of view, he was already out of the game?

Or because of something still alive and lingering from their relationship in Northern Ireland?

In any case, for whatever reason, she'd left him the freedom to move again.

Or maybe that note on the table changed all that, he thought.

He pushed himself from the doorway and across to the table. He moved the glass that was distorting the letters in the centre and read without lifting the paper.

The same doctor will call again at nine tomorrow morning. I've given him spare keys I found in a kitchen drawer. I'll contact you myself some time afterwards. Don't leave the flat. Ring me at the following number to leave a message.

It was six-thirty by then.

Stafford folded the note and carried it with him back to the bedroom, killing the light in front as he went.

He'd take the doctor's attention and the doctor's advice and the doctor's antibiotics in the morning, he decided, but he wouldn't take any more of the doctor's sedatives.

He needed to be awake the next day.

203

PART FOUR
Friday

ONE

1

When Dixie McDaid was roughly woken, he had no idea what time it was.

As a matter of fact, he wasn't even sure what *day* it was any more. They'd taken his wrist-watch and wouldn't answer his questions and kept the electric lights permanently on in his cell.

In the beginning, when they'd brought him in from the farm-house in Hertfordshire, he'd tried to make an effort, to keep a rough estimate based on patterns he'd heard about from other volunteers in Northern Ireland. A four-hour interrogation session. Maybe twenty minutes' sleep before he was woken. Another four hours' questioning. A third of a day already gone.

It seemed important. Knowing how long Sean had been out there, on the run. Calculating how close he was getting to his target.

Not any longer, though. Right now, Dixie didn't give a damn about time. If Sean succeeded, he succeeded. That was *his* area. Nothing Dixie could do about it. *His* job was to concentrate on keeping his mouth shut.

And he was happier with that. Staying silent while they grilled him. Staring at the wall. And picking his nose.

So he didn't complain about the ill-treatment, the exhaustion and the lack of basic facilities. He didn't point out that they were breaking their own laws by denying him access to a legal representative. He didn't even bother trying to be smart any more.

The process of deep interrogation had managed to reduce Dixie down to his essence. All he really felt now was hatred of the English. But even that he kept to himself.

The only thing that made him nervous from time to time was the prospect of physical pain.

He didn't want to be hurt again.

He tried not to think about it. But his mind kept going back to those cigarette burns Junior Doherty had made on his cheeks. He knew how close he'd come to talking because of them.

So far, though, the English detectives had only shaken him or pulled his head upwards by the hair, just to keep him awake.

Best and most encouraging of all, Dixie guessed that his strategy was working. The last few sessions, the cops didn't have the same enthusiasm about them. They were getting ragged, dropping the pace, not putting the same effort in. They were starting to believe that he didn't really know anything about Sean's intentions and getting around to stitching him up on some trumped-up charge just to sweep him out of their lives.

So, for the first time, Dixie came to the Interview Room a little cocky now, leading his guards instead of being a weight on them, trying a swagger despite his weariness.

And then the door was opened and he sauntered in, and saw immediately that something was different.

The usual crew of tired detectives weren't waiting inside. Instead, a big, old-fashioned copper, in a suit the same colour as his muddy brown hair, was sitting at the table. Beside him was the young public schoolboy type who'd been at the farmhouse in Hertfordshire. And sitting over on a window ledge

208

was the woman with short, black hair who'd been with him.

The schoolboy had a folded tabloid newspaper on the table in front of him. Dixie could see almost half the back page. The headline had something about Eric Cantona, the French soccer player.

2

June Maybury looked uneasily at Dixie McDaid. She'd expected much the same character as she'd met a couple of days before, much the same volatile mixture of shapes and fears, postures and uncertainties. She'd been looking forward to playing on his self-regard again.

It wasn't there now.

Two days of physical neglect and intensive interrogation had succeeded only in stripping away his weaknesses. With his dead eyes, his pale, blotchy skin and unshaven beard that grew in ridiculously untidy little tufts, Dixie knew that there was nothing left of him that was in any way attractive. And he didn't care.

When Gilston told him to sit, he didn't move. The detective who'd brought him took his arm and forced him across the room and into the chair, before going back to stand guard at the door.

For no better reason than to leave his victim guessing, Gilston started with Dixie's expulsion from Northern Ireland. He seemed to be amused by the idea of Dixie being helpless, seemed to dwell on the image of Dixie being humiliated by Jody Stafford while dangling a couple of broken arms.

Dixie said nothing. He picked a spot on the wall somewhere above Gilston's head and found it fascinating enough to hold his interest. After a while he used his right index finger to explore his nostrils and take out dried mucus that he rolled between the finger and thumb.

Gilston suddenly switched from statements to questions.

'How long have you lived in the house on Kilburn High Road, Dixie?' he asked.

There was no answer, no response.

'Have you always rented the same flat there? What's your landlord's name? Do you know many people in the local Irish community? What's your next-door neighbour's name?'

Dixie's reaction to the last question was minuscule. He simply stopped rolling the mucus between his thumb and forefinger.

It wasn't visible from the other side of the table. But June Maybury, sitting on a window ledge to the side of Dixie, saw it immediately. She made her own small gesture, folding her arms, to indicate a hit to Gilston.

Gilston quickly took it up. 'Mary Cassidy,' he said, as if just recalling it. 'Is that the name of the girl next door? How well do you know her? Do you visit her often? Have you ever taken her out? She's Irish too, isn't she? Have you spent some time in her flat? While she was there? While she was out, even?'

By then, Dixie's thumb and forefinger were pressed so violently together that the tips of both digits were white from lack of blood. All his tension was contained in that right arm and hand. Otherwise he looked unconcerned.

Maybury unfolded her arms and stepped down to the floor, leaning back now against the window-sill.

She said, 'We know it would have been necessary for your brother Sean to visit your flat, Dixie. We know why it would have been necessary. What we don't know is exactly what part your friend Mary would have played in all this. She says she's entirely innocent.'

Dixie frowned, not only worried about his neighbour, but

210

also troubled by the tense being used. *Would have. Would have.*

Maybury didn't let him settle on it, didn't let him work him-self round to the belief that they were only winding him up. She walked across to the table and took the newspaper from Bromley. She unfolded it and laid it flat on the table in front of Dixie, with the front page up.

Dixie tried to keep staring at the wall, but he couldn't resist glancing downwards.

The headline made little obvious sense to him. CLUB OF DEATH.

But under it, to the left of the page, there was an old pho-tograph of his brother, so enlarged that it had almost lost its definition.

He read the report.

Convicted IRA killer and self-styled military commander, Sean McDaid (34), was savagely clubbed to death by two of his own 'soldiers' in a London house last night. Police named the assailants today as Danny Boyce, another convicted IRA mass murderer, and Denis Reilly, sentenced to life imprison-ment for the murder of Constable John Trelly. The pair, along with McDaid, were among four prisoners who blasted their way out of Whitemoor Prison last Tuesday night and gunned down two unarmed local constables in their flight the next morning. According to the police, the so-called revolutionar-ies were squabbling over blood money embezzled from IRA funds . . .

It's over, Dixie thought. Without Sean, it was over.

He felt crushed by the news and by the way the bastards had broken it to him, no longer able to fight off the pain and the tiredness.

There were stinging tears in his eyes and he furiously wiped his left cheek as a bead broke and trickled down his face.

211

For a moment he was six years old again. It was just a few days after his mother's death in 1972, and he was screaming and struggling to escape again the smothering hold of Maisie Connolly while watching his brother Sean, only twelve at the time, walking away with Jody Stafford, out of his life.

The first time Sean had ever abandoned him.

'I'll be back for you, Dixie.'

And he was, six years later.

He was always true to his word, Dixie thought. Always true. But not now. Not any more. He wouldn't be back any more.

Dixie also felt enraged. And when the first wave of grief passed, that's what took hold of him. He was used to obscenities from the English yellow press. But he didn't think they had a right to gloat and sneer over a dead man's corpse.

'Where's the body?' he demanded suddenly.

His voice was hoarse. He cleared his throat and repeated the question.

No one answered. Gilston and Bromley looked away from him, down at the surface of the table.

What did it mean, Dixie wondered, that they couldn't even look him in the face. What were they trying to hide?

'Where's the fucking body?' he shouted.

June Maybury, still standing beside him, touched his shoulder with her hand. 'It's all over, Dixie,' she said. 'Sean never made it to your flat. The others are dead, too. Jennifer Crooks. Woolly Barr. It's Boyce and Reilly that we –'

'Where are they?' Dixie interrupted.

Gilston coughed and raised his head. 'The Metropolitan Police are confident of apprehending Danny Boyce and Denis Reilly at an early stage of the murder investigation –'

'You don't have them!' Dixie cried.

'Our understanding of their intentions', Maybury said, 'is that they will attempt to complete the operation your brother Sean began.'

212

Dixie was vigorously shaking his head. 'No. No.'

'Don't believe everything you read in that newspaper report,' Gilston advised. 'Your brother didn't die instantly. And they don't necessarily want the money for their personal use.'

'I said Sean *would have* needed to visit your flat,' Maybury added. 'Yesterday morning, disguised as a tramp, Denis Reilly actually did so. And managed to escape afterwards.'

'No. No.'

'What do you mean?'

Dixie didn't answer. He kept shaking his head.

'Two of a kind,' Maybury advanced.

Dixie started. 'What?'

'Two of a kind,' she said again. 'Denis Reilly and your brother.'

The effect on Dixie startled her. He stared at her stupidly, his eyes almost closed, his mouth drooping, terrified of what she was going to add. The phrase obviously had some vital significance for him.

She tried to think of possibilities while still talking calmly to him.

Two of a kind. A pair? Two active service units? A target with two separate parts?

She said, 'It's possible that Reilly and Boyce may have set out to *sabotage* your brother's plans. We don't believe so. Our information is that your brother died in a leadership dispute.'

Dixie struggled to concentrate. Against the pain. The irritation. The tears. The droning voices.

He wanted Reilly's head. And he wanted Boyce's head. He knew Sean himself mightn't have agreed with him, but he felt that certain things were more important than politics. For over twenty years Sean was the only family he had. The only comfort. The only true friend.

But he knew that he wasn't going to claim any heads while lying in a cell in God knows what police station.

213

Unless he gave the cops the details of the operation.

Unless the cops lay in wait for Boyce and Reilly and cut them down before they reached the target. Compliments of Dixie McDaid, lads.

Obviously, he thought, the police already knew the overall plan. Two of a kind, he repeated to himself. Two of a kind.

But he wondered what Sean would have thought. What Sean would have wanted.

To give himself time, something to distract him from the cops' insistent voices, he flicked through the newspaper in front of him.

The rest of the story of Sean's death was on pages five and six. Photographs of Pa Daly's house in Harlesden. One disgusting shot of Sean's blood-soaked hand visible under the cloth that concealed the rest of his body. The usual sensational story of Sean's past.

He moved on.

The TV feature was on some nature programme by David Attenborough.

The sports headline on the back page was about the French footballer Eric Cantona fighting a spectator.

Dixie flipped the paper over and started again. Still uncertain. Still torn by grief and revenge.

He got as far as page three. And then it struck him. Dully at first. As if his tiredness was cushioning the impact of strong impressions.

He went back to the front page to check the date and found then that this was his third day in custody. It seemed about right. Wednesday. Thursday. Friday.

But when he turned the paper over again and read the main sports story, it was something he already knew about, something he'd read about maybe a week before.

For a long time, fighting against the increased barrage of questions from the others, knowing from their agitation that

214

he was on to something, he struggled to make sense of it all.

The back page was a week old.

The front page was today's.

And then he laughed. With ease. Without control. With tears, this time of relief, now streaming down his reddened face and into his sparse beard. He laughed until the sound drowned out and killed off the questions from the police and he kept on laughing through the silence that followed.

3

Geoffrey Gilston tapped a pencil against the surface of the table and slid his fingers down the barrel to turn the pencil upside down and start all over again, tapping it on the table.

June Maybury sat on the window-sill, staring vacantly outwards.

Bromley was moodily looking through the tabloid newspaper.

Dixie McDaid had been taken back to his cell a few minutes before and the silence between the three was heavy with unspoken regrets and accusations.

Eventually Bromley muttered, 'I'm dreadfully sorry. I should have checked.'

'You're damned right you should've checked,' Gilston snarled.

'I had a number of editions, you see,' Bromley explained lamely. 'I was using them for pasting mock-ups while preparing. I'm afraid I inadvertently left in an old back page.'

'Why the hell couldn't you just use *today's* back page, man?'

'It doesn't matter,' June Maybury began.

'Of course it bloody matters!' Gilston snapped.

'I mean', she explained stiffly, 'that there is nothing we can do about it now. At least we know that Dixie –'

'He was on the point of bloody telling us where and when his brother was going to move.' Gilston held up a trembling hand and almost closed his thumb against his forefinger, leaving the smallest of gaps. 'We were that close to wrapping it up. That close!'

Maybury looked with a little more sympathy at the shame-faced Bromley, though accepting that she herself had to take some of the blame.

It was her idea, after all. A good idea. It had almost worked. But she should've overseen the final mock-up for the false newspaper. Her suspension, of course, had prevented her showing herself at Headquarters. And since Bromley had worked through the night without Rawlings's knowledge, what could you do but accept his apologies?

She said honourably now, 'It's my responsibility.'

Gilston made a dismissive, dissatisfied sound.

'Did you get the rest of the material out?' she asked Bromley.

Bromley nodded, still unhappy. 'I placed them last night, before anything was out to bed.'

'Good.' She paused, not wanting him to linger with his melancholy any more. 'What are you supposed to be doing right now?'

'The best cover being the truth, I'm actually officially interviewing Dixie McDaid,' he said. 'I'd better get back, I suppose.' He stood up and laughed nervously. 'To report the lack of progress.'

When he was gone, softly closing the door of the Interview Room behind him, Gilston said simply, 'I don't like that chap.'

'You don't like *anyone* in the Service,' Maybury pointed out.

Given a less dour nature, he might publicly have made an exception of herself. Instead he confined himself to a grunt.

'No one in Special Branch actually *likes* anyone in the Service,' she added.

216

'The younger they are and the closer to the centre of power, the less I like them,' Gilston admitted. 'Bromley has a combination I can't take at all.'

In the silence that followed, Gilston took the newspaper and read the racing returns inside the back page from more than a week before. All it achieved was an unwelcome reminder of old losses.

He knew that part of his irritation with Bromley had a more local cause. Bromley had arrived before Maybury that morning, carrying the false tabloid and all set for the interview with Dixie McDaid. Rushing things. All boyish eagerness. Forcing aside the agreed meeting between Gilston and Maybury.

As if reading the Superintendent's mind, Maybury said now, 'Last night. What did you tell George Rawlings?'

Gilston set his stolid face in neutral. A man who liked talking about the failings of others, but not much given to public explanations of his own behaviour.

He said finally, 'I haven't always seen eye to eye with you on things. I still don't where Jody Stafford is concerned. The fact is, I didn't end up in that flat in Neasden because my men picked up Stafford's trail. I was told you were going there and who you were with. There was a phone call to my office.'

'Someone is running up expensive telephone bills,' she observed.

'It came from your own Headquarters. And like you said yourself, I'm not too comfortable about getting into bed with you people.'

He reddened a little, embarrassed by the ambiguity of the last phrase.

But her mind was elsewhere.

She said, 'So what did you tell Rawlings?'

'I told him what I've just told you, that I received a telephone call informing me that you had located Jody Stafford in a flat in Neasden. But I also told him that the call was

217

merely a hoax and the house empty.'

'Why?'

'If the telephone call was made on Rawlings's own instructions, he would expect a report from me. If it wasn't, the chances were that he also received a call. I had to cover myself.'

'That's not what I meant. Why didn't you tell Rawlings the truth?'

'We prefer to arrest our traitors. More embarrassment for you lot. We haven't had one since Bettaney in 1983.'

She said, 'It still doesn't explain much. Why risk your own neck to save mine?'

'I don't care about your neck,' Gilston admitted ungallantly, recovering his gruffness. 'You can put it through a wringer, for all the interest I have in it. I care about my work. Whoever rang my office was serving their own interests by attempting to put you out of the game. Their interests are not mine. If you're a danger to them, I'd rather have you sitting on this side of the fence. The question is this. Who knew where you were going yesterday?'

She'd already chewed over that and said immediately, 'My secretary took the call.'

'Well, you'd better run the rule over her, hadn't you?' He took up the pencil again and went back to tapping it in slow time on the table. Then he asked, 'Did you know that Rawlings's private secretary is queer, by the way?'

'Orrinsmith? But he looks too . . .'

'Too queer to be actually queer.'

'Gay,' she said with exasperation. 'The decent word is gay.'

'I'm afraid there's damn all that's gay about being homosexual and working in intelligence,' Gilston said bluntly. 'And you don't get blackmailed for gaiety. You get it for queerness. Rawlings has a reputation as a womaniser, doesn't he?'

Maybury shrugged. 'So I've heard.'

'So everybody's heard,' Gilston pointed out. 'It's a carefully planted story. All he needs to do is wink to keep the myth alive. But did you know that you can't find an Englishwoman he's supposed to have . . . had relations with? East Germans. Russians. Poles. All of them while he was serving in MI6. Very convenient, don't you think? A girl in every port, except the ones we have jurisdiction over.'

'What you're suggesting is absurd.'

'I'm not suggesting anything. I'm asking a question. Have you ever actually *seen* him with a woman?'

She shook her head. 'No.'

Gilston sighed and shifted noisily in his chair. 'If I seem a little crabbed this morning, it's because I was awake last night, digging all this up. You had much better accept it, you know. You have a mole in MI5, working on Sean McDaid's side, burrowing away at the foundations of the IRA's peace process.'

'I thought you didn't believe in their ceasefire,' she challenged.

'I don't,' he admitted. 'But my scepticism is a long way from one of your people giving the IRA ammunition. You'd better start with your secretary, by the way.'

Maybury came off the window-sill and walked across to lean on the table, opposite Gilston.

'I'll lay a bet', she challenged, 'that I'll know within twelve hours exactly where Sean McDaid is.'

Gilston raised his eyebrows, a dubious look in his eyes.

'Twelve hours?' he repeated. 'I hope you're right. You want my best guess? From the time of the jailbreak? From McDaid's movements up to now? Her Majesty is attending a charity performance at the Barbican tomorrow night. It won't be a bomb, though. There's no way he could have placed a bomb with a delayed timer anywhere in there or near the approaches. No. It has to be a marksman's rifle. But where has he got the equipment? Not Dixie McDaid's flat. We've taken that apart.'

219

Maybury smiled and held up a confident index finger.

'Try Mary Cassidy's flat next door,' she suggested. 'Nothing to do with the girl herself. Just an impression I got from Dixie.'

4

Sitting on the edge of his bed, gently bathing his damaged lip, Sean McDaid looked out through the open bedroom door at the hunched figure of Danny Boyce trudging wearily up the stairs with a newspaper in his big paw.

Another gloomy face, McDaid thought irritably, wondering what the hell was biting the big oaf now. Something in the newspaper, he guessed. Five minutes before, Boyce had gone down to collect it, and he'd been in reasonable humour then.

The clock in the living-room below chimed out the hour as Boyce reached the landing. Three o'clock.

McDaid grunted with annoyance. Bill Enright was already three hours late and obviously wasn't going to make it now. From midday, when he was supposed to report to Maisie Connolly's house, McDaid had telephoned his flat every quarter of an hour, getting a disconnected tone every time.

It was worrying. Enright knew their address. If he was lifted . . .

But it wasn't only that.

It was more that the whole operation seemed half blessed and half dogged by luck.

McDaid could happily accept the breaks. He believed that God was on his side. But he wasn't troubled by consistent adversity, either. God, the most demanding of allies, was only testing him. To his superstitious mind, though, the *uncertain* struggle between good and evil in his fortunes was disturbing.

That morning, for instance, the weatherman had been fore-casting more rain and strong northerly winds, just the conditions McDaid had hoped for to launch his first attack. But waiting for Enright had drained his confidence and made him short-tempered and fatalistic again.

Enright wasn't only essential as a replacement for Reilly. He also had the explosives and the detonators and the plans they needed for continuing the campaign after taking out the first target, by bombing towns and villages along the south coast on a daily basis until they were all either killed or captured.

As for Reilly . . .

McDaid swore savagely, ignoring the hang-dog Boyce who had just entered the bedroom and was standing in front of him, offering the newspaper.

Reilly spent sleepless nights thinking only of women and money, McDaid reminded himself. It had started on Tuesday night in Jennifer Crooks's house. It had continued last night, when Reilly had been creeping around until early morning, test-ing the locks on the bedroom doors, trying to get a hand on the locked briefcase that was supposed to contain thirty thousand pounds. Planning and dreaming and sweating in the dark.

Just a petty criminal, McDaid decided again. The kind that was lucky to escape with kneecapping back in Belfast.

Did he lose sleep because a part of his country was still occu-pied by Crown forces, or because his people were dying in the struggle for freedom? No. Women and money. Women and money.

'You asked for the newspaper, Sean,' Danny Boyce was saying.

McDaid looked up. Boyce was slumped, his face long with misery.

'What the fuck's the matter with you?' McDaid demanded.

'Nothing,' Boyce muttered. He shrugged. 'Too much wait-ing around, I suppose.'

'Anything in the paper?'

'Naw.'

McDaid took the newspaper and threw it on the bed. 'Tell Reilly there's a briefing in five minutes. Down in the front room,' he added.

He didn't want Reilly casing out the bedroom for a sneak attack.

Boyce slouched off, closing the door behind him.

McDaid sighed and shook the newspaper open. The front page had a model claiming she'd been groped by a politician, more about the footballer Eric Cantona, and down in a box in the right-hand corner a dripping charity appeal. *This is Ru. She desperately needs your help.*

Scandal and sex, sports and charity, McDaid thought with disdain. It just about summed up the Englishman's shrunken empire.

Of the three, the charity appeal annoyed him most. He didn't believe in disability.

The world was divided between the fighters and the self-indulgent, he thought. His own code was simple. You didn't whine. You didn't put your hand out for alms. You didn't go under with booze, like his old man had done back in Northern Ireland. You picked up whatever weapons you could lay your hands on and you fought back.

He waited until he heard the others going past on the landing and descending the stairs. Then he took the briefcase with him and followed.

Reilly, sitting in one of the armchairs at the fireplace, looked first at the briefcase. The same hungry way he always looked first at a woman's body and not her face, McDaid thought with disgust.

McDaid sat in the armchair opposite Reilly and put the briefcase to one side on the floor.

For the past hour or so, he'd been trying to think of an angle

222

that would keep a link between the money and what he wanted Reilly to do.

He said now, 'We move out tomorrow at 1800 hours. Danny and myself will go together.' He gestured to Reilly. 'You'll go with Bill Enright. You'll both –'

He stopped as he heard the old woman, Maisie Connolly, in the front hallway outside, fumbling at the umbrella stand. He waited, through a minute of silence, until she opened the front door, went out and pulled it closed after her.

Still not satisfied, he checked from behind the curtains of the window. And only then continued.

He said, 'You'll both take the unit's funds and conceal them where Bill has arranged and where we can collect them before moving on to the next target area.'

'Where do we link up again?' Reilly asked. 'I mean, I suppose we're operating as a unit tomorrow night. Right?'

'I'll give you the full details at the briefing tomorrow morning.'

'Fair enough.'

'Right now we have another problem,' McDaid explained. 'Bill Enright can't travel by himself with the equipment he has. One of us will have to organise transport, preferably a Hiace van, and get across to him.'

'I'll go,' Boyce volunteered.

McDaid frowned, wondering about the motive, the eagerness. And then about his own perceptions. A week before he would've accepted Boyce's enthusiasm as normal.

'You've never met him, Danny,' he pointed out. 'You wouldn't even know what you're looking for.'

'Well, you'd better go yourself, then,' Boyce suggested moodily.

McDaid shook his head. 'Too risky after yesterday. You go, Denis.'

Reilly pouted like a child, thinking about the money that

was supposed to be in McDaid's briefcase. Thinking that he didn't want to stray further than arm's length away from it, and certainly not as far as Neasden.

McDaid didn't give him a chance to work on his objections. 'Don't take chances,' he advised. 'Leave now. Return in darkness. Park the van around the back of the house. You and Enright will have to sleep in it tonight. You can collect blankets and pillows when you come back.'

He got up and bustled Reilly out of his seat, clapping his hands. 'Come on, let's go!'

To Danny Boyce, left sitting on the settee while McDaid went with Reilly to the street door, it seemed that Reilly's attitude was still too uncertain to be trusted. So he was happy to see the back of him for a couple of hours.

Boyce picked up the paperback spinechiller he'd brought down with him and opened it on the last page he'd read. When McDaid stuck his head in the door on the way back, Boyce had his legs up on the plastic stool and was holding the open book close to his face.

'I'm going up to get some sleep, Danny,' McDaid said. 'I missed out on it last night. Call me if the phone rings. Or if Reilly comes back too early. Call me at six anyway.'

'Right, Sean.'

For fifteen minutes, Boyce stayed exactly as he was, his legs stretched out, the book raised, the door still open behind him. He wasn't reading, though. He was repeating in his mind the telephone number from the charity appeal on that newspaper he couldn't check any more because it was now lying on McDaid's bed. And he was listening to McDaid's movements in the room above.

When he was satisfied that McDaid slept, he got up himself, very quietly, and went into the front hallway.

Maisie Connolly was still out, probably shopping in the local supermarket, and there was no other phone in the house. His only threat of detection came from McDaid himself, and McDaid would have to swing out of a creaking bed and pull open a noisy door to look down from the landing.

Boyce listened another minute, then picked up the telephone receiver. He dialled the number from the charity appeal. A young woman's chirpy voice answered almost immediately, before the first ringing tone had ended.

'Good afternoon. May I help you?'

He said, 'I'm calling about Ru.'

'We've had many concerned calls about Ru today, sir,' the woman told him smoothly. 'Is there anything special you feel you could contribute?'

Boyce hesitated, every step an agony of indecision and uncertainty for him; but he finally said, 'I'm Danny Boyce.'

There was a sharp intake of breath at the other end. Obviously, it was the first thing the woman had been told to hope for, and the last she expected to hear.

In the silence that followed, Boyce's doubts almost overwhelmed him.

But he had something stronger than doubt inside, so he hung on, until a man's upper-class English voice said, 'You're calling about Ru, sir.'

'Where is she?' Boyce asked bluntly.

'I'm afraid you'll have to inform us, in the first instance, sir, exactly how you would see your relationship with Ru.'

'Deirdre is my wife. Her maiden name was Ruane. Ru was her nickname before we married.'

'I see. Would you have her date of birth?'

'The thirteenth of August 1950. You said she was in hospital and suicidal. Where is she?'

'She's in good hands, Mr Boyce.'

'You tell me where she is or I'll hang up this fucking phone right now and you won't hear from me again.'

'I don't think that would be wise or in your own interests.

225

However. Your wife is being cared for at a private house in Dublin, run by some of our own people.'

'You bastards!' Boyce exploded. Carelessly. Forgetting where he was, who was in the bedroom above him. 'You bastards! You've kidnapped her.'

'It's always possible that one of our less careful staff members might inadvertently tell her that you were killed by the security forces in –'

'Shut up!' Boyce raged. 'I want a deal!'

'You understand that there is no question of not serving out the sentence imposed –'

'I told you to shut up! First of all I want Denis Reilly and another guy, Bill Enright, out of my way. Reilly has just gone to meet Enright at a flat on North Circular Road in Neasden, where Enright is living under the name Bob Dalton.'

'Yes, yes,' the voice said wearily. 'Actually, what we're more interested in at the mom——'

Boyce suddenly slapped down an index finger to disconnect.

A trace, he thought. The guy was stalling him, deliberately getting him annoyed and confused, to give the technicians time to trace the call.

Had they had enough time already? He didn't think so.

But he wasn't very good at this, he decided. He'd already given them Reilly and Enright for nothing. The only thing he had left was McDaid himself. And if he was going to trade again, he'd have to do it from outside, maybe the booth at the corner of the road.

He'd heard that they sometimes tapped all the public phones in Irish areas during an IRA hunt. But Woolwich wasn't Irish.

How to manage the negotiations, though?

He thought of fantastical plans. He'd have to see Deirdre and their daughter free somewhere, Paris maybe, before he made the final call. They'd all have to move quickly. The British. The agents in Dublin. Himself. The next

226

couple of hours . . .

It was all a confusion. His brain crammed with conflicting images of light and dark. His daughter in his arms again. His wife dead or deranged.

But he finally made up his mind. He'd give them McDaid only if a deal was struck. Only if he could dictate the terms of the deal.

He was turning away from the telephone table towards the street door, replacing the receiver he still held in his hand, when he caught a blur of darkness from inside the front room through the open door. He stopped and focused.

And felt an ache of surprised pleasure in his stomach. Because McDaid's briefcase was still sitting in there on the carpet.

Money, he thought. Thirty grand. With it his passage to freedom, to France. And with him gone, out of the picture, the Brits would have no more reason for holding Deirdre.

He changed direction and headed back to the front room.

Just as his foot hit the threshold, he heard from above a creaking of the bed, and then, as he froze, the bedroom door opening on its squeaky hinges.

McDaid came out on the landing, bleary-eyed, woken from a short sleep. He was carrying his revolver lightly in his right hand.

Boyce, unarmed himself, thought that if he could lure him down the stairs . . .

He looked quickly around. He saw that the only weapon was a heavy stick in the stand by the street door.

McDaid leaned on the banister. He peered downwards and groaned. He said, 'The damned thing woke me up.'

Boyce moved back into the hallway, towards the stand. 'What?' he asked.

'The briefcase,' McDaid said. 'I left it below. I forgot about it. Bring it up to us, will you?'

227

Boyce went back to the front room, sketching a new plan. All he had to do was carry the briefcase up, use *that* as a weapon as soon as he was next to McDaid.

He was climbing quickly, eagerly, already on the eighth step, hugging the briefcase tightly to his chest, when McDaid laughed.

'No need to be so careful with it, Danny,' McDaid said. 'There's nothing at all in it. Or only a few office papers or something. The money was just a story to keep Reilly sweet. I don't want him to find it if he gets back, though.'

Boyce felt suddenly sick now in his stomach, the pleasure churning into acid. He gagged a little. He almost struck out anyway with the case, from sheer rage and frustration, from despair.

McDaid, his hand outstretched, noted it all silently. And decided to stay awake.

5

Jody Stafford woke in the dark from a bloody nightmare with a stench in his nostrils. The smell was of stale blood and rotting flesh.

But it wasn't the corpse of Bill Enright that had brought the dream and the sensations to him in his sleep. It was his own injured left hand, lying by his face on the blue pillow.

He worried immediately about how long he'd slept. He hadn't intended dropping off at all.

Maybury's doctor had come that morning to change the dressing and force him to eat some breakfast. A round little man with glasses, who hardly talked.

The bastard, Stafford thought suddenly then. The doctor.

228

He'd given an injection, claiming it was just a local anaesthetic. But it must have been another sedative.

Stafford patted along the top of the bedside cabinet for the lamp switch and then searched the chair on the other side for his wrist-watch. The strap was caked with dried blood and the face had been damaged in the struggle with Enright. The digital display was stuck on 1:27:09.

He got out of bed, weak and light-headed, his muscles stiff and his joints aching. He knew that he should spend a few minutes stretching and warming, but he was too anxious. He struggled across to the window and pulled open the curtains.

It was dusk outside. Beyond the house's back garden, he could see street lights and the headlights of cars. The traffic was heavy and slow-moving. It must be rush hour, he realised. Early in the evening.

He went outside to the other room, switching on the light there, and found a working clock on the electric cooker in the kitchen area. It said that the time was ten minutes past five.

He'd slept through the entire day, for nearly eight hours.

All his plans had been disrupted. And all his projections were now irrelevant.

McDaid had been expecting Enright at midday. What would he have done when Enright didn't show? Move house? He was unlikely to have another lined up so handily. Chances were he'd send someone to investigate.

Stafford calculated. The same calculations he'd run through the night before.

When someone doesn't show, you wait an hour for them, making excuses. Bad timekeeping. Heavy traffic. After that you accept there might be a serious problem. But you don't take the risk of *acting* on it until you're certain. Another hour or two.

But how far away was McDaid? How long would it take to reach Neasden?

He wondered if anyone had called while he slept. He thought not. McDaid's messenger boy wouldn't have left again without forcing an entry and checking the place.

He had to dress quickly now, Stafford decided. He had to act on the strategy he'd already worked out for dealing with the inevitable caller.

Still weak, too weak for a fight, Stafford went back to the bedroom to dress. He checked the magazine in the Beretta and carried the gun with him when he returned to the outer room. He unlocked the front door and left it ajar after pulling it to from the hallway outside.

Going down the stairs he passed a youth in blue overalls coming home from work who stared at him with his mouth open. In the lobby below, he saw his reflection in the hat-stand mirror. He was deathly pale and looked seriously ill.

It was dark in the street by now, and raining heavily. Across the road there was a small pizzeria whose windows offered a clear view of the house. Stafford sat on one of its high stools at a fixed table and ordered.

The way his luck was going, he reckoned he mightn't even get a chance to taste the food. But he'd finished the pizza and salad and was into his fourth coffee and already attracting added attention from the staff before it finally happened.

A beige Hiace van pulled up to the footpath outside the house and Denis Reilly, his red face and country manners too obvious for a job like this, got out and pushed the driver's door closed behind him. No keys to lock it with. A stolen vehicle.

Stafford had already paid for everything except the last coffee. He dropped a pound coin in the saucer and left.

Reilly, pressing on the bell to Enright's flat, didn't notice his approach. He wasn't expecting a threat from behind. In fact, it seemed as if he wasn't wary of threats at all.

Stafford pushed the Beretta into the small of his back and reached painfully around with his damaged left hand to

230

dangle a set of keys in front of Reilly's face.

'Open up, Denis,' he said. 'Leave the keys in the door. When you step inside, take three paces forward and stop again.'

Stafford collected the keys and closed the street door behind them before ordering Reilly up the stairs and into Enright's flat.

There, Reilly stared at the blood-stained table and picked the opposite side of it when told to sit down and place his hands on the surface.

Stafford sat on the wooden chest and covered him with the Beretta from there.

He said, 'You know who I am, Denis?'

They'd met twice before in Belfast, but it was better not to leave these things uncertain.

Reilly looked sullen and sulky, aware now that he'd walked into a trap, but not knowing yet if Sean McDaid had any part in setting it. Everything was always thwarting him, he thought savagely. Life, always promising something, never delivered.

He twisted his mouth into a bitter expression. 'Yeah, I know you.'

'Good,' Stafford praised. 'Now for something a little more difficult. Do you still recognise me as your superior officer?'

He hardly expected an answer and didn't get one.

After a while, he said, 'You've got two choices, Denis. We're liaising with the English police –'

'So I've heard,' Reilly sneered.

'Don't knock it until you hear it,' Stafford advised. 'If you don't want to co-operate, I'll just hand you over. No qualms. You're not a volunteer any more, just another deserter. If you want to help, I'll get you out of here through the network.'

Reilly thought about it.

He had two choices, all right, he reckoned. But they weren't the ones Stafford described.

He could make a play here, he thought, and probably end

231

up dead. Or he could feed Stafford a false address and double back himself to take McDaid and the money by surprise in Woolwich.

He had to start with something tasty for Stafford, though. Something to win him over. And maybe even help to clear things up for himself while he was doing it.

But he was learning, too. He didn't dive right in for what he wanted. And he didn't act the patriot too much, either.

He said, 'I don't mind helping you. Just as long as I don't have to go back to prison, that's all. McDaid is going to set off a bomb somewhere tomorrow night. I don't know where.'

'Is that right?' Stafford asked. 'Where is he going to get explosives?'

'They're already there.'

'Where?'

'Wherever. I don't know, do I?'

'Something with a timer on it? Why would he have to escape for that?'

'I don't know. He said his brother Dixie planted the stuff about a year ago.' Reilly took a breath, reckoning this was the best opening. 'He has the money Dixie ripped off from you in Belfast. That's what he's using for equipment.'

Stafford frowned. But he was worried about concealed bombs, not embezzlement.

'Money?' he said absently.

'He says about five thousand,' Reilly added. Probing. Wanting to be told it was worth risking his neck to go back for.

Stafford's frown deepened as he focused on what had been said.

'Dixie?' he repeated. 'Dixie fiddled the bar in one of the Belfast drinking clubs out of a couple of hundred quid. We threw him out without a penny. Sean had to stand him a few quid over here until he got work.'

In the silence, Reilly could feel his face getting hotter and

232

redder. With shame. With rage. With the *certainty* now that McDaid had taken him for a ride again.

He swore violently and hissed, 'He said fucking thirty thousand!'

'Thirty? You were giving me five.'

Stafford laughed, and then had to use the Beretta to wave the infuriated Reilly back to his seat. He saw in the youth's contorted face the stupid greed that McDaid had played on. But he also saw a terrible lust for revenge.

'So where's McDaid now?' he asked confidently.

6

Superintendent Gilston parked his car in Neasden Lane and walked the short distance from there to Bill Enright's flat.

On the way, he dropped fifty pence into the hands of a beggar who was sitting cross-legged in a shop doorway. He didn't usually indulge in charity. But when he was in sunny humour those around him sometimes came in for unexpected benefits. It was just an accident that the beggar happened to be the first person he met after leaving the car.

Earlier that afternoon, Gilston's men had lifted the floorboards in Mary Cassidy's flat and found two Kalashnikov assault rifles, one stun grenade, three revolvers and several hundred rounds of ammunition, as well as detonators and fuses. Not a sharpshooter's equipment, certainly, but a significant blow to Sean McDaid's unit and enough to put his brother Dixie away for quite a long time.

Admittedly the credit wasn't entirely Gilston's. Maybury, he accepted, had first pointed in the right direction.

But the arms find was only half the reason for the

Superintendent's celebration.

Thirty minutes before, the detectives outside the flat in Neasden had reported Denis Reilly's arrival. And no kudos for Maybury or MI5 this time, Gilston thought. The collar was exclusively the result of Special Branch surveillance.

He hadn't contacted her. He hadn't yet told *anyone* in MI5 about the development. The damn place was as leaky as a sieve.

Personally, he didn't hold out much hope of discovering whether it was Rawlings himself or Orrinsmith or Maybury's secretary or someone else who was passing information to the terrorists. He reckoned that McDaid's unit would be picked off and mopped up and that the mole would just burrow out of sight again.

It couldn't be ideological motives that drove the mole, he decided. An MI5 agent doubling for the IRA? No. It had to be blackmail, some sort of personal hold.

There was another reason for his silence, of course. Ever since the murder of John Fowler in Dixie McDaid's flat, the hunt for Sean McDaid had a more personal edge for Special Branch.

Gilston's relative good humour survived for exactly eight minutes after he'd dropped the coin in the beggar's hand.

It lasted through the report from the two detectives who had originally observed both Stafford waiting in the pizzeria and Reilly arriving in the Hiace van. It hung on through his instructions to the force of officers now assembled at the scene.

'No one knows precisely what Stafford's role is in all this,' he advised. 'The fact that he seemed to hold a gun on Reilly may be nothing more than mere caution on his part and does- n't mean that he's not trying to establish contact with McDaid with a view to co-operation. I don't want any arrests. Not yet. One or other of those two will lead us to McDaid himself. If they leave together, we follow. If they leave separately, we follow both. The command car is Inspector Peters's, who'll give you your positions now.'

And for a short while afterwards, as the men were being deployed, Gilston's outlook was still bright.

Up to the moment a red BMW came up from Dudden Hill to North Circular Road and turned into the Avenue where he was standing in the shadows. And June Maybury stepped out of it after killing the engine.

As soon as she opened her mouth, she asked, from his point of view, the most exasperating question possible.

'Were you trying to contact me?'

'No,' Gilston said dourly.

'Oh? Why not?'

'What are you doing here?' he asked testily.

Feeling that their relationship was slipping back to mutual antagonism and distrust, she realised that this must be its real nature, that it only struggled occasionally into co-operation from that base.

She said quietly, amicably, 'About three-thirty this afternoon, Danny Boyce took the bait about his wife and rang the number. He told us that Reilly was on his way here to contact Bill Enright –'

'Who's Bill Enright?'

'One of McDaid's and Stafford's old active service unit in Northern Ireland. He's living in London as Bob Dalton.'

'The flat Stafford is in now?'

'Yes.'

'Where is he?'

'Who knows? In any case, Boyce was on the point of telling where *McDaid* is, but something disturbed him. I've heard the tapes and –'

'More than I have,' Gilston interrupted coldly. 'Why wasn't my office informed?'

'Your office *was* informed.'

235

'Don't you think I know what goes through my own bloody office?'

'Then why are you here?' she demanded irritably.

His voice grew louder, his tone sharper. 'Because my own bloody men spotted Reilly arriving less than an hour ago and contacted me. Who contacted you? You're suspended from duty.'

'Well, I decided to spend the afternoon in Personnel after all. It was the easiest way to keep an eye on things, although I didn't get out until now. I had someone monitoring the calls.'

'Who was supposed to inform us?'

'Bromley cleared the arrangements with Rawlings, passing the scheme off as his own idea. So the ultimate responsibility, the decision, must have been Rawlings's . . .'

Gilston sighed heavily, but otherwise left it all hanging there in the silence. Until Inspector Peters, a young man dressed almost entirely in denim and sitting in the front passenger seat of the Branch car directly in front of Maybury's BMW, lowered his window and called softly out, 'Movement, sir. Denis Reilly has just left the house and is heading for the beige Hiace van he arrived in.'

'Alone?' Gilston asked.

'Yes, sir.'

It wasn't the action Gilston had really expected, but he'd still prepared a response to it. The jury was still out on Stafford, he conceded. But Reilly was definitely one of McDaid's unit. Reilly was moving. Stafford wasn't.

He said to Peters, 'You stay here and watch Stafford.'

'I'll stay with him,' June Maybury put in.

'Miss Maybury here will keep you company,' Gilston added drily. 'I'll see to Reilly. Keep in touch.'

'Yes, sir.'

7

The irony was that Denis Reilly felt free for the first time in his life.

He'd never had the sensation before. There was a roominess about it, he found. A sense of relief, of weightlessness. He didn't feel tense any more. He didn't feel tight in his muscles. He didn't feel pinched in his mind. The space inside the Hiace van and the sight of the road opening out in front of him were comforting.

And then he realised that all these things had come to him because he was alone for the first time in his life. He was by himself, with no one to hassle him. No one had sent him. No one was with him. And no one was waiting for him.

He couldn't remember a time like that before. All his memories were of jails of one sort or another.

His sullen resentment as a child against his loud, drunken father and against his mother's whining blackmail.

His rage at being stopped and searched by British troops as a teenager on the streets of Belfast. Their rifle butts and their batons in his body, their foreign accents ordering him about. Keep your mouth shut, Paddy. Do what you're told, Paddy.

It was why he'd joined the IRA. To get shut of the English bastards.

They were supposed to be freedom fighters, weren't they, the Republicans? The fight for Irish freedom.

But he was wrong. The fucking IRA was more tight-assed than anyone else. More than his old man. More than the British squaddies. Keep your mouth shut, Reilly. Do what you're told, Reilly.

And all it led to was a narrow cell in a special secure unit inside a thirty-foot wall in Whitemoor Prison.

Some fucking freedom.

And then McDaid, the mad fucking priest. No women. No money. No gambling. No bad thoughts. Just rosary beads and revolvers and dead patriots watching you like prison screws.

But now he was free, Reilly knew. And just because he'd taken the decision to be free. By himself. It was as simple as that. His only regret was that he hadn't known how to do it before.

Jody Stafford had given him some money and new orders back there in Neasden. He was happy to accept the money, but he wasn't taking orders any longer. He was his own man now.

Driving up the A5 beyond Dollis Hill, he thought he'd keep heading north while the darkness lasted. Make it to Liverpool. See what the chances were of getting across to Dublin on the ferry.

The cops were expecting an attack in London, he knew. Maybe they weren't so vigilant at the northern ports. And he could always work on making a disguise. Just like McDaid.

He drove on through light, misting rain, dreaming to the rhythm of the windscreen wipers, and didn't really start to feel uneasy until Edgware.

He thought at first it was just the old anxiety, just the old guilt. You grew up with a violent old man and a pious mother and you always felt dirty and nervous whenever you happened to find yourself having fun. Fun was sin. So sin was fun. And the only way you could manage it was to get your kicks from crime, since everything you did was always going to be wrong anyway.

But the old anxiety still clung to him, even now. Sin. Hell. Damnation. And eternal suffering. They all clung to him. Vague feelings of shame.

238

Clung to him like . . .

Like those headlights in his rear-view mirror, he thought suddenly. They'd been bothering his eyes for a mile or so and now they were troubling his mind as well.

Maybe they weren't always the same car. Maybe they were someone travelling in the same direction.

Maybe.

But when you started feeling uneasy, *everything* got infected.

He flicked the indicator switch and pulled over to the foot-path and stopped there, with the engine idling.

The car behind overtook him. He glanced across at the occupants and didn't like what he saw. Two young men, look-ing straight ahead at the road in front of them, with no interest in him at all.

He stayed a while, checking on the rest of the cars that passed. Couples, singles, sometimes two or three men together again. Like the first pair, no one bothered to look across at him.

They all might be cops, he thought. And none of them might be cops.

He felt confused. Uneasy inside, he still had nothing out-side his own nervousness to confirm or deny his fears.

He rejoined the line of traffic, but a little further on pulled in to a McDonald's car-park.

He killed the lights and the engine and sat there in the dark, checking on the cars that followed him in. All of them spewed out families, mostly a single parent with two or three kids.

His nervousness eased a little. But he didn't feel so relaxed inside the van any more. He felt enclosed.

He got out, checked that no one could see him not being able to lock the driver's door, and walked across and through the restaurant's entrance.

He knew immediately that it was a stupid mistake. The neon lights. The bright open spaces. The clatter of plates and things. The plastic everything. The people looking at him. People who might recognise him from the news photographs.

He should be in the dark. By himself. On the road.

But he'd already joined the queue, forced into it by kids pressing inwards from behind.

He let two young boys scurry past him, then broke from the line and turned back to the exit.

The first thing he saw was the two men who'd overtaken him in that first car back on the road. They still weren't looking at him. But everyone else in the place seemed to be staring in his direction.

He lifted his hand to shield his face and found that he was holding a plastic tray. He couldn't remember having picked it up. He dropped it without thinking, as if the surface was hot. As it hit the steel railing and clattered to the floor, he looked around desperately and ran towards the restaurant's side entrance.

A laughing fat woman carrying meals to a table stepped right in front of him. She went down as he hit her, her burgers and her fries and her drinks jumping into the air and raining on him as he stepped over her body while it was bouncing off the floor.

When he saw the two other cops coming in the side entrance he decided he was either going to shoot his way out or die. He'd meant what he'd said to Stafford. No more prison.

He pulled out the .38 revolver. The gasps and clucking he'd heard when he'd barged the fat woman turned to screams now. People scattered in front of him. They stretched out along the narrow seating in the booths and tried to hide under the ludicrous little plastic tables.

All except a blonde, long-haired child who scurried across the floor in front of him after her free mobile McBurglar toy.

He tried to avoid her. Swerving left, he knocked his hip against one of the fixed tables and lost his balance. When he went down, his right arm jarred against the railing around the counter area, jolting the revolver from his hand.

240

The gun skidded away from him, but then hit the base of the counter and came spinning back across the polished floor towards his outstretched hand. Mere inches from his fingers, a brown suede shoe stamped on the gun and stopped its progress.

Instantly, then, someone else's gun was jabbing into the back of his head. A voice was shouting in his ear. And hands were pulling his arms behind him and locking them together with handcuffs.

He saw nothing of his passage back through the restaurant and into the car-park again. His eyes were filled with tears of rage and frustration.

They pushed him into the rear of a big car outside and piled in on either side after him.

A dull, brown-haired character, looking like someone's old-fashioned uncle, turned to him from the front passenger seat, asking, 'Where were you heading, son?'

'Fuck off!' Reilly shouted.

He wanted them to hit him, to punish him for his own stupidity. But they didn't.

The old-fashioned character turned back to listen to messages from the police radio.

Reilly, still shouting, picked up snatches, and then gradually fell silent as the details became clearer. Something about Jody Stafford, he heard. Someone following Stafford across London, heading south-east. And he understood. Stafford was leading the cops to McDaid in Woolwich.

Reilly, gaping vacantly as he struggled to figure it out, whether McDaid would get his tonight as well, suddenly realised that the old cop in front was staring at him, seeing in his expression what was in his mind.

The cop smiled and got out of the car, then bent down to say, 'Take him in and question him. I'll be in to see him later. With some of his friends.'

8

In Woolwich, in the upstairs front bedroom of the house opposite Maisie Connolly's, Inspector Peters and June Maybury
had set up a temporary command post, where they sat immobile now in the darkness, staring across the road.

The owner, the elderly widow of a former army major, had
insisted on extending her hospitality to refreshments. But her
tea was stewed and sour and her soft biscuits had obviously
been opened for Christmas, four weeks before, and neglected
ever since.

'Stafford left the house in Neasden about half an hour after
Reilly,' Peters reported, when Superintendent Gilston, coming across from the north-west after Reilly's capture, finally
caught up with the others. 'He walked a mile or so before hail-
ing a taxi.'

'Why didn't he ring for a taxi from the house?' Gilston
wondered.

'The telephone is out of order. It was vandalised yesterday.
Possibly by Stafford himself. And something else about the
flat, sir.' Peters drew a breath and said, 'There's a dead body
in a wooden chest up there.'

'Bill Enright,' Maybury put in.

'Have you seen it?'

'No, the descriptions fit.'

'Have they moved it?'

'No,' Peters said again. 'They've left everything as it was.
Just in case.'

'Good,' Gilston approved. 'What about the situation here?'

'The house is owned by a Mrs Connolly, apparently a

retiring woman, living alone. Originally from Northern Ireland, it seems. We haven't questioned any of the neighbours yet, apart from our hostess. We don't really know who else is in there with her. Stafford simply knocked and was admitted.'

Gilston was starting another question, an ironic one this time, about reassessing Stafford's role and motives, when Maybury said sharply, 'Wait! Look!'

They turned and watched the street door of Maisie Connolly's house opposite.

It opened slowly. For a moment no one came out and no one was visible in the bright hallway. Whoever had unlocked it and pulled it backwards was now standing behind it, shielded from view.

Peters was reluctant to issue instructions over the two-way radio. Apart from the men distributed around the street and at the rear and in neighbours' houses, he had four officers among the bushes in each of the adjoining gardens. The crackle of static or his own voice might be overheard through the open door.

He raised his eyebrows towards Gilston and realised then that the enquiry couldn't be seen in the dark.

But he was spared a decision. The figure of Jody Stafford suddenly appeared in the hallway and walked briskly through the doorway and down the garden path. By the time he'd reached the little wrought-iron gate at the front of the garden, the door had closed again behind him.

Even from a distance they could see that Stafford was still weak and unsteady on his legs. Under the sleeve of the black leather jacket he wore there was a bright-red stain in the bandage around his left arm.

On the other side of the gate he paused for a second, grimacing with pain, then turned right and walked away.

'Put a team on him,' Gilston instructed.

While Peters conveyed the orders, Gilston fretted about his dilemma.

He could sit where he was, he thought, withdrawing the more conspicuous of his men to better cover when morning came, and wait for those inside Maisie Connolly's house to make their move. It had the virtue of greater safety. Unless alerted, the terrorists were unlikely to come out into an English suburban morning with guns in their hands.

Or he could announce his presence and invite surrender. After a delicate siege, of course. He reckoned that there were now two terrorists left inside and that only one, Sean McDaid himself, was desperate. As Maybury had predicted, Danny Boyce no longer had the stomach for a fight.

Gilston hadn't even approached a decision, was still laying out the preliminary pros and cons in his mind, when the door opposite opened again and, this time, Maisie Connolly herself stepped down to the garden path and stooped to release a brindle cat she was carrying. The animal didn't really fancy any of the damp January night and squirmed desperately to escape back to the warmth indoors.

It was, Gilston decided instantly, too good a chance to pass up.

'Take it! Take it!' he shouted suddenly.

And Peters, unconsciously parroting, repeated not only the words, but the tone and the accent as well. 'Take it! Take it!' Before adding his own, 'In! In! All units in!'

The four officers in the adjoining gardens burst through hedges and bushes, in behind the astonished Maisie Connolly, and rushed through the open door, led by the agile cat. As they disappeared down the hallway, two women detectives reached Mrs Connolly. To calm her. To silence her. To draw her away from the scene. Others, sharpshooters, covered the front windows of the house from the street below.

A minute passed.

Another thirty seconds.

And there was no movement in or behind the curtains of the house.

244

There were no shouts. No gunshots. No struggle.

And no terrorists, Gilston realised gloomily, as he watched his officers coming back from the house to the front garden and showing their empty hands upwards to him.

He swore violently and knocked his fist against the back of a nearby chair.

'What is this?' he demanded of June Maybury. 'More of MI5's early warning system?'

She gestured through the window, across at Maisie Connolly. 'Ask the woman.'

Gilston strode angrily away from her, down the stairs, past the startled widow of the late major. Out of one house and across the street and into the other.

By then, Maisie Connolly, pale and shaken, was huddled by the fire in her own front room. She'd already admitted who her recent guests were.

'But they've gone,' she kept repeating in a pleading whisper. 'They've gone.'

As if that was going to save her from the attention of the police.

'Gone?' Gilston repeated gruffly. 'When? When?'

Maybury, coming behind him, felt sorry for the older woman. She guessed what had happened here, because she'd seen it too many times in Northern Ireland. An innocent woman made to choose by coercion. Not between police and criminals, though. Those weren't the words or the concepts. But between her own people and foreigners.

Maybury said nothing, however. Things were not as complex for Superintendent Gilston, she knew. To him, the Irish were the foreigners.

'When?' Gilston repeated now. 'When did they leave?'

'The young fellow,' Maisie Connolly stuttered. 'With the red face . . .'

'Denis Reilly?'

'Reilly. Aye, that's right. He'd left before I got back from shopping, around four. The other two went off at five.'

'Are you sure of the time?'

'Five,' she said again. 'I know that. I'm sure. I was going to make them dinner, you see. They didn't want it. They won't be coming back, you know.'

Maybury and Gilston shared a look. Five o'clock. At least two hours before either of them had an inkling that McDaid was holed up in Woolwich.

It wasn't a leak from MI5. Not this time.

But still Gilston asked, 'Did they get any phone calls before they left?'

Maisie Connolly shook her head. 'Not today. None I heard today. They'll not be coming back, you know.'

'Yes, we know that.'

'I heard them, you know. They were in here, in this room. I heard them when I was on my way out shopping.'

Gilston softened a little with the prospect of information. 'What did you hear, Mrs Connolly?'

'They didn't know I was out there in the hallway. I heard young Sean . . . I lived beside his family, you know. Back in Belfast.'

'Yes. What did you hear?'

'I heard him say they were moving out tomorrow. That's how he said it. Eighteen hundred hours. Young Sean and the big lad together. That Reilly chap to go with someone else.'

'Would it be Enright?'

'Enright, that's it. Bill Enright. So they won't be coming back here.'

Tomorrow, Gilston's mind echoed. The Queen. The Barbican.

He could see it happening, Her Majesty's death, without knowing how it was done. Like watching a conjurer perform a magic trick.

He could see it happening, the Queen's death, and he was

powerless to stop it. Like being forsaken in a nightmare.

Frustrated, he turned on June Maybury as they left Maisie Connolly's house. 'So much for your confidence. Twelve hours. Is that what you said?'

She didn't rise to his ill temper. She said levelly, 'I wouldn't rule out the possibility of Danny Boyce contacting us again.'

'This is what is wrong with the way you people do business,' Gilston said bitterly. 'Your best bet is always some toe-rag at the bottom of the pile. You *cultivate* them. Danny Boyce will go the same way Woolly Barr went. And Barr, if you can remember, was your last best bet. The same way. With two bullets in his head. Don't you think that if *you* can play on Boyce's weakness, the other side can too. You never seem to learn that. You never seem to realise that they're *better* at it than you.'

Inspector Peters, waiting for them at the garden gate, had fresh, but insignificant news.

'Jody Stafford took another taxi from here and appears now to be heading back to the flat in Neasden.'

'Keep an eye on him,' Gilston ordered wearily. 'Keep a team on him.'

He wasn't going to admit it, not with Maybury standing beside him, but he hadn't the same interest in Jody Stafford any more. The man wasn't a part of McDaid's plans. He was floundering in the dark. Just like the rest of them.

'Let's hear what Reilly has to say for himself,' he suggested. 'And take the woman in. You never know what else she overheard.'

But he'd already guessed the answer to that one.

Nothing! Or nothing McDaid still wanted under wraps, anyway.

9

Less than three hundred metres away, in a cul-de-sac off Burrage Road, Sean McDaid was sitting on a low stool in a child's bedroom, holding a gun on a woman and her daughter.

The two hostages were in the girl's bed, fully clothed under the covers, and locked together in an anxious embrace. The child was dozing feverishly, waking with a whimper every so often. The mother was awake, but kept her eyes closed. Both of them were shivering with fear.

McDaid was indifferent to their terror. The woman was English. The daughter too, of course. They meant nothing to him.

A while back, the child had screamed for a few minutes, suddenly flying off into hysteria, and he'd found it grating on his nerves, tempting him into violence to shut her up. Now he hardly thought about them, unless they asked for something or moved too much or too suddenly.

The mother was the blonde woman who'd avoided him as a tramp the day before and then smiled at him when he was dressed in a suit. The girl, brought to and watched home from the nearby school, was her only child.

And McDaid's guess about the father had been right. He was long gone, off somewhere the other end of the country with some younger woman.

You could always tell, McDaid reckoned. Kids with no father to look after them were always weaker. Always whining. Never sure of themselves.

It irritated him. The whole trend of families breaking up and churning out whinging kids irritated him.

248

Almost everything irritated McDaid now, though. His painful lip and side. The creaking bed. The low stool he was sitting on. The silly posters of pop groups and cartoon characters on the walls.

He was tired. Very tired. He'd slept only fitfully the previous night, guarding the empty briefcase against Reilly's attentions. And he'd managed only half an hour before waking again this afternoon.

Now he was facing the prospect of another full night without sleep.

Danny Boyce was in next door, in the woman's bedroom, waiting on his chance.

For what?

McDaid still didn't know. He only knew that he couldn't trust Danny. Not until tomorrow, anyway. Tomorrow he'd happily rely on him, but not before then.

And through the long night, with nothing to do but watch and think, McDaid was confident that he'd figure out exactly what was eating away at the big fellow.

Because there was a pattern to Danny's moods. Chirpy one day. Gloomy the next. Then sunny again. Just like the weather. Bright and breezy one day. Sullen the next.

It had to be something outside him pulling at the strings, something McDaid himself had experienced as well. They'd shared everything since breaking out of Whitemoor.

A long night ahead, then.

But McDaid didn't mind the physical pain or the mental effort. He prided himself on endurance. He'd often boasted he could take as much and do as much as the toughest special forces soldier in the British Army.

And knowing he could match them, he felt superior to them. They had the unit and the regiment and the Crown to lean on and take strength from. McDaid was denied these things.

As he'd always known would happen, everyone else had

either betrayed or deserted him. They lacked the strength or the will, the courage or the conviction. They lacked the faith.

Woolly Barr, who was always too weak.

Reilly, damned by his own greed for pleasure.

Danny Boyce, corrupted by something yet unknown.

Of the ones McDaid might've trusted, might've built a new organisation with, Dixie and Bill Enright and Jennifer Crooks were clearly either killed or captured by now.

But it didn't matter now that they hadn't lived. What mattered was their deaths, and the manner of their deaths. He himself would go out tomorrow and die too after completing his mission. But he'd leave behind a sacrifice and a symbol as powerful as the General Post Office in Dublin in 1916, where Pearse had proclaimed the Irish Republic against impossible odds.

In the end, he knew, it wasn't rational thought or mutual respect or understanding that drove men's actions; it was the raw emotional appeal of gestures like his own, out of which myths and slogans and war cries were created to nourish the next generation.

McDaid's act of destruction was intended not only to provoke England, but also to remind the Irish of the rich heritage they seemed to be throwing away in this current capitulation to the British Crown.

He felt at peace with himself.

If anything still troubled him, it was what had niggled at his mind for a day and a half now, the memory of an educated English voice warning him over the phone in Dixie's flat that his capture was imminent. Not that he worried about it affecting his plans. But it didn't fit properly into his view of the world. It was like a growth on an otherwise perfect body.

And he would've liked to remove it before dying. So that, when the future generations paused to consider his bequest, his gift to them would be pure, unstained by foreign taints.

PART FIVE

Saturday

ONE

1

It was all a matter of timing, Sean McDaid knew.

It had *always* been a matter of timing. From the break-out at Whitemoor, through the days of keeping out of sight, right up to now, waiting to give the order to move in, when it came down to a question of judging the hours and the minutes.

But there were problems. Things he hadn't expected and hadn't allowed for.

By a quarter to five that Saturday afternoon, when he sat down to watch the television news, he calculated that he'd slept a total of three hours from the previous thirty-six. Part of his anxiety was wondering how much longer he could last without making mistakes.

Most of the day he'd suffered from a throbbing pain, right at the base of his skull. His mind was clouded and unfocused at times. He couldn't really decide any more whether or not it was better to kill the hostages.

The kid had been fretful all day, off her food and whimpering constantly. The mother too was getting strung out, drifting further and further away from controlling the child.

McDaid had snipped the telephone wires the night before. Since then, no one had come near the house. No neighbours. No delivery people. Not even another child.

Saturday afternoon, he thought disdainfully, and the kid had no playmates looking for her.

At least he'd chosen well. Although it hadn't been difficult. Any mother who led her child the long way round a harmless-looking tramp in broad daylight had to be reclusive and over-protective.

Quarter to five, he locked the two of them in the bedroom and went downstairs to turn on the television.

He sat through the news and the sports results and the weather and the regional sports reports, and only then decided that the time had finally come.

He got up and went to the open doorway.

'Danny!' he called. 'Down here!'

Boyce, alone with his troubles in the main bedroom upstairs, took a while to respond to the summons.

McDaid passed the time in the front hallway, staring at himself in the mirror hanging from the wall. He hadn't washed or shaved that morning and his light stubble irritated him. His eyes were black and hollow and his short, curly hair was dull from lack of care.

When he heard Boyce's step on the landing above, he turned and went back to the living-room, sitting in a flowery armchair at the low coffee table to wait.

Boyce came in and slumped in the matching armchair opposite. He had a dark, unhappy look on his face, his lips set tightly together, his eyes averted. As if there was something he'd decided to get off his chest.

McDaid didn't give him the chance to talk. He wasn't interested in Boyce's irrelevant angle on things.

'We're moving tonight, Danny,' he said. 'There's only the two of us now, so you've got to do the work of a couple for me.'

Boyce still looked uncertain, but he finally asked, 'Where are we going, Sean?'

'You know the Barbican?'

254

'I do, yeah.'

McDaid took photographs and diagrams from his water-proof folder and spread them on the coffee table. He pointed with the tip of a pencil.

'This is the front entrance to the Arts Centre. This is the rear. Here's the front again on the diagram.'

'I know the place, Sean.'

'Good,' McDaid said crisply. 'There's a première on there tonight that the Queen's attending. The proceeds are going to the War Widows Fund. A coincidence, isn't it?'

'Right.'

'I want you to approach the place from here, through Holborn and up Aldersgate Street. The security's going to be very tight, but only around the direct approaches to the centre. Get as close as you can, maybe at the corner with Beech Street, and create a diversion for me here at eight-thirty-five exactly, while the show is in progress. Have you got that? Eight-thirty-five.'

'A diversion with what, Sean?' Boyce asked wearily.

McDaid held up his hands in apology. 'I know, Danny, I know. You should've had Reilly and Bill Enright with you. You should've had Kalashnikovs and a couple of stun grenades. But the lads are taken and I didn't manage to get the gear out of Dixie's flat. There's nothing we can do about it. There's only us left, and whatever weapons we have.'

'Kalashnikovs?' Boyce repeated.

'Three of them.'

'So that's what you went to Dixie's for, then?'

'That's it. No use crying about them now, though. Have you got your revolver?'

Boyce indicated with a flick of his head. 'Upstairs.'

'Ammo?'

'Enough, I suppose.'

'I don't want anything spectacular, Danny,' McDaid assured him. 'Just draw their attention at the right moment.

255

Eight-thirty-five.'

Boyce nodded reluctantly. 'How long are we going to take to get there?'

'I'm leaving shortly, after I've cleaned myself up. You go twenty minutes after me.'

Boyce raised his eyes towards the ceiling. 'What about the woman and kid?'

McDaid shrugged as he stood up. 'We can't take a chance on them, Danny. You'll have to kill them before you leave.'

2

Danny Boyce stayed sitting in the armchair in the living-room. He listened to the sounds of Sean McDaid cleaning himself in the bathroom overhead and to the thinner, more penetrating noise of the child crying in the small bedroom beside the bathroom.

The girl cried without pausing, but also without energy and without hope. An unbroken wail. Like the keening of the damned.

Boyce's daughter had once suffered an ear infection as a child and whimpered through a whole night like that. He'd found the noise unbearable then. And it stretched him to breaking point again now. It kept making the same pathetic demand on you, he thought. Kept accusing you of cruelty. Kept reminding you just how helpless you were.

To take his mind off it, he started wondering why McDaid was always solemn and silent in the bathroom.

McDaid never sang while he washed. He never hummed. He never impersonated anyone.

Boyce tried to remember if he knew anyone who washed

256

like that; but he didn't. It struck him as unnatural.

McDaid was fifteen minutes in the bathroom.

When he came back down he was dressed in black jeans and a black leather jacket, items from among the clothes they'd taken with them from Jennifer Crooks's house.

He didn't linger. He just stepped into the living-room to say goodbye.

'Wait twenty minutes,' he ordered. 'Then leave. Eight-thirty-five in Aldersgate Street. Not before. Good luck, Danny.'

Boyce's response was dull. He couldn't even summon the enthusiasm to fake it any more.

'Good luck, Sean.'

He stood up and walked to the window to watch McDaid leave.

Once the black figure had disappeared into the gusting wind and heavy rain, beyond the corner of the cul-de-sac, he turned away and plodded upstairs. He took his revolver and its ammunition from the main bedroom and walked from there along the landing to the child's room.

He pushed the handle to open the door, but found it locked.

He searched for the key, but couldn't find it anywhere outside. Not in the lock itself. Not on the carpet. Not on the small table in the landing.

McDaid had obviously taken it when he'd closed the door a while back and put it somewhere.

Boyce tried the bathroom. He looked in the pockets of the clothes McDaid had changed from. He looked in the wash basket and under the toilets and on the shelves of the cabinet.

Not finding it, he went back downstairs to check where McDaid had been sitting, in and around the floral armchair.

And didn't find it there, either.

By then, five of Boyce's allotted twenty minutes had already passed.

He went back again to stand at the child's bedroom.

Inside, the pair had fallen silent, worrying about the uncertain sounds and waiting in dread of what they thought was to come.

Boyce stepped back a pace on the landing and threw his broad shoulder against the door.

The wood cracked and shattered and then the lock gave. The door flew inwards. The woman and child screamed in terror and pressed back against the wall as the big man hurtled helplessly towards them.

But he stopped himself in front of them and drew quickly back into the doorway again.

He raised his hands and said, 'I'm not going to hurt you.'

The woman was violently hugging her daughter. 'Well, let us go then!' she shouted at him. 'Let us go! For God's sake, let us go!'

He shook his head. 'I can't. Not yet. He might still see you.'

She had no idea what he was talking about, because she didn't know that McDaid had left. She stared at him, at the revolver in his raised hand, her eyes as wide with fear as her daughter's, not understanding him and not trusting him.

'Can I use your phone?' he asked.

The woman laughed then. Out of control. Not from relief, but because the politeness of the request was so insane in the circumstances.

He said, 'You don't have to stay in this room. But don't leave the house yet, please.'

He waited a few moments in the doorway, but she wouldn't move. As if the distance still between them somehow protected her.

Boyce smiled helplessly and turned to go down the stairs again.

In the front hallway, he stooped to reconnect the telephone wires McDaid had cut the previous night.

When the phone was working, though, he found that he

258

couldn't remember the number he'd rung the day before. Twice he tried what he thought were the digits, but only managed a dry cleaner's and someone's answering machine.

Once more he plodded up the stairs, checking on his watch again. He was going to ask the woman if she had a copy of the same newspaper, but it occurred to him that they must've put the advertisement in all the previous day's papers. No one could've known which paper he read or which he'd buy. They wouldn't take a chance like that.

'Did you buy a paper yesterday?' he asked the woman. 'Have you still got it?'

They were a little more relaxed, a little less terrified. They hadn't yet come off the bed, but they were sitting on the edge of it.

She said, 'Downstairs. In the rack under the television.'

'Thanks.'

He smiled again.

But he felt a terrible sadness when he found the advertisement and looked once more at his wife's nickname in print there. He knew now that they might never live together again. He knew that the British would put him away for even longer this time.

Unless they agreed to and honoured the deal he'd try to shake from them.

He wondered who had betrayed him, who had told the British about himself and his wife.

Woolly, he thought then. Woolly Barr.

The same girl with the same line in courtesy answered him again today. 'We've had many concerned calls about Ru, sir. Is there anything special you feel you could contribute?'

'This is Danny Boyce again,' he said dully. 'Put me through to the person I was speaking to yesterday.'

3

'I don't know, do I?' Denis Reilly said again. 'I just don't know.'

And Superintendent Gilston, looking at the transcripts from nearly a day's interrogations, some of which he'd led himself, was finally starting to believe him.

Reilly was bitter and angry and resentful. But the cops he abused were only a conduit for his rage; it was really directed against Sean McDaid. He seemed to be searching for some way of revenging himself on his former leader. So far, he hadn't found it.

As for Maisie Connolly, Gilston's other main witness, she grew more confused with every question, more confusing with every answer. Her constant refrains were pathetic justifications. *I didn't invite them, you know. There was nothing I could do about it. They won't be back, you see.* Otherwise she offered little sense.

Maybury had felt sympathy for the woman. Gilston didn't. Only impatience.

A mood that was dominating his exchanges with Reilly also.

'It doesn't make sense,' he said again now. 'If the bomb is fitted with a timer device, why break out of prison?'

'I don't know.'

'If it's not fitted with a timer, how does he expect to set it off?'

'I told you. All I know is that he said Dixie put it there a year ago.'

'We have records of Dixie McDaid's employments in this country. He never worked anywhere that might be considered a bombing target.'

260

'Not legally, maybe. It doesn't mean he wasn't there. Builders don't always ask for your social security number.'

'What arms did you have?'

'All I saw were some revolvers.'

'Nothing high-powered?'

'No.'

'Tell me what you remember McDaid saying.'

'I already told you that.'

'Where he said it. How he said it.'

'I told you.'

'You're missing things.'

At six-fifteen, somewhere in the middle of this endlessly repeating cycle of questions and answers, Gilston was summoned from the Interview Room to take a visitor.

An unfamiliar black-haired woman, young and a little nervous, was waiting for him in his office.

'Superintendent Gilston?'

'Yes?'

'My name is Karen Grant. I spoke to you last Wednesday, you may remember, when we intercepted a call to a farmhouse in Hertfordshire from Northern Ireland. I was the one who conveyed the information to you.'

'Yes, of course,' Gilston said vaguely. 'Miss Grant. What is it?'

'I was instructed by June Maybury to monitor incoming calls on the line reserved for the advertisement placed in yesterday's newspapers. I have a report to make to Miss Maybury, but I'm unable to find her at the moment.'

'I'm not surprised,' Gilston muttered.

'In the event of being unable to trace her, I was instructed to report immediately to you, sir.'

'And to anyone else?'

'No one else, sir.'

'I see. What is it, then?'

'Danny Boyce called again, sir. This time from a house close to Mrs Connolly's in Woolwich, where he and Sean McDaid held a woman and her child hostage last night and earlier today. According to Boyce, McDaid's plan is to attack the Barbican tonight. Boyce's role is to create a diversion in Aldersgate Street at eight-thirty-five.'

'Where is Boyce now?'

'Waiting at the other end of the line for instructions, sir. His message has been passed on to Director-General Rawlings.'

'I see,' Gilston said again. 'Is that it?'

'Yes, sir.'

Gilston thanked her. When she was gone, he sat behind his desk and tried to take them one at a time, the doubts and questions that were flitting through his mind.

His message has been passed on to Director-General Rawlings, Grant had said.

Was that sufficient, Gilston wondered.

No, he decided. Possibly not. And why take a chance on it?

He picked up the receiver and pushed a button to get through to his own superior in Special Branch.

But Deputy Assistant Commander Michael Lammas, not too pleased with Gilston's performance the last few days, only snapped at him crustily, 'I've already been informed by the Director-General of MI5 of this latest development. In fact I was on my way out the door to a meeting of those concerned when your call brought me back. What did you imagine? That the information would be ignored or dismissed?'

When the line went abruptly and noisily dead, Gilston held the receiver in his hand and thought again.

It still didn't make much sense, he decided. Any of it. How could they have known a year ago, when the bomb was supposedly planted, that the Queen would be attending the Barbican tonight?

But assume that the bomb story was just a red herring, he

thought. Assume that McDaid had a marksman's rifle with telescopic infra-red sights buried somewhere he could dig up handily. Then the attempt on the Queen's life would have to be made while she was either entering or leaving the Barbican Centre.

So why order a diversion for eight-thirty-five, with the play in progress and the Queen already seated?

He became aware of the bleeping telephone receiver and put it back on its cradle.

He checked his address book for June Maybury's home number and rang it. All he got was an answering machine.

He looked at his watch. Six-thirty. Two hours before McDaid's planned diversion at the Barbican.

It occurred to him now that he hadn't been invited. Not in the best odour, of course, after recent failures. *A meeting of those concerned*, as Lammas had just put it. But he'd probably amble down there anyway, see it through to the end.

He tried June Maybury's number again.

This time, listening to her boy-friend's stilted instructions again, he decided to leave a message on the machine.

He was at the tail of it, signing off, when the receiver was suddenly lifted at the other end.

'Tim Aston speaking,' the voice said breathlessly. 'Yes?'

'Mr Aston? I don't know if I have the correct num—'

'You're looking for June. I've only just come in. Wet to the skin. Dreadful night. I haven't seen her since morning.'

'Do you know where she is?'

'Yes, she left a note. Could I ring you back, please. Just security, you know. New Scotland Yard, isn't it?'

When Aston finally got through again, several minutes later, he said, 'According to the note, written two hours ago, you'll find June in the Cat and Cage. I should think it's right. It's where she usually retires to brood, you know. I'm not allowed to intrude myself.'

4

Three grey-haired men in dark suits sat in silence around a circular table, waiting for news.

Time was running out for them, but not so quickly that it could force them to shake off their usual reticence and rivalry.

A clock ticked loudly in a corner of the room, setting their nerves on edge. It was almost seven o'clock.

On the hour, as if by arrangement, a door opened and admitted the gloomy Home Secretary, dressed in formal evening wear for the première at the Barbican. He remained standing to address the trio.

'I'm afraid Her Majesty quite refuses to cancel her engagement this evening, gentlemen.'

George Rawlings tapped the base of his cane on the floor and grunted his approval. 'Quite right, too.'

The Home Secretary looked dubious.

'What we have is a threat,' Rawlings pointed out. 'Nothing more. If we are to respond to every threat by diving immediately into the bunker, then we may as well abandon the defence of the realm and arrange our forces around the bunker itself. The question of a cancellation would not have been countenanced by the previous administration.'

'Different times,' Tremmell, the Commander of Scotland Yard's Anti-Terrorist Squad muttered. 'Different PM.'

'Quite!' Rawlings agreed brusquely.

Deputy Assistant Commander Lammas, the Head of Special Branch, tried to keep the steering straight. Difficult, he knew, with three pairs of hands on the tiller.

'One can't imagine an explosive device inside the Barbican,'

264

he suggested.

'Don't look at me, Michael,' Tremmell said petulantly. 'Scotland Yard hasn't been kept quite up to date on this one.'

'Not the occasion for a turf battle, Bernard,' Rawlings reproved him. He glanced significantly at his watch. 'And I doubt if we have the time quite to resolve it.'

'No, it's not the place for quibbling,' the Home Secretary agreed. He paused. He bit his lip, quite obviously out of his depth. 'But MI5', he added, recalling his advisers' prompting, '*has* been given rather a free hand on this one, George. You have the responsibility. You insisted on taking the lead in mainland operations against the IRA. It's a valid question as to where it has all led.'

'Or where it will lead us tonight,' Tremmell put in.

'What is important', Lammas tried again, 'is the safety of Her Majesty and Her Majesty's subjects. Could we return to that, please?'

'Of course the Barbican is currently being swept again for suspect devices,' Rawlings assured.

'Well, let's do it properly this time,' the Home Secretary snapped, gaining in confidence. 'One still remembers the horror of Brighton in 1984, when the entire Government was endangered. As I recall, the IRA planted their bomb on an upper floor of the hotel, *knowing* that the security would be slacker as it got higher.'

'1984?' Rawlings repeated. 'I was in East Germany in 1984.'

'Oh, for God's sake!' Lammas groaned.

'The Barbican *is* rather a nightmare,' Tremmell advanced. 'The sheer size and complexity of the place. Notoriously like a maze inside.'

Rawlings looked again at his watch. 'And McDaid hasn't left us a generous amount of time, has he?'

Tremmell flicked with his fingertips at a photocopy lying on the table in front of him. 'What of these drawings?' he asked. 'Taken from Jennifer Crooks's house and car, weren't they? Any particular assistance yet?'

'The consensus is that they probably represent a section of the Barbican,' Rawlings told him. 'But the scale is too large to locate it precisely. Perhaps a small area of the auditorium. We still don't know.'

'What about Boyce?' Lammas asked.

'I suspect we'll rather have to allow him a free hand,' Rawlings proposed.

'Is that wise? Can you trust him?'

'He's currently under heavy surveillance and on his way in towards Aldersgate Street. There's no question of taking any risks with him. Of course, if we want to flush out McDaid, we'll have to allow Boyce to follow instructions, even to the extent of shooting at eight-thirty-five.'

'Are you mad?' Tremmell enquired.

'There's no question of any danger. He has already been disarmed and will be firing blanks.'

'I wasn't thinking of the danger in Aldersgate Street,' Tremmell said. 'I was thinking of the threat to the Royal Box. Boyce's shots will signal McDaid's attack. It is not good policing, George, to invite the commission of a crime in order to apprehend the criminal. Better to ensure safety, even at the expense of not catching McDaid.'

Rawlings smiled thinly. 'Can't agree with you there, I'm afraid, Bernard. As I say, if you wish to flush out McDaid you must give him the illusion of opportunity. Leave him go now and he will create a real opportunity in the near future.'

'You're using Her Majesty as bait, man!' Tremmell said indignantly.

Rawlings clucked with disapproval at the intemperance of the language.

The Home Secretary bit his lip, undecided again.

'After all,' Rawlings pointed out, 'as we know precisely the time of Boyce's diversion, we couldn't be better prepared for it. Hardly a question of facing a surprise attack.'

The Home Secretary bit his lip a little more. And then he nodded. Very slowly. Very reluctantly.

Rawlings allowed himself a miniature flourish of his cane. As if in triumph.

5

The Cat and Cage was a dimly lit, fashionable pub on the south bank of the Thames in Bermondsey, a short walk from June Maybury's apartment.

At seven that evening it was quiet. The afternoon drinkers seemed to have broken for a meal. The evening crowd hadn't gathered yet. No doubt waiting and hoping forlornly for the storm outside to abate.

June Maybury sat by herself in a spacious booth in the quietest corner. She had a newspaper and a book and a glass of vodka and white lemonade in front of her. But she wasn't either reading or drinking.

She looked up as Superintendent Gilston came in and stood inside the doorway with his back to her, shaking the rain-water from his umbrella back into the night outside, and then turning again and trying to adapt to the light. She watched him finally locate her and walk across and sit down opposite, leaving the umbrella at his feet. But her eyes didn't register either surprise or greeting.

She wondered, though, even before he spoke, if she should tell him now about her affair with Stafford in Northern Ireland. She should tell someone, she'd already decided. Otherwise she'd never rid herself of it. And Gilston was the only one whose judgement she trusted.

She realised now that she was tired of being a section head in MI5. There was too much dull administrative work.

She wanted a transfer to MI6 and a posting to some trouble spot. Iran, maybe. Iraq. Somewhere with excitement and complications, like Northern Ireland used to be. Somewhere she could pick up the pace of her life again.

It might never come. If she confessed to being a traitor – and that's what it really was, wasn't it – it definitely wouldn't.

Forced to look back over her life by the events of the last few days, she saw now that she got into complications for the fun of it and got out again simply by leaving them behind. She wasn't the untangling, resolving kind. She *liked* the knots and the problems, until they became too dangerous.

So the urge to confide in the gruff Superintendent quickly passed. And as quickly turned into a defensive curtness.

She only said, 'Can I get you a drink?'

Gilston shook his head. 'No. I only came in to let you know you were right, you know. Your, ah, boy-friend told me where you were.'

'What was I right about, Superintendent?'

Gilston acknowledged her coldness with a slight nod. 'Danny Boyce rang again,' he said. 'But I was right also. McDaid's target is the Barbican tonight.'

'Why aren't you there, then?'

'Instead of here, you mean? Bothering you.'

She took up her drink and sipped the vodka. 'More or less.'

Gilston shrugged and got up.

He'd half intended mentioning that he knew she'd taken Stafford as a lover in Northern Ireland.

He supposed he liked her for some reason. He must do. Because he couldn't remember when he'd last disapproved so strongly of someone's actions without lecturing them.

But the way to sensitive conversation was too difficult now,

268

too complex and too well defended. The small affection he felt, denied any room to grow, didn't make it worth the effort.

He said, 'I'm not an official part of the investigation any more.'

'And you think that makes us similar, do you, the fact that we're both out in the cold?'

'No,' Gilston said sadly, a little hurt. 'I don't think it makes us similar at all, Miss Maybury. Good evening.'

'See you.'

When he was gone, diving into the heavy rain outside with his umbrella left behind at her feet, she finished her drink and called for another.

And only then, as the irritation died and the private emotion sank back into her, only then remembered that there was a model of the Barbican Centre in Dixie McDaid's flat.

Too late to summon Gilston back to her.

Unless he returned for his umbrella.

But of course he already knew about that, she told herself. They'd have itemised and checked everything in Dixie's place.

And the models were only shells, without interior detail.

But still . . .

Hadn't the Special Branch detective, John Fowler, been killed by McDaid beside that particular model of the Barbican?

One of the barmen approached her table, carrying her drinks on a tray.

She stood up before he could serve.

She said, 'I've changed my mind, John.'

Her car was back at the apartment. A five-minute walk, she knew. About six or seven miles up to Kilburn, she calculated. If she was lucky, if the traffic was light . . .

She stooped to pick up Gilston's umbrella, not having brought one of her own. It hadn't been raining when she'd left the apartment.

6

From a coin box on North Circular Road in Neasden, Jody Stafford looked through the rain at the window of a nearby electrical shop. Inside the shop there was an array of television sets still switched on. All of them were tuned to ITV's *International Gladiators*. The programme was scheduled to finish at seven-fifteen.

In ten minutes' time, as Stafford confirmed, trapping the telephone receiver between his shoulder and the side of his head and raising his right hand to check the watch that had once belonged to Bill Enright.

His left hand, still bandaged, was almost powerless now. He carried it as if in a sling, tucked tight against his stomach.

Ten minutes.

And if his call didn't get through before then, he guessed it would already be too late.

The line was to Northern Ireland, his last chance to play a role in Sean McDaid's desperate, and still unclear enterprise.

All day Stafford had ransacked Bill Enright's flat, searching for leads. Just as he'd gone through Maisie Connolly's house the night before after getting there within an hour of leaving Neasden, only to find the too-elusive McDaid out of his reach again.

All he'd picked up from Maisie Connolly was the certainty that McDaid and Boyce intended moving out at six o'clock and striking somewhere this evening.

Enright's flat had yielded nothing up to twenty minutes before. And then only an old photograph that had triggered a memory that suggested the possibility of a break.

270

Enright shouldn't have brought the photograph with him at all, of course. He was now living as someone else. But everyone has sentimental attachments.

It showed him as a youth in a hurling team. Bottom row, second from the left. Two places on was the only other character Stafford recognised, a man who later became Brigade Commander of the Belfast IRA and who afterwards took control of the mainland bombing campaign.

Nally. Dermot Nally.

According to Denis Reilly, Dixie McDaid had planted explosives somewhere more than a year ago. The semtex could only have come from his brother, who could only have got it by going through Dermot Nally with an operational plan.

Maybe not the scheme McDaid actually intended embarking on before his capture, the scheme he'd resurrected now.

But still . . .

'Jody?' Nally asked uncertainly from the other end of the line. 'Is that you? Give us the word.'

Stafford supplied the password and got through some more tests of his local knowledge and finally, impatiently, put his question.

He could *hear* Nally scratching his head in the silence on the other side.

'I don't know, Jody,' Nally said then. 'I mean, McDaid's unit was just sent over on a bombing campaign a year ago. Once he got there, the targets would be his own choice. He wouldn't be telling me.'

'Shit!' Stafford swore.

'I'll tell you who might have a better idea, though.'

'Who?'

'Brennan.'

'Brennan?' Stafford repeated. '*Tommy* Brennan?'

'Brennan was supposed to go over with McDaid for the first job, but he didn't make it. Just as well for him. You know the two lads who travelled with McDaid got killed, one of them in prison? Well, somebody had a go at Brennan over here after McDaid was picked up. One of McDaid's other cronies. Got shot himself a few days after and couldn't come back for a second bite.'

'This wouldn't be in Belfast.'

'No, Derry. Brennan went to live in Derry for a while last year. If you want him now, though, you won't be the only one looking for him. The RUC are scouring the place for him. They say he raided a bank last week, trying to get money to get out of the country. Maybe he knew McDaid was going to break out.'

'Maybe,' Stafford agreed. Knowing it was true.

'They couldn't be looking for him that badly for just a bank raid, though, could they? I mean, the place has been saturated, you know. Just like the old days. Looks like provocation to me, to test the ceasefire.'

Brennan, Stafford thought after he'd finished the call.

Tommy Brennan.

The little bastard had been holding out on him all this time, feeding him a little when he knew he had to, like the address of Jennifer Crooks's house. What was he playing for? McDaid's death? Stafford's death? Both of them? Leaving him free to live easily on the proceeds of a bank robbery.

What luck, Stafford thought, that he hadn't kneecapped the bastard back there in Belfast last Tuesday night. What luck that he was still in IRA custody.

He checked his pockets and reckoned that he hadn't enough change to stay on hold while waiting for Brennan to break under torture. He'd give them the number from the booth and get them to ring back.

Hopefully no one else would need the phone and he'd be able to stay in out of the storm.

7

This time there was crime scene tape across the front doors of Mary Cassidy's and Dixie McDaid's flats and two officers on guard in the corridor.

A bit late, June Maybury thought.

She wasn't interested in Mary Cassidy, who was still being questioned about the small-arms dump found under her floorboards.

She got the key to Dixie's flat, unlocked the door and ducked under the tape. She went to the bedroom, leaving wet footprints behind her on the carpet, and switched on the light. And then she stood in front of the model of the Barbican Centre, dripping water on to the floor.

It was, she thought again, an odd choice for an attack.

The Queen was there tonight, of course. But the Queen was in a hundred different places in a week, and most of them were more promising than the Barbican for an assassin.

That model had to say something, she decided. Shell as it was, showing only the main structural features and without interior detail, it had to say something.

Otherwise it wouldn't be there. The McDaids wouldn't risk drawing attention to their target with a *useless* model.

Sean McDaid might or might not have come for the guns under Mary Cassidy's floorboards. But he'd also come to look at this model of the Barbican.

With Dixie in custody before he could get to him, the model had to talk for Dixie. And it had to say something vital enough to risk being captured for.

Tell Sean the hobby still keeps me interested.

She remembered that.

The only *instruction* Dixie had given to Woolly Barr on his visit to prison. Everything else just conversation, just stuff Woolly would pass on as a matter of course.

She lifted the structure to check underneath and found only the same base plate as the other models. No markings. No additions. Nothing concealed.

She checked for recent damage to the material that might indicate an opening where a message had been hidden. There weren't any.

She ran her fingers over the surface, looking for inconsistencies. But found none of those either.

Frustrated, feeling in the *presence* of something significant, but not able to understand it, she started comparing the Barbican with the other models, searching for differences in design, in execution.

8

They watched the Royal Family's arrival on a monitor in the control room at the Barbican Centre, George Rawlings irritating his colleagues in Special Branch and Scotland Yard by pointing his cane and offering a commentary on the images, as if he were a television presenter.

In a late change, the Queen had agreed to use a side entrance, where only security personnel expected her.

Another of the screens showed the Centre's front lobby, with its red carpet and its formal reception group and the loyal crowds still waiting outside in the driving rain for a glimpse of Charles, or Andrew, or Anne.

In a few minutes, when the Royal Family was safely in the

royal box, the welcoming group would be told that their vigil was only a decoy, thanked for their contribution and asked to take their seats for the performance. And assured, of course, that they would meet Her Majesty afterwards, back stage with the cast and crew.

Rawlings and the others followed the Royal Family's progress from one monitor to another as they were guided through the Centre's draughty walkways towards the theatre.

Most of the time, it wasn't really clear where exactly each of them was. The Duke. The Prince of Wales. Princess Anne. The protection around them was so dense that they were often lost to the cameras.

Once she entered the royal box, though, the Queen stood briefly to acknowledge the applause of the audience and to take the royal salute.

In the control room, it was thought that she made too visible a target while standing.

But for what?

It was clear to everyone now that there were no explosives inside the Barbican.

And no weapon could possibly have got through the detectors.

'But of course they said that about Whitemoor, didn't they?' Tremmell remarked. 'Before the escape.'

A greater fear was that a gun had been so densely packed and so deeply buried somewhere in the Centre that it had been missed by the sweep.

For the most part, the detectors were at the outer defences. What if the weapon was already inside that ring?

'Seven-fifty-two,' Rawlings noted as the Queen sat.

The reception group hurried from the lobby. Watching them, the crowd in the rain-swept streets outside grew restless, asking the uniformed constables for explanations.

A minute later the house lights went down.

In the darkness, the cameras inside the auditorium switched modes, offering the same views, but with a little less clarity and much less colour.

News came through that Danny Boyce had entered Holborn, on the approach to Aldersgate Street.

As the curtain came up on the opening act of the play, those in the control room searched for Boyce's image on the monitor fed by the hand-held camera outside.

The IRA man wasn't yet in shot, though.

Snatches of the exchange between officers co-ordinating street security and the detective holding the camera were overheard.

But no, the detective hadn't located Boyce yet.

Rawlings again travelled along the row of monitors that were offering wide angles on the walkways and the approaches to the theatre.

He settled for a moment on the screen filled by the royal box.

Then he shifted to the images from the stage itself. Without being able to hear the dialogue, it was difficult to catch the drift of the piece. A man with a football supporter's scarf around his neck seemed to be searching the ground, either for something he had lost or something he hoped to find.

It was odd, Rawlings thought. He had forgotten to ask the title and the author of the play.

'There's Boyce now,' Lammas observed quietly.

The IRA man wore a tweed overcoat, its raised collar offering him little protection against the driving rain. He seemed cold and miserable, like most who were on the streets tonight.

At the corner of Aldersgate Street and London Wall, he paused for a few moments, resting by the Museum of London. He looked nervously, jerkily, at his wrist-watch.

'Eight-ten,' Rawlings announced for the others.

Boyce put his hands back in the pockets of his overcoat and

went up Aldersgate Street, stooped against the wind, to the corner of Beech Street.

He stopped there, a little uncertain, and seemed for a moment to consider retracing his route.

If he did, he was going to attract attention by the repetition, going to draw down on himself some ill-informed constable who might cart him off before the vital time.

But he steadied himself. On Beech Street, he mingled easily with the waiting crowd, without ever trying to hide. An umbrella, carried by an old woman wearing her late husband's military decorations, was offered to him as shelter.

The minutes ticked away.

The drama on stage became more and more inexplicable, a mime that no one could interpret.

Until Rawlings coughed and said, 'Eight-thirty. Does anyone know when the first act ends, incidentally?'

The silence hung.

And then Tremmell, not answering the question, but merely reading his own wrist-watch, added, 'Eight-thirty-one.'

9

June Maybury still stood in the bedroom of Dixie McDaid's flat. Still baffled. Still convinced that there was something here for her.

The comparison hadn't yielded anything, of course. There were no marked differences between the Barbican and the other models.

Two of a kind, she thought then.

Because her mind was running on similarities and differences.

Two of a kind.

277

The phrase had rattled Dixie McDaid when she'd used it casually during interrogation.

It meant a lot to him. He feared the discovery of its private meaning. Just as he'd feared the discovery of Harlesden under earlier interrogation.

She knew him. She knew his moods and his reactions. And just as Harlesden had almost brought her Sean McDaid, so *two of a kind* might also . . .

Also fail to bring her Sean McDaid, she realised.

Always a step ahead of her, McDaid had been. Always controlling her informants like distant mouthpieces, when she imagined that *she* was in control. Always feeding her the wrong information.

Woolly Barr. His brother Dixie. Denis Reilly. And now Danny Boyce.

She didn't doubt that Boyce was telling the truth. He'd told the truth about Reilly going to the flat in Neasden to visit Bill Enright.

But McDaid had *wanted* him to spill that. Because McDaid had wanted Reilly out of his hair.

What Boyce didn't know while he was telling his truth was that he and McDaid weren't going to be in Maisie Connolly's house when the cops came looking for them.

And if McDaid had set up Danny Boyce the previous night as the false prophet, as the misinformed supergrass . . .

The realisation had an unpleasant physical effect on her, like a cold sweat.

She thought: *Danny Boyce has no idea precisely what Sean McDaid's intentions are tonight.*

10

Eight-thirty-three.

Danny Boyce again checked the digital display on his wrist-watch. But this time he kept staring at the face afterwards, counting off the seconds, and wiping away the raindrops.

The revolver was in the right-hand pocket of his overcoat. Every time he finished drying the face of the watch, his hand went back to the pocket to feel the gun.

They'd given him blanks to fire. But he tried to forget that the gun was useless. He had to act as if he were still firing live rounds. Otherwise it would *look* like the game it really was.

He wondered where McDaid was waiting and what his plans were. He wondered if McDaid could see him at that moment. He had to assume that he could.

What would he have done, Boyce asked himself, if he had live rounds and orders for a real diversion.

But what kind of diversion? A quick flurry to distract attention? Or a running battle to keep attention away from somewhere else for a long period. McDaid hadn't specified.

Eight-thirty-four.

Boyce finally selected his victim.

The old woman with the umbrella had gone regretfully home, too cold and too wet to endure standing there in the open much longer.

And elsewhere, too, the crowd had thinned between himself and the Barbican.

But many had stayed. Some under shelter. Most of them not.

One of them was a young woman carrying a miniature Union Jack. She seemed to be with two or three women friends

279

of her own age. She was already a little drunk, her guard a little lowered.

An easy target, he decided. She wouldn't struggle much when he grabbed her.

He could fire a couple of blanks, he thought, and then hold her for say, five or ten minutes. Much better than letting off a quick round or two before being overpowered.

It worried him slightly that the idea seemed to be influenced by the knowledge that he was already under arrest. Free, and looking to the possibility of escape afterwards, he would hardly have lumbered himself with a hostage.

He wondered then if the authorities would react badly to him involving an innocent bystander. Another crime to chalk up against him.

He wondered if the woman herself might afterwards bring charges. He worried that she might be injured.

Eight-thirty-five.

Confused by his doubts, Boyce was paralysed for a moment or two after the alarm sounded in his wrist-watch.

He noticed a number of men nearby, looking at him oddly, and wondered if they were cops, impatient with his delay.

The young woman he'd picked as a hostage, standing only a couple of metres away from him, turned to the sound of his bleeping alarm. He shut it off nervously. She smiled at him, an easy, familiar smile on a wet, cheerful face, before turning back to her friends to laugh at some joke they shared.

The rain dripped from his hair to the nape of his neck and ran under the collars of his overcoat and shirt in little streams between his shoulder-blades. His toes felt bitten by the damp cold. His eyes blurred from the moisture on his lashes.

Sodden and miserable, he suffered again the thoughts that had made him useless as an IRA volunteer for a long time back. Somewhere the young woman had parents. A few years younger, and she could have been his own daughter.

He moved away to get her out of his sight.

Abandoning the idea of a hostage, he simply took the revolver from his pocket. To his right, one of the men he'd noticed earlier immediately drew his own hand-gun and adopted a firing stance.

'Armed police!' he called. 'Throw your weapon to the ground! Armed police!'

Like a tide receding over pebbles on a beach, the screaming crowd scampered away from Boyce and left six or seven armed policemen in isolation around him.

But Boyce's instructions were to make some noise. So he aimed the revolver into the night sky and fired twice.

Understanding what he thought everyone else understood. That he was firing blanks. That he had the approval of the security forces. That he was in no danger himself.

He saw it all as a show, as contrived as the performance *inside* the Barbican.

And for a second he was pleased with the response. A lot of noise. A lot of wild movement. The neat rows of domed umbrellas suddenly breaking apart as their owners struggled to escape. Some of the umbrellas being whipped by the winds and shooting free like parachutes into the air. Others getting their sharp spokes entangled in clothes and flesh. The nearer crowds retreating in fear, the further ones being sucked inwards by curiosity. Collision. Confusion. Panic. For a second Danny Boyce was the centre of London.

But as he was lowering his arm, intending to throw the gun to the ground, he realised that he had made a stupid mistake. He saw it in the fierce face of the young detective standing opposite him. Saw that he'd wrongly trusted the British. That he'd abandoned the very first lesson he'd learned as an IRA volunteer.

The cop's hard, wind-lashed face showed nothing but the resolve to disable a terrorist before being shot at himself.

Obviously, no one had told him of Danny Boyce's private deal with MI5. No one had told *any* of the cops in the street.

Before the bullet actually hit him, Boyce already knew that he was dead.

His last thought was of his family, illegally imprisoned, as he imagined, by the British in a Dublin house.

A second later and he might have realised that this too was just a fabrication, that this too was only another stupid mistake of his, and that his wife and daughter must really be in France by now, waiting forlornly for him.

But he was spared the extra twist.

Two bullets hit him simultaneously from different angles, one in the right thigh and one in the heart.

And he died instantly.

11

Eight-thirty-five.

Sean McDaid finished the last of his whisky and left the pub, nodding to the barman on the way.

Outside he pulled up the collar of his black jacket against the wind and the driving rain and kept his head down as he walked.

He hadn't intended sitting out the early evening in a bar, risking recognition. But the weather was foul. And he hadn't found any other shelter that wouldn't have made him even more suspicious a figure.

No one had challenged him, though. No one had recognised him.

His photograph had been in the newspapers and on television the past few days. But he knew that people didn't identify the wanted from photographs and artists' impressions, unless they already knew them. What makes the ordinary punter doubtful is odd behaviour. Furtiveness. Fear. Haste. A man sitting alone in a pub is less remarkable than a man hanging around corners to no good purpose on a filthy night.

After leaving the cul-de-sac earlier in the evening, though, he'd stayed in a bus shelter near the top of Burrage Road, watching for Boyce's departure.

Not that he doubted Boyce. Rereading the previous day's newspaper and ringing the dubious advertisers that invited the generous to help Ru, he'd figured out the pressures they were putting on Boyce and what Boyce was up to.

A bonus really, he decided. They'd convinced themselves that they had a reliable man inside. Through Danny he could have fed them dog food and they'd have found a sauce to eat it with.

He'd stayed on Burrage Road because he didn't really have far to go from there and didn't want to spend too much time over too few drinks in an empty bar.

Leaving the pub on Woolwich Road now, he turned immediately right down Warspite Road and kept walking until he heard the Thames, sounding rough and wild tonight, crashing away at the river bank in front of him.

12

June Maybury paced between the two rooms of Dixie McDaid's flat.

The logic of her conclusions making her anxious and restless.

Not only did Danny Boyce have no idea of Sean McDaid's intentions, she told herself. In itself his ignorance wouldn't be

283

a threat. The problem was, *half* of what he thought he knew was inaccurate. *Half* of everything he passed on was misleading.

Sean McDaid was going to strike tonight. Yes. But not at the Barbican Centre.

Sean McDaid hoped to disrupt both the peace process in Northern Ireland and the internal stability of the United Kingdom. Yes. But not with an attack on the Queen and the Royal Family.

Then how? And where? And who?

Finding herself in the outer room, she hurried back to the bedroom again.

The model of the Barbican was now irrelevant, she decided. McDaid hadn't come here to look at that.

Then what had he come for?

She glanced over the rest of the models.

Eliminate the obvious ones, she thought. Those in Northern Ireland. Queen's University. The Guildhall. Those in Dublin. Arbour Hill.

It left . . .

It struck her as a rapid sequence of words and phrases crowding her mind.

Two of a kind, she thought. Animals. Noah. The ark. The Flood. It must have been their code name. Sean and Dixie. Two of a kind. And Maisie Connolly's house in Woolwich. And the timing of the break from Whitemoor.

She clicked her fingers to snap her mind out of the recurring sequence.

She went quickly back outside to the telephone on the table near the front door.

An operator finally got her through to the Controller of the Thames Barrier in Woolwich.

It took a while to introduce herself, a while for the Controller to accept and understand the introduction.

She asked then, 'What significance would damaging the

Barrier have tonight? Particularly tonight.'

'That's rather odd,' the Controller observed. 'I was just asking myself the same question. Hypothetical, of course. You see, we're about to close it. In three hours.'

'Close it? You mean for repairs?

'No, not at all. *Raise it* would perhaps be more a layman's term. In any case, to seal off the upper Thames.'

'Why?'

'Because there is a warning of a dangerously high tidal surge.'

'How do you know?'

'Because the East Coast Storm Tide Warning Service at Bracknell has informed us. And our own computer analysis –'

'How do *they* know? The East Coast whatever.'

Like all experts, he imagined that the particular area of his expertise should be common knowledge. He sighed impatiently. He said, 'Because surge tides occur under certain meteorological conditions, which now prevail. Storm force northerly winds are driving a surge southwards from the North Sea and this enormous mass of water will reach the Thames Estuary within the next twelve hours.'

'So what happens if you don't close the Barrier?' she asked.

'Worst or best scenario?' he enquired.

'Worst.'

'Well then,' he said. He took a breath and cleared his throat. 'Catastrophic flooding in the tidal parts of London. Thousands of deaths in the affected areas. Paralysis of the city's centre, including Parliament and Whitehall. London Underground no longer operating. No electrical power. No gas. No telephone communications. No fresh water. No sewage system. Perhaps an entire year to have London functioning again as it is tonight.'

'*Could* the Barrier be damaged?'

'Unlikely to any serious extent. The gates are steel. Enormous structures. Each weighs almost four thousand tonnes.'

285

'With a bomb?'

'Superficially, perhaps,' he conceded. 'I don't see how a bomb could be planted on the river bed, though.'

'Who operates the gates?'

'We do, from the control tower on the southern shore.'

She saw immediately that this was where the weakness was. The control room. The mechanisms operating the Barrier.

If McDaid was going to attack, he'd strike there, paralysing the Barrier for the vital period.

'How long does it take you to close the Barrier?' she asked.

'Thirty minutes.'

'Will you do something?' she pleaded. 'Don't wait two or three hours. Close it now.'

'I'm afraid I can't do that.'

'I'll take full responsibility.'

'It doesn't matter what responsibility you take, Miss Maybury, I can't do it. Shipping on the river must come safely through. Warnings must be issued. Notice boards upstream and downstream must be illuminated. Information –'

'Yes, yes,' she interrupted. 'Look. Do this, then. Double-check your security there. Secure the control room itself. Check the area outside and the perimeter.'

'For what?' he enquired.

'For intruders. Just do that for me. You'll have police with you as soon as I can get them there. Do it now!'

She disconnected and immediately rang MI5 Headquarters.

'Is Karen Grant there?'

'No, ma'am.'

'Shit! Ahm . . . David Bromley?'

'I'll put you through to Mr Bromley, ma'am.'

Bromley sounded edgy when he came on. Why? Waiting for news from the Barbican.

'Yes?' he enquired brusquely. And then, 'Oh! Good evening, ma'am.'

286

'Listen carefully, please,' she said. 'I know that everyone is at the Barbican. But Sean McDaid is not going to attack the Barbican. He's going to attempt to disable the Thames Barrier. Do you understand?'

'The Thames Barrier? Yes, but why –'

'Don't ask,' she ordered. 'There's no time. Just do this. Get a rapid-response team out there now. Now! Do you understand?'

He seemed cowed by her sharpness, her authority. 'Yes, ma'am.'

'See what the local police station can offer in the meantime. And contact Superintendent Gilston at the Barbican and let him know.'

'Yes, ma'am. Are you –'

'I'll see him there. In Woolwich. At the Barrier.'

She hung up again and looked at her watch.

Eight-thirty-five.

Probably already too late, she thought darkly.

Cursing an oversight, she had to run back to the bedroom to check again on the model of the Thames Barrier.

But a few moments later she was through the front door of Dixie McDaid's flat and into the hallway, demanding of the startled detectives outside, 'Do you have a siren?'

13

Sean McDaid, too wet now to worry about the rain and spray that the savage wind kept dashing into his face, cut across Harrington Way from Warspite Road and stopped on Unity Way to consider his target.

The Thames Barrier.

Stretching away from him for over five hundred metres

across the swelling Thames.

The six enormous rising gates, each, he knew, over twenty metres high and weighing almost four thousand tonnes, were still out of sight in their recesses on the river bed. Only the piers that supported them were in any way visible, like great hulking hunchbacks in the darkness, their bodies slashed by red navigation lights. Massive concrete structures that disappeared downwards into the raging river and reared up as steel domes and bright-yellow cranes and rocking beams.

It looked impregnable.

Tonight, though, McDaid only scoffed at its pretensions.

He moved a little, into the arc of a street light, to study his diagrams.

Directly in front of him, at the end of Unity Way, was the Thames Barrier Visitors Centre. Closed, of course, for the weekend now.

Beyond it, back towards Warspite Road, was the Control Building, and beyond that again the Generator and Workshop. All functional, unappealing structures, like cheap factories in a modern industrial estate.

McDaid had picked his route, had folded the sodden diagram and put it away again, when he heard the sounds. Shouted commands and guard dogs yelping with excitement.

He drew back quickly to the shadows and watched.

Inside the Barrier compound, security guards scurried about on lightning patrols, checking walls and entrances, fencing and doors, and all with a speed and thoroughness that had to be more than just routine. A man holding a hard red hat to his head against the efforts of the howling wind, his white overalls at first spotted and then covered with rain, came to issue instructions to a guard, his free arm waving frantically into the darkness of the night.

A man from the Control Room, McDaid guessed. Maybe even the man in charge.

McDaid wondered. And worried.

And yet, the fact that there were no cops in sight and no sirens to be heard calmed him also.

But still . . .

He thought again of the phone call he'd taken while in Dixie's flat. Something he'd lived with for two days now without understanding. It made him uneasy once more.

What, he asked himself now, if someone in British Intelligence had been double-guessing him all the way, *wanting* him to arrive here at the Barrier.

But why? How could anyone on *their* side be served by leaving him free?

He didn't like to think about it. For two days he'd ignored it, and nothing had happened. It was too late now. Thought would only delay him.

His world was one of brutal opposites. Oppressor and oppressed. Occupier and occupied. Tyrant and freedom fighter. Complexities had no validity for him.

Restless, he trudged back along Harrington Way and went to the river end of Warspite Road, where he waited anxiously for a full hour, hidden from view, counting off the minutes, but still not reflecting on much, until the security was finally scaled down inside the Barrier compound.

They seemed suddenly to decide that the threat was only imaginary after all.

Maybe it had just been a general alert at every installation, McDaid thought. Because of what was happening at the Barbican.

He waited another ten minutes. No more jumpy guards. No more barking dogs. No more torches or searchlights.

So he stepped out, into the light again, and walked briskly down towards the buffeted river bank, but away from the compound.

Eighteen months before, while working with a company

responsible for the maintenance of the steel gates and operating machinery at the Barrier, Dixie had hidden forty pounds of commercial explosives behind a dummy panel in the Barrier Control Room. Not a big package. Only about a foot square. But enough to disable the sophisticated equipment that controlled the Barrier and enough to sever the power supply to the gates themselves.

The bomb had been wrapped in a great deal of cellophane to hide its distinctive smell. And it had been fitted with a remote-control device taken from a model aircraft.

At first, Dixie had thought about putting a timer on it to avoid having to return for the explosion.

But the impossible problem was predicting the right weather conditions so far in advance. And blowing the Control Room without the threat of flooding would only be a temporary nuisance.

So the new plan was to bury the device that was to detonate the bomb. Bury it nearby, with unopened packs of batteries, and wait for the right conditions to set it off.

The first, they hoped, in a series of major bomb offensives in the south-east of England carried out by the active service unit led by McDaid.

But bad luck had dogged the unit from the start.

Tommy Brennan, who might or might not have picked up enough to blow the plan, had cried off before leaving Belfast, admitting himself to hospital with a perforated ulcer.

It couldn't have been just coincidence that the other members of the unit, including McDaid himself, had been picked up, one by one, as they'd entered Britain.

And of course Dixie had been under surveillance for a long time afterwards. Brought in for questioning. His flat searched.

But worst of all, left with the problem of how to convey the location of the buried detonator to Sean without giving the whole game away.

Simple enough, as it turned out.

He'd shown it on the model of the Thames Barrier in his flat.

Tell Sean the hobby still keeps me interested.

The surveillance on Dixie had eased the past few months, ever since the ceasefire in Northern Ireland. He'd hoped to slip away after the jailbreak and contact Sean in Jennifer Crooks's house.

If he failed, he was to lead the cops away on a wild-goose chase, so that Sean could get into his flat and check out the model, using a tramp's welcome in Mary Cassidy's place if necessary.

McDaid stopped walking now and turned towards the river to find his bearings. He closed his eyes and concentrated on Dixie's model. Then he took out and checked his diagram again.

Beyond the Generator Buildings and the Workshop, beyond the Barrier compound itself, in the bottom right-hand corner of a green area of the river bank, the detonating device was buried.

That too had been heavily wrapped in cellophane.

He had no spade for digging, and no prospect of getting one now. But the soil was soft after the recent heavy rains. Anything would do, he thought. A strip of wood. An iron bar. Even a flat stone.

What bothered him more was the time.

Nine-forty-five, as he saw when he glanced at his watch.

Already an hour behind his own tight schedule.

14

It was nine-forty-six when June Maybury hit the Woolwich Road in her red BMW.

She turned off early, impatiently, towards the Thames, down Penhall Road, but then got lost in the tightly packed streets and had to come back.

Slowing to turn again as she approached Warspite Road, she was surprised that there was no one on duty at the corner.

Maybe it was already over, she thought. A damp squib. McDaid taken without fuss.

But she drove to the car-park at the Visitors Centre and still found no security presence. Even inside the Barrier compound no guards were visible.

What had happened to the alert, she wondered. What had happened to the rapid-response team? What had happened to the local cops?

More importantly, what had happened to the bomb? And the bomb squad.

If there was a bomb.

If she hadn't been duped again by McDaid.

She threw open the car door and was stepping out, trying to avoid the puddles under her feet, when the headlights of another car that was entering the car-park caught her and blinded her for a moment.

15

With the wind howling down at him from the north, and the river apparently stretching to drag him into itself, and now hailstones biting at his hands and face, Sean McDaid stooped in the darkness to lift another portion of watery soil with the strip of plywood he'd found. He stopped for a moment then, not to rest, but thinking what he hadn't dared to worry about before, that the remote-control device mightn't have survived the landscaping along the banks of the Thames.

And when he stopped, he heard a noise.

The sucking noise that heavy mud makes when a buried shoe is violently pulled back out of it.

It was slightly behind him and over to his right, he thought. Much the same direction he'd come himself.

Maybe twenty metres away, he reckoned. Maybe. The wind seemed to be inside his head. The hailstones seemed to be hammering at his eardrums. The Thames itself was in a tantrum, pounding away on the other side. It was difficult to judge.

He held his breath and listened.

And heard the sound again.

Still stooping, he went carefully backwards, skiing along the surface of the mud instead of stepping into it, until he met the wall at the Barrier compound car-park. Bracing himself against the support behind, he flung the plywood back out to where he'd been digging.

The plopping noise brought the prowler more quickly to the scene.

He was a tall man, dressed in a dark overcoat, very wet, and carrying a gun in his left hand.

A detective, McDaid guessed, although he could see nothing but the shadow and the outline.

Too many questions bothered him. What was an armed detective doing here? Was he alone? Hadn't the alert been called off?

All of them irrelevant, he decided. Deal with this. Then take what comes.

As the cop slithered down on his haunches to examine the hole and the mound of sodden earth beside it, McDaid tried to approach him silently from behind. But the heavy mud betrayed him too.

The cop swivelled, spinning fast in the mud.

And McDaid had to shoot.

The gunshot echoed like thunder along the water, gathering volume as it travelled, disturbing dogs and cats and birds. A sudden cacophony of barking and caterwauling and flapping wings mixed and argued with the wind and the water.

McDaid, unbalanced by the gun's recoil, lost his footing in the mud and went down, landing on his back. For a moment, as his hand skidded off the ground and shot helplessly away, he thought he'd lost the gun also. But his fingers held their grip.

He struggled, like a beetle on its back, unable to turn over immediately.

And he saw that he hadn't even killed the man. He'd shot him in the left shoulder, knocking the gun from his hand. But the gun had fallen close to him, settling into the earth by his side, and the cop was trying to drag himself round to take it with his good arm.

McDaid searched desperately for a hold in the slime underneath him and finally found something solid, a rock beneath the surface, to pull himself towards.

On his knees, advancing on the cop, he held the pointing automatic with both hands. But he didn't want to shoot unless he had to. Didn't want to risk another explosion of sound. Didn't want to waste another bullet.

The cop wasn't going to make it anyway, he saw. The pain from his wounded shoulder was making him faint.

McDaid stretched out and snatched the detective's gun and threw it backwards, over his own shoulder. After that he ignored the wounded man. His suffering. The look of bafflement on his face. The fear in his eyes.

He found the plywood and dug furiously while still on his knees, his back to the river now, facing the wounded cop and the direction he'd come from, his own automatic lying handily beside him.

When the wood struck something that resisted it he used his right hand to explore the bottom of the hole he'd dug. The mud and water went up past his wrists, seeping into the sleeves of his jacket and shirt.

But as his fingers fastened on something solid, something in waterproof wrapping, he knew at once from the texture and shape that he'd found the detonator.

He was grunting with relief, staring straight into the wounded cop's eyes, like a snarling dog with a new bone, when he heard that sucking sound again.

But from behind him this time.

16

June Maybury heard the gunshot as the approaching car drew up beside her in the Visitors car-park and as she stooped to look through the passenger window at the anxious face of David Bromley.

Bromley killed the engine and got out, staring across the

roof at her, his hand shielding his face from the hailstones being driven into it by the wind coming off the river. He was trembling slightly. But whether from the cold or fear or discomfort . . .

He shouted, 'Did you hear –'

His question bitten off and carried away by the wind.

'Over there!' she shouted. She pointed, beyond the Generator Building and the Workshop. Everything, words and gestures, broader and larger and cruder because of the elements. 'Are you armed?' she shouted.

He nodded vigorously. 'Yes!'

'Bring it! Have you a torch?'

'Yes!'

She set off in front of him, sprinting through the pools, the water kicking up from her heels on to the back of her jeans and up beyond her waist. As she ran she tried to figure the quickest route to the gunfire, knowing that it had come from the area marked with a miniature harp embossed on Dixie McDaid's model.

When Bromley finally came alongside her again, still trying to keep on his toes through the water, still trying to save his face from the stinging hailstones, she demanded, 'Where the hell is everyone?'

He was already breathless. 'What?'

'Everyone! Where?'

He worked his left hand, as if rapidly casting a fly with a fishing rod. Jabbing towards the area the shot had come from. 'There! Must be! There!'

'Did you get through to Gilston?'

'What?'

'Gilston!'

'Yes!'

17

The sound of someone wading through the mud, much clearer than the last time, because now it was carried towards him by the wind, still didn't make Sean McDaid reach down for his own automatic. He knew that he had no chance of finding it and turning to fire without being shot first himself.

Instead he pretended not to notice the newcomer's approach.

Still on his knees, he worked furiously, trying to release the remote control and its batteries from the cellophane wrapping, hunching over the package to keep it hidden by his body. Some of his fingers, cold and lifeless and bitten by the hail, were already bleeding.

He wondered what distance it was from there to the bomb in the Control Room. Not so far, he reckoned, that he couldn't trigger it without having to move any nearer.

He had the remote control already free and his numb fingers were pressing frantically along the perforation in the pack of batteries when he felt the coldness of a gun barrel against the back of his head.

He glanced up quickly into the eyes of the wounded cop. And he saw that the man was puzzled, not relieved. And understood from his reaction that it wasn't another detective behind.

McDaid ignored the gun.

He fumbled at a catch on the back of the remote control and finally managed to prise it free to knock off the cover of the battery housing.

He braced himself for a blow from the gun, deciding that he'd act, chopping backwards at the legs behind him, the moment that barrel left his head.

But it was a voice that came at him. And startled him.

'Put it down, Sean!'

A voice from his childhood. When he was twelve years old. Wide-eyed with wonder and picking up a real Armalite rifle to play with. The same voice. The same tone. The same phrase.

'Put it down, Sean!'

Jody Stafford.

McDaid forced himself to keep his silence.

To argue is to lose strength, he told himself. Discussion and dialogue are weaknesses. Nobody fears you when they only have to listen to you. Open your mouth and you eventually talk yourself into a ceasefire.

He said nothing.

Instead, with his raw, bleeding fingers he took a battery from the pack and inserted it in the remote control.

Man is defined only by his actions, he told himself. To keep his mind occupied. To keep the fear at bay. Let Jody Stafford express what he is and where he stands, he thought. Pull the fucking trigger or back off.

He felt the gun barrel pushing harder into the back of his skull and he felt heartened by that. It was, he knew, only another warning. And that was a form of dialogue.

He took the second of the four batteries and pressed it in beside the first.

18

It seemed to Jody Stafford that either his own thoughts were being caught by the gales and whipped into a frenzy of speed, or that Sean McDaid, with his numb and muddied and bleeding fingers, was fumbling in slow motion. So much passed through Stafford's mind while the younger man's hand moved the short distance with a battery.

But he knew that both perceptions were illusions.

He knew that for four years his conclusions had been painfully slow and that McDaid's actions had been unhesitating.

And now he envied McDaid the simplicity of his politics. The way you envy the simplicity of your own past. The way he envied Rawlings and others their simplicities. Us and Them. Right and Wrong.

For Stafford, who had once loved one of Them, and probably still loved her despite the bitterness, and who had once loved and reared McDaid as a boy, there were no simplicities any more.

The oldest of the old divisions in the Republican movement, he thought, stretching back to 1916 and beyond, was that between the gun and the ballot box.

And he was still a part of it.

Because here he was, indulging in debate, while Sean McDaid calmly inserted the last of the batteries.

19

Maybury and Bromley were already on the river bank beyond the Barrier Workshop, their pace slowing as the wind hit them with its full force across the river and the open ground and their feet slithered and sank in the mud, when they heard the second gunshot and saw the brief flash of its light.

Quite close, they could see. And straight in front of them. Difficult again to judge with the howling and the insistent patter of hail and the reverberations off the water, but it seemed only fifteen, twenty metres away.

Bromley foolishly shone his torch, risking more gunfire at his own exposed position. Through the slanting sleet, its beam almost immediately picked out and held the little tableau ahead.

An officer down, as Maybury saw at once, clutching his left shoulder. The body of Sean McDaid fallen across a freshly dug hole, as if trying to enter a grave that had been cut too small for him. And Jody Stafford, standing with his back to her, an automatic pistol in his right hand, his hidden left apparently reaching towards what was clearly a remote-control device lying near McDaid's body.

She instantly rewound the action in her mind.

And got it wrong.

Stafford and McDaid had come together to blow the Barrier and flood the city of London, she thought. The detective had surprised them and killed McDaid. Stafford had disabled the detective. And now Stafford was going to detonate the bomb.

To her right, on the periphery of her vision, she noticed that Bromley had advanced and that his arms were extended, his

300

right pointing the hand-gun at Stafford, his left underneath the other for support. The hail bounced off the metal and off the surface of his dark raincoat. His eyes seemed to have trouble keeping themselves clear of water.

Stafford moved. But not downwards towards the remote control. He half turned, raising his left hand to shield his eyes from the torch.

And then she was reminded. And curiously elated.

Stafford's left hand was useless, damaged by a bullet from Bill Enright's gun, the same pistol Stafford himself was dropping to the ground from his right hand now.

She yelled, 'No! Hold your fire, Bromley!'

Certain that she was in time. Certain that Bromley heard, despite the whistle of the wind and the pounding of the Thames along the bank. Because he glanced for a moment back at her. Certain that a long pause, almost thirty seconds, followed her call.

And yet, when those thirty seconds were gone, when Stafford had turned to face them fully, a smile of recognition on his face at her voice, that broad, careless, mischievous smile that she'd fallen for in Belfast and hadn't seen in almost four years . . . When all of that, Bromley fired anyway.

Three times. Very rapidly.

The first bullet caught Stafford in the chest and kicked him up and backwards. The second missed. The third shattered the side of his head as he was falling.

June Maybury cursed and screamed and ran past Bromley. Some instinct, useless now, telling her to put her body between the gun and Stafford.

But Stafford was already dead before he hit and slithered grotesquely in the mud. The third bullet had taken his temple away.

With nothing saner to do, she turned furiously on Bromley. She stood there, her face contorted, her raised fists clenched

against the pellets of ice pouring down from the sky. And she
started. Shouting. 'I told you to hold your fucking fire, you –'

But something instantly silenced her rage and her grief.

Not Bromley's face. She couldn't see it. His torch still blinded her. Maybe that. Maybe the fact that herself and the
wounded detective were still caught in the strong beam, like
helpless prey.

When he spoke, there was no longer any doubt.

'Move away!' he shouted. 'Move away! Over to your left!
Three paces!'

She did it, slipping on the slight incline, thinking hard as
she worked to balance herself.

Was this part of someone's precautions, she wondered. Did
they know of her old relationship with Stafford? Did they think
she was going to do the terrorists' work for them?

Bromley called again, however. 'Stop!'

She noticed then that his torch hadn't followed her movement, that the beam still trapped both herself and the
detective.

And she began to question. And to understand. At last,
began to understand. The full horror of it finally striking home
as Bromley gestured with his gun at the fallen detective and
shouted, 'You too! Move over beside her! Move!'

The horror only deepened by her failure to grasp the reasons, to make sense of it all.

Because it must have been Bromley, she realised now, who
had telephoned a warning to Sean McDaid in Dixie's flat.
Bromley had been working at Headquarters when she'd rung
from Kilburn and must have had the call intercepted for him
by someone else.

And Bromley, of course, who had fouled up the newspaper
with those faked reports of McDaid's death and who had relied
on Dixie to spot the deliberate error.

And Bromley who had warned the escaped prisoners at

Jennifer Crooks's house, perhaps. He'd had the opportunity there, too. He was the first to receive the report of the officer who had intercepted the call to Stafford in the farmhouse.

And Bromley, of course, who took that noble stand against Rawlings and made himself privy to everything that passed between Gilston and Maybury.

Bromley who had never requested a rapid-response unit or notified the local cops tonight. Bromley who wanted her and the wounded detective out of his way now, so that he could reach the remote control and detonate the bomb.

She knew then that she was going to die.

Bromley was going to kill her and the wounded detective, just as he'd killed Jody Stafford.

But not quite, she saw, as she watched him reaching with his foot for the automatic pistol Stafford had used. *That* would be the weapon to finish her and the detective off.

Because there couldn't be any witnesses. The story would have to be told by Bromley alone. How Stafford and McDaid had killed Maybury and the detective in the raging storm along the banks of the Thames before blowing the Barrier with semtex. How Bromley himself had arrived too late to do anything but stop the terrorists escaping.

Had he guessed yet, though, as she had, that it must have been Stafford's gun that had killed McDaid? Would the ballistic reports finally nail his story and hang him?

It was her only hope.

Otherwise she felt sad and sour.

The bitterest thing, she thought, was not having lost the only person she'd ever really loved. She hadn't loved Jody Stafford. She'd needed him. Enjoyed him. And felt for him.

But not the other.

And that was the bitterest thing, knowing that she was incapable of love, of accepting the difference in another.

No one working in the intelligence service was capable of

303

love, she thought morosely. Only of intrigue. of secrecy. Distrust. Isolation. Of fantasies of order and chaos. And an unquestioning loyalty to intrigue and secrecy, distrust and isolation, and fantasies or order and chaos.

All the poorer half of human nature.

She'd lived like that. And now she was going to die like that.

As Bromley juggled his torch and his gun in his right hand and reached with his left for the detonator, she wondered if Jody Stafford had ever really broken out of his own intolerance and blindness, if he'd ever really loved.

The fact that she'd never asked, never struggled to find out, and now would never know, seemed the real waste of her life.

Epilogue

ONE

1

George Rawlings and Superintendent Geoffrey Gilston stood up at the same time in the darkened room, while the video was still running, and found their way to the aisle and out the door.

They walked in silence to Rawlings's office.

The scenes they'd just witnessed on the screen were harrowing. The roofs of double-decker buses barely visible above the flood waters. The Houses of Parliament and Westminister Abbey, even as far back as Downing Street and the Foreign Office, accessible only by river craft. The bodies of the dead still floating on the surface.

For Gilston, the plump, effeminate cheeks of Nicholas Orrinsmith, Rawlings's private secretary, couldn't have offered a more irritating relief.

He would never develop now beyond his old-fashioned ways, Gilston accepted. Nor did he want to. He simply didn't like effeminate men, no more than he liked the hard-nosed, functional career women he often met in MI5.

Orrinsmith brought a tray with tea and biscuits when the two senior men were seated. And then he left, closing the door behind him with the loud discretion of a funeral attendant.

'Ah!' Rawlings exclaimed, as if surprised. 'Tea, Geoffrey?'

He put aside his cane, crooking it on the desk, to pour and serve.

And the ice having been broken by the beverage, he said then, 'Sad to hear about old Lammas resigning. I always thought him a fine head of Special Branch. Will you be applying for the vacancy yourself?'

'Yes,' Gilston said in his blunt way.

'You'll need solid references, of course.'

Gilston was silent, wary of an offer.

But Rawlings didn't make one.

'I'm delighted to see *someone* coming out of all this with a reputation enhanced,' he said. 'It's claimed so many careers, hasn't it? Prison Governors. Even talk of the Junior Minister at the Home Office. And, ah, I'll be stepping down myself in a few months. Did you know?'

'Better than being dead, sir,' Gilston observed. A little sourly. Thinking of the policemen who had fallen.

'Quite,' Rawlings agreed.

He stirred a melting sugar lump into his tea and tapped the spoon on the rim of his china cup before placing it in the saucer. He said, 'About Bromley . . .'

Gilston's reaction was almost automatic by now. 'I never liked the chap.'

'Clever you, Geoffrey,' Rawlings conceded. Half envy. Half irony. 'Clever you.'

As if he realised then that no amount of analysis or explanation could reverse the clock or restore his job, he said nothing more.

Gilston, never one to waste time on useless formalities, finished his tea quickly and stood up. 'If you don't mind, sir –'

But Rawlings seemed reluctant to be left alone, seemed to crave a little company.

'Dreadful video,' he muttered. 'Didn't you think? Quite harrowing stuff.'

308

Only a simulation, as he knew. Part of the advertising campaign in the late 1960s when the Greater London Council was lobbying for the construction of the Thames Barrier at Woolwich.

But still harrowing.

And its effect seemed to linger in his mind like guilt, nagging him about his failures in the case.

'If you don't mind, sir,' Gilston said again, 'I'd better return to the office.'

This time, Rawlings smiled faintly and offered a regretful little wave. 'Of course. Of course.'

2

Geoffrey Gilston didn't return to New Scotland Yard, though.

He drove along the south bank of the Thames, through Southwark, and into Bermondsey, where he found her, as she'd promised, in the same booth of the Cat and Cage as before, and again drinking vodka and white lemonade.

For the first time in decades, since his early twenties, he discovered that he was conscious of his dull appearance as he walked across to her.

Not ashamed. No. He hadn't drifted as far as that in his liking for her. But conscious.

He sat beside her and one of the table staff brought him the beer he ordered.

'He's resigning,' he said. 'Rawlings.'

June Maybury nodded. 'I wouldn't have expected anything else.'

'Will they offer it to you? Or something else? Deputy Director-General?'

'Possibly. But I won't be in a position to accept. I've already applied for a transfer to the Firm.'

'To MI6?'

'Yes. Field work. Something the Service is running woefully short of. And it's my own particular forte.'

'I don't see why you shouldn't . . .'

He tailed off, disappointed that the pleasure of working opposite her was never going to be his again now.

'Why?' she repeated. 'Because I didn't see it either. That's why. No more than Rawlings did. I didn't see Bromley as a threat. You know why? Why none of us could see it?'

'Because you were too close to him.'

'Exactly. Because Bromley was the perfect Service man. The career intelligence officer. Socially adept. Extremely secure. No problem with alcohol. Positive vetting at every session. In the best traditions of the Service.' She paused and drank. And then she added, 'It seems the best tradition of the Service might be mere self-preservation, though.'

Gilston frowned. 'Come again?'

June Maybury smiled, a wry acceptance of her own recent blindness. What she had to tell him was the result of a top-secret internal enquiry. But she felt he was entitled to know. Particularly if he was going to head Special Branch for the next few years.

'There is a small, powerful element within the Service', she said, 'who are just as scathing about the IRA ceasefire as Sean McDaid was. Bromley was one of them. I can see the hand of my old mentor, Sir Andrew Pinnington, in all of it somewhere. But nothing can be proved. If Pinnington had been left in place as Director-General, there would be no ceasefire.'

'Hawks, then,' Gilston said. 'A hard core of hawks.'

'Oh, sure,' she agreed. 'They're all married to the belief in a military solution in Northern Ireland. But it's not quite as simple as that, either. Because deep down, their actions are guided by an arrogance that's toppled over into madness. There are no Soviets to monitor any more. No Cold War. And now they're suddenly deprived of Northern Ireland as well. What work is to be done? Nothing. The Service is threatened with being redundant.'

'It's faced disbandment before,' Gilston pointed out. 'In the early Nineties.'

'True. But it was saved by claiming the lead in the fight against the IRA. More officers were sent to Belfast. More were thrown into intelligence gathering and counter-terrorism on the mainland. More were recruited. But now, since the cease-fire, it has no reason for its own existence at all. Consider the diagnosis. For if the only protector of British virtue is allowed to wither, then Britain itself will surely die from impurities. The Service must survive. At all costs. Even if it's the only survivor. The irony is, these people are as religiously wedded to their cause as the most fanatical Republican terrorist is to his. The longer the ceasefire holds, the more these people will work to subvert it. They have to destroy the peace, so that they can win the war that will follow. And it doesn't begin with Pinnington and end with Bromley, either. There are others in the Service, the ones who monitored calls, the ones who passed information on to Bromley. All gone to ground now, of course.'

'And the hawks in the IRA?' Gilston wondered.

'Gone to ground, too. For the moment.'

'I was wrong about Jody Stafford,' he conceded.

'Maybe not,' she said. 'They have codes that are just as rigid as ours. If Stafford couldn't execute McDaid himself, maybe he was willing to acquiesce in what he did. Stafford didn't co-operate with us.'

But it was a public posture only.

She thought again, sadly, of Bromley shooting Stafford, blaming herself, as she would always blame herself, for the

311

death, for not knowing her own people as well as she should have. Racked with guilt about it all – another part of that religious upbringing by her maiden aunts in Dublin – she'd almost welcomed her own death as punishment.

But as Bromley stooped to pick up the remote control, another gunshot suddenly broke through the noise of the storm. The bullet hit Bromley in the chest, knocking him sideways, away from the remote control. Falling, he dropped his own hand-gun and the torch.

The torch spun on the wet surface and then settled to illuminate the newcomer. A young man. Red-haired. With two or three days' heavy growth on his face. Dressed in jeans and a brown leather jacket.

Still covering Bromley, he kicked aside the various weapons and picked up the torch, after removing the batteries again from the remote control.

He said, 'I'm sorry, ma'am. I don't know if I should have fired without warning. It's just –'

'No, no,' she assured him. 'You were right. You had no time. You couldn't risk it.' She paused and looked from the man on the ground to his companion and asked, 'But who are you?'

'DC Perkins, ma'am,' the wounded man said. 'Special Branch.'

'DC Wise, ma'am.'

'How did you get here?'

'We were on surveillance duty, ma'am. Jody Stafford in Neasden. Superintendent Gilston's orders. We followed Stafford to a phone booth earlier this evening, where he made and received a number of lengthy calls. Afterwards we tailed him over to here. We got the impression that he was waiting for someone, and then following someone else. But we saw no one, and then we lost him in the dark when he came on to the river bank here.'

312

Perkins, the wounded man, at last got back on his feet. 'We split up to search,' he explained. He pointed to the hole McDaid had dug. 'I stumbled on that. The next I knew, someone had shot me from behind.'

'I'd gone to the other side,' Wise said, gesturing through the dark. 'It took a while to find you all. It's hard to know precisely where a gunshot is coming from so near the water.'

'Have you radioed for assistance?' Maybury asked.

'Not yet, ma'am, no. No chance.'

'Better do it now.'

Bromley was already dead, however, by the time help arrived.

The wounded Special Branch detective had surgery that night and was recovering in hospital.

'Rum thing,' Gilston said now, considering the last of his beer in the bottom of the glass. 'The expert opinion is that the device wouldn't actually have triggered the bomb.'

'The expert opinion from the British Embassy in Kuwait in 1990', Maybury countered, 'was that there was no serious threat of invasion from Iraq. Remember? A couple of days later Saddam Hussein's tanks were rolling across the border and the Gulf War was on.'

She finished her vodka and said, 'I owe you a drink, don't I? And an umbrella.'